What Reviewers Say About BOLD STROKES Authors

ॐ

KIM BALDWIN

"*A riveting novel of suspense* seems to be a very overworked phrase. However, it is extremely apt when discussing Kim Baldwin's [*Hunter's Pursuit*]. An exciting page turner [features] Katarzyna Demetrious, a bounty hunter...with a million dollar price on her head. Look for this excellent novel of suspense..." – **R. Lynne Watson**, *MegaScene*

"*Force of Nature* is an exciting and substantial reading experience which will long remain with the reader. Likeable characters with plausible problems and concerns, imaginative settings, engrossing events, and a well-tailored writing style all contribute to an exceptional novel. Baldwin's characterization is acutely and meticulously circumscribed and expansive. It is indeed gratifying to see a new author attempt and succeed in expanding her literary technique and writing style. Kim Baldwin is an author who has achieved both." – **Arlene Germain**, reviewer for the *Lambda Book Report* and the *Midwest Book Review*

ॐ

ROSE BEECHAM

"...her characters seem fully capable of walking away from the particulars of whodunit and engaging the reader in other aspects of their lives." – *Lambda Book Report*

"When Jennifer Fulton writes mysteries, she writes them as Rose Beecham. And since Jennifer Fulton is a very fine writer, you might expect that Rose Beecham is a fine writer too. You're right...On the way to a remarkable, and thoroughly convincing climax, Beecham creates believable characters in compelling situations, with enough humor to provide effective counterpoint to the work of detecting." – *Bay Area Reporter*

RONICA BLACK

"Black juggles the assorted elements of her first book with assured pacing and estimable panache...[including]...the relative depth— for genre fiction—of the central characters: Erin, the married-but-separated detective who comes to her lesbian senses; loner Patricia, the policewoman-mentor who finds herself falling for Erin; and sultry club owner Elizabeth, the sexually predatory suspect who discards women like Kleenex...until she meets Erin." – **Richard Labonte**, *Book Marks*, Q Syndicate, 2005

"Black's characterization is skillful, and the sexual chemistry surrounding the three major characters is palpable and definitely hot-hot-hot. If you're looking for a more traditional murder mystery, *In Too Deep* might not be entirely your cup of Earl. On the other hand, if you're looking for a solid read with ample amounts of eroticism and a red herring or two, you're sure to find *In Too Deep* a satisfying read." —**Lynne Jamneck**, L-Word.com Literature

GUN BROOKE

"Course of Action is a romance...populated with a host of captivating and amiable characters. The glimpses into the lifestyles of the rich and beautiful people are rather like guilty pleasures....[A] most satisfying and entertaining reading experience." – **Arlene Germain**, reviewer for the *Lambda Book Report* and the *Midwest Book Review*

"*Protector of the Realm* has it all; sabotage, corruption, erotic love and exhilarating space fights. Gun Brooke's second novel is forceful with a winning combination of solid characters and a brilliant plot." – **Kathi Isserman**, *JustAboutWrite*

JANE FLETCHER

"*The Walls of Westernfort* is not only a highly engaging and fast-paced adventure novel, it provides the reader with an interesting framework for examining the same questions of loyalty, faith, family and love that [the characters] must face." – **M. J. Lowe**, *Midwest Book Review*

❧

Lee Lynch

"There's a heady sense of '60s back-to-the-land communal idealism and '70s woman-power feminism (with hints of lesbian separatism) to this spirited novel—even though it's set in contemporary rural Oregon. Partners Donny (she's black and blue-collar) and Chick (she's plus-sized and motherly) are both in their 50s, owners of the dyke-centric Natural Woman Foods store, a homey nexus for *Sweet Creek*'s expansive cast of characters….Lynch, with a dozen novels to her credit dating back to the early days of Naiad Press, has earned her stripes as a writerly elder; she was contributing stories to the lesbian magazine *The Ladder* four decades ago. But this latest is sublimely in tune with the times."
– **Richard Labonte**, *Book Marks*, Q Syndicate, 2006

❧

Radcly*f*fe

"…well-honed storytelling skills…solid prose and sure-handedness of the narrative…" – **Elizabeth Flynn**, *Lambda Book Report*

"…well-plotted…lovely romance…I couldn't turn the pages fast enough!" – **Ann Bannon**, author of *The Beebo Brinker Chronicles*

❧

Ali Vali

"Rich in character portrayal, *The Devil Inside* by Ali Vali is an unusual, unpredictable, and thought-provoking love story that will have the reader questioning the definition of right and wrong long after she finishes the book….*The Devil Inside*'s strength is that it is unlike most romance novels. Nothing about the story and its characters is conventional. We do not know what the future holds for Emma and Cain, but Vali tempts us with every word so we want to find out. I am very much looking forward to the sequel *The Devil Unleashed*."
– **Kathi Isserman**, *JustAboutWrite*

Too Close
to Touch

Visit us at www.boldstrokesbooks.com

TOO CLOSE
TO TOUCH

by

Georgia Beers

2006

CREDITS
EDITORS: JENNIFER KNIGHT AND STACIA SEAMAN
PRODUCTION DESIGN: STACIA SEAMAN
COVER DESIGN BY SHERI (GRAPHICARTIST2020@HOTMAIL.COM)

Acknowledgments

I am very lucky to have a terrific band of proofreaders/friends. My sincere thanks to Stacy Harp, Steff Obkirchner, and Jackie Ciresi. Their suggestions, nitpicks, and general opinions continue to help me make my stories into the best they can be, and their warm and loving encouragement keeps me going whenever I falter. I couldn't ask for better cheerleaders.

I owe special thanks to my good friends in the medical profession: Amy Ziberna, Nancy Valentage, and Radclyffe, for answering the questions I had regarding medical details I know nothing about.

Thank you to Jennifer Knight, editor extraordinaire, for her valiant attempts to teach me the ins and outs of point of view, her lessons on smoothing out the flow, and her suggestion that characters nodding seventy-eight times in one book might be construed as overkill. I'm working on them all, Jennifer. I promise.

Gratitude upon gratitude upon gratitude to Radclyffe and the amazing staff of Bold Strokes Books. I'm a very lucky woman who is honored to be included in a group filled with such talent, determination, and love for the genre.

My eternal, loving gratefulness to my partner and wife, Bonnie Mowry. She is the most loving, sacrificing, and supportive partner any woman could want and she treats my dream of being a full-time writer as her own, working and forgoing in order to make it happen. It is by no small effort from her that this book is in your hands now.

Dedication

To Bonnie
My heart, my soul, my inspiration . . .

CHAPTER ONE

The Black Widow in Rochester, New York, was a pleasant surprise as lesbian bars went, and Gretchen Kaiser was happy to have found the place. It had a classy feel to it that many such establishments lacked, and the crowd seemed a bit more sophisticated than the average bunch of local college-age dykes. The bar itself was made of wood and brass, and the stools were actually *not* riddled with scratches or falling apart.

Gretchen suspected that happy hour during the week might feature more than a handful of business suit–clad women, an opportunity she might want to check out once she got settled in. Despite its air of refinement, the Widow still boasted the standard lesbian bar necessities: the pool table in the back, postage stamp–sized dance floor across from the bar, jukebox blaring Melissa Etheridge in the corner. Gretchen felt welcomed, warm, at home.

She sipped the last of her Dewar's on the rocks in unhurried relaxation and watched Christy, the pretty bartender, as she took care of a group of four women she obviously knew. It was fairly early on a Saturday night, but the crowd was slowly increasing in size and Gretchen was glad she'd commandeered the corner stool. The view was perfect. She was able to enjoy her drink, appreciate Christy's need to bend over and retrieve beer from the under-the-counter refrigerators, and take in the lesbians of this new city. Her new city.

"How you doing on that, hon?" Christy's auburn hair was pulled back into a ponytail, rebellious wisps wafting around her face. Her complexion was peaches-and-cream smooth, with a sprinkling of freckles that trailed across her nose and surrounded a little diamond stud in her left nostril. She looked pointedly at Gretchen's near-empty rock glass. "Can I get another for the birthday girl?"

"That would be great, Christy. Thanks." Gretchen smiled at the title.

She'd arrived over an hour ago and the bar was practically empty, so she'd started up a conversation with Christy. It hadn't been long before the scotch had loosened her tongue and she was pouring out her story in typical dump-it-on-the-bartender fashion. The fact that the entire day had passed and her father hadn't called to wish her a happy birthday in her new place was something she was trying hard to forget. She felt like a child for even caring. She was well over forty now; birthdays weren't supposed to matter anymore. Her father apparently agreed.

Bothered by the sting, she had welcomed the attention from Christy, who promptly did a celebratory shot of tequila with her. Now, Gretchen caught herself wondering if it would be possible to talk Christy into going home with her. Judging by the constant attention Christy paid her even as business picked up, she was pretty sure it would.

Still smiling, Gretchen scanned the room and realized the group of women down the bar were surreptitiously looking her way. Her heart rate picked up. Being checked out was not an unusual occurrence. Gretchen knew she was an attractive woman and attention wasn't something she had trouble getting, but it still brought a slight flush to her cheeks.

Christy stopped near the bunch on her way to fixing Gretchen's drink. When she returned and set the scotch down, she gestured at the women with her head. "This one's on them, hon."

Gretchen looked past her toward the group. All four women held up their glasses and toasted, "Happy birthday!"

Gretchen saluted in return, her grin splitting her face, and mouthed a thank-you. She shot a knowing look at Christy, who winked at her. As two of the women headed for the pool table, the other two sauntered toward Gretchen. One was tall and handsome, a big, muscular woman who carried herself with confidence rather than trying to hide her size. The other was a young, feminine blonde who seemed either lost in, or bored with, her surroundings; it was hard to tell.

The taller woman gestured at the stool next to Gretchen. "Mind if we join you?"

"Please do," Gretchen said. "Thanks for the drink."

"Hey, it's your birthday," the woman replied by way of explanation. She held out her hand. "I'm Mick."

"Gretchen." Mick's hand was thick and strong, her skin unexpectedly soft. Her handshake was firm, but not overpowering.

"This is Tina." Mick introduced the blonde, who smiled but didn't offer her hand. "Did you want to play pool?" Mick inquired.

"Oh, no. I try not do anything I'm not good at."

Mick smiled knowingly. "Forgive the cliché, but I haven't seen you around here before." She took a swig of her beer, the bottle virtually disappearing in her hand.

Gretchen chuckled. "That's because I've never been here before."

"That would explain it."

"I'm going to go to the little girls' room," Tina chimed in, squeezing Mick's arm.

"Okay, babe." Mick watched her go and Gretchen took the opportunity to take a good look at her new acquaintance.

Mick had to be close to six feet tall, looked to be in her late thirties, and definitely lifted weights. Gretchen was glad they were sitting or, at five foot four, she would have felt completely insignificant and dwarfed by the sheer presence of this woman. Mick's hair was chestnut brown, the cut simple, short, and stylish. Three silver hoops of varying sizes adorned her left ear, one dangling the symbol for female. Her wardrobe was neat and unpretentious, but not inexpensive. Her jeans seemed tailored for her body, showcasing well-worked muscles and gently cradling her curves. The white T-shirt was saved from being too masculine by the v-neck cut, which showed enough bronzed skin to make Gretchen curious about what lay underneath the fabric. A rainbow tattoo peeked out from under her left sleeve.

When Mick turned startling green eyes back in her direction, Gretchen almost laughed aloud at her own blatant appraisal and quickly pretended to be studying her drink. *Not at all my type*, she thought. *But certainly not hard on the eyes.*

"So tell me, Gretchen," Mick said. "Why haven't you been to the Widow before?"

"Because I'm the new kid in town."

"Yeah? Where are you from?"

"Poughkeepsie."

"Ah. A big-city girl. And you've been in our little city how long?"

"I just moved in on Wednesday."

"Wow. You're the *really* new kid. That's cool." She took a long pull from her bottle. "Apartment or house?"

"Apartment for now. We'll see how it goes."

"City or suburbs?"

"Near Park Avenue."

"Ah. That area is always a good choice. Well, I think you'll like it here. It's a pretty cool spot."

The conversation flowed easily and Gretchen felt immediately comfortable talking to Mick. That was something that didn't often happen to her when the setting wasn't work related; she was generally a reserved and private person and didn't converse effortlessly with strangers unless it had to do with her job.

When Tina returned from the bathroom, Mick bought them all another drink, waving off Gretchen's attempts to catch the round. "No way." She pushed Gretchen's money back across the bar. To Christy, she said, "The birthday girl isn't allowed to buy."

Gretchen found the dynamic between Mick and Tina interesting. She didn't think they were partners, but they were definitely there together—maybe just for the night? Tina held possessively to Mick's arm, her hand, her thigh, as if marking her territory for Gretchen's benefit. Gretchen merely smiled in amusement and intentionally let her eyes wander over Mick.

The evening passed loudly. The other two women in the original foursome wandered down after their pool game and were introduced as Lori and Kathy, partners for a hundred years, according to Mick. The five women chatted, joked, and drank, keeping Christy busy with orders and flirtatious comments. Knowing she needed to drive herself home, Gretchen consciously slowed her own alcohol consumption after Mick bought her yet another drink. She was having such a good time with these women, these new friends, the last thing she wanted was to allow herself to become too intoxicated. No better way to alienate new acquaintances than to force them to feel responsible for getting you home and pouring you into your bed.

As if reading her mind, Christy set a glass of water down near Gretchen's scotch and squeezed her hand. Gretchen made a mental note to double her tip. Her head swimming just slightly, she then directed her attention to Lori, who was asking her a question.

"So, G. Why here? Why'd you leave Poughkeepsie to come way upstate?"

"Honestly? I needed to put some distance between me and my family." It was the truth. Maybe not the whole truth, but Gretchen was nervous about starting her new job on Monday and didn't want to conduct a postmortem on her reasons for making the change. She was having such fun, so she avoided the subject altogether and put her focus elsewhere.

Lori gave her an understanding look. "I hear that. Do they have a problem with you being gay?" She was a cute, athletic blonde in capris and a green tank top, and Gretchen was surprised to feel a pull of attraction, despite the fact that Lori's hand was in the firm grip of her partner's.

First the bartender, now the married chick, Gretchen's inner voice scolded with amusement. *Cut it out.* Aloud, she replied, "They have a problem with that, among other things." The tone of her voice must have indicated the subject was closed, because Lori left it alone.

Midnight came and went and the crowd at the Black Widow began to thin out gradually as lesbians of all sizes, shapes, and colors trickled out into the night like slow-flowing water. Lori and Kathy said their good-byes first.

"It's been ages since we've been out past ten and we may turn into pumpkins at any minute." Lori tugged on Kathy's hand. "Ready, love?" Kathy nodded through a yawn, causing them all to laugh. "I'm sure we'll see you again, Gretchen."

"It was nice meeting you," Gretchen replied. "Thanks so much for the drinks and the company."

"Our pleasure. Happy birthday."

"We need to go, too, don't we?" Tina's voice had a slightly bored quality to it as she laid her head on Mick's upper arm in a childlike fashion.

"I suppose we do," Mick replied. She held her hand out to Gretchen. "Birthday girl, it was a joy spending the evening with you." When Gretchen placed her hand in Mick's, Mick pulled her forward and kissed her cheek sweetly. In her ear, so only Gretchen could hear, she whispered, "I hope to see you again."

Gretchen smiled, feeling her cheeks flush pink.

As the four women departed, Christy took the empties away and dropped Gretchen's glass into the sink full of suds beneath the bar. "You certainly charmed her," she said with nonchalance.

"Who?"

"Mick."

"Oh. I don't know about that."

"I do. I know her pretty well. She was quite taken with you."

Gretchen arched an eyebrow and propped her forearms on the bar, studying Christy with a smirk. "Well. She's not really my type."

"No?"

"Oh, no. She's way too butch for me. I'm more partial to…pretty, as opposed to handsome."

"Really."

Lowering her voice so Christy had to lean close to hear it, she said, "I like curves and long hair and softness more than muscles and power."

"Mm-hmm."

"Actually, *I* prefer to be the muscle and power."

"I see."

Gretchen drained her water glass and set it down in front of Christy. Christy mirrored Gretchen's stance on her own side of the bar and they held eye contact for several long seconds.

"Can I get your number?" Christy finally asked, her voice low.

"I think that could be arranged."

CHAPTER TWO

K ylie O'Brien was nervous and it was pissing her off.
She'd gotten into work two hours early, just to make sure everything was in order. She'd straightened up her own desk—not that it wasn't always so impeccably organized she got picked on by her coworkers, but she wanted to be sure to make a good impression on her new boss.

It was true that Kylie had been working for Emerson, Inc. for more than ten years. It was also true that she was a damn good executive administrative assistant, but none of that would matter if she and the new boss didn't hit it off. If their styles clashed or if they had trouble communicating, all it would take was a phone call to the powers that be and Kylie could find herself transferred. Or worse: out of a job. The ability to snap your fingers and change the landscape was the only thing Kylie thought might be appealing about being the boss. For the most part, she was happy behind the scenes.

She missed Jim already. He'd retired only a week ago, but it felt like months. He'd been her boss for nearly seven years, pulling her up with him as he rose through the ranks of the company. She knew him better than he knew himself, and that had always made it easy to be sure things ran smoothly in his office. She kept him on track, gave him the appearance of being organized, though they both knew better, and he was generous in his support of her, both within the company and through personal bonuses. With Jim Sheridan as her superior, she'd never felt taken for granted. She wasn't looking forward to starting over with somebody she hadn't even met.

She gave her cubicle another once-over, then poked her head into the large office opposite her area and gave that a quick look as well. It was clean and spacious and ready for its new occupant. Satisfied, she headed down the hall toward the ladies' room to give herself a final once-over. It was still about forty-five minutes before the masses would begin to pour in.

Kylie wasn't exactly a morning person; she preferred to work late rather than come in early. She was much more productive when the phones weren't ringing off the hook and people weren't demanding her attention every minute. Things tended to really quiet down after five, but she was finding that being in early had the same perks. It was very quiet and she could actually hear herself think.

She smiled at an unfamiliar man as she passed him in the hall. It seemed like an entirely different group of people came in early. She recognized only a handful of those she'd seen so far. It occurred to her that while she shared her penchant for evening hours with a select handful of Emerson employees, there must be a similar group of "morning people."

The cell phone on her hip rang as she pushed open the door to the ladies' room, the sound annoyingly loud in the quiet hush of the morning. Kylie grabbed it and flipped it open quickly, knowing who it was before she even looked.

"You've got a lot of nerve calling me this early," she said, hiding a grin. She smiled and nodded at a small brunette who came out of a stall and headed to the sink.

"Who do you think you're kidding?" Mick replied. "You're in early so you can make a good impression on the new boss. Think I don't know you like the back of my hand?"

"Damn you." The smile in Kylie's voice was clear because Mick was right. She knew Kylie inside and out. She should. They'd been friends since the second grade.

As Mick said something about the weekend, Kylie leaned back against the counter and tried to be subtle about watching the brunette woman. Her subject was extremely attractive. The woman's dark hair was a mass of curls that fell down around her shoulders, and her smartly cut black pantsuit made her seem much taller than her petite frame actually was.

Pulling her eyes away proved to be difficult, but Kylie managed to turn aside before she could be caught staring. "The weekend… yes. How was it?" she asked Mick, trying to focus on the topic of conversation.

"The usual."

"Let me guess. You went out Saturday night, you took some babe home, ditched her by Sunday afternoon, and went to the gym. How'd I do?"

Mick chuckled. "Not bad. Not bad at all. But I only went to the gym because you were being too good to do something with me on Sunday."

"Hey, I told you I had things to do." She watched the stylish brunette out of the corner of her eye, enjoying the sight of her bending toward the mirror to touch up her mascara. Kylie's eyes drifted down over the curve of hips and nicely shaped behind. "Preparations to make."

"For new boss day."

"Exactly." A toilet flushed and an older woman with gray hair and a friendly smile joined the brunette at the sink, blocking Kylie's view.

"You sound nervous," Mick commented.

"I *am* nervous. I have to learn a whole new person starting today."

"You'll be great. As soon as he sees how terrific you are at your job, he'll be thanking his lucky stars. And if that doesn't work, we'll go to the mall and buy you some tighter clothes."

"It's a she."

The older woman dried her hands and left. The brunette was now applying lipstick. She blotted her lips together and ran a precise fingertip over each corner, tidying. Kylie swallowed.

"What's a she?" Mick asked.

"My new boss. It's a she, not a he."

"Even better."

"Funny. What if she doesn't like me?"

"She will."

"Oh, God. What if I don't like her?"

"Would you stop with the panicking already? It's all good. Everything will be fine. Just relax and do your job. She's going to love you."

Kylie sighed. "Okay, okay. You're right. Listen, I've got to go. I need some strong black coffee to calm my nerves."

"Your logic is bizarre, Ky."

"It's one of the many reasons you love me. Hey, wait. Who was the date Saturday night? UPS Girl?"

"Nope. Post Office Chick."

"You're a dog."

"I wasn't the one doing the howling, babe."

Kylie couldn't help but laugh. "Ugh. You disgust me. Do you know that?"

"It's one of the many reasons you love me."

Kylie snapped her phone shut, still grinning, and turned toward the mirror. She tucked her dark blond hair behind her ears and neatened her eyeliner with her finger. She took a deep breath and let it out slowly, hoping to relax at least a little. Then she smoothed her hands over her hips, willing away the wrinkles in her navy blue skirt.

Next to her, the brunette snapped her purse shut. As she passed Kylie, she smiled, her dark eyes sparkling. "Have a great day," she said in a voice that was so deep and husky, it made Kylie raise her eyebrows in surprise.

"Thanks. You, too." As the door shut, she muttered to herself, "Wow. That was fun to look at."

She spent another ten minutes in the bathroom emptying her nervous bladder, fixing, reapplying, and adjusting her make-up, and fussing with her hair. The level of her anxiety was disconcerting and she had to give herself a little pep talk before taking a final, cleansing breath and heading back to her cubicle.

She stopped dead in her tracks and stared when she saw the steaming cup of black coffee perched on her desk. Turning slowly, she looked toward the office opposite her area and saw the brunette from the ladies' room unpacking her briefcase behind the large mahogany desk Kylie herself had dusted earlier that morning.

Crap. Picking up the coffee cup, she took a too-large sip, hoping to bolster her nerves, but only succeeding in burning the roof of her mouth. *Time to face the music, O'Brien.*

She crossed the hall and rapped her knuckles lightly on the door frame. "Morning," she said.

The brunette looked up and smiled. "Hi there." Her eyes pointed at the cup. "Strong enough for you?"

Kylie felt a blush rise in her cheeks as the sensual timbre of the woman's voice hit her low in her belly. "It's perfect. Thank you."

The brunette held out her hand over the enormous desk. "Gretchen Kaiser."

Kylie stepped toward her and placed her hand firmly in that of her new boss. "Kylie O'Brien." Despite her smaller hand, Gretchen's grip was a combination of softness and power. Kylie hoped hers gave the same impression.

"Not Irish at all, are you, Kylie O'Brien?"

"Maybe just a touch." Kylie smiled, still too unsure to be charmed by the easy banter and still tingling from the zap of embarrassment knowing Gretchen had heard her voice all her fears and worries in the bathroom.

"It's nice to meet you."

"Same here."

"They tell me you're my right hand, that I can rely on you to keep this department running smoothly."

"I've been here a long time. I know this company very well."

"Good. Being the new kid on the block, I'm going to count on you for your expertise. You okay with that?"

"Absolutely."

"Excellent. The first thing we need to do is to set up a meeting of all my sales reps."

"All of them or just the ones here in Rochester?"

"Rochester, Syracuse, Buffalo, Albany, and anywhere in between. I want them to see my face so they can picture who's screaming at them through the phone when their numbers are down."

Kylie winced inwardly at the thought of the reps being yelled at. Jim had been a gentle manager, and verbally berating his people would never have crossed his mind.

Gretchen interrupted her thought process. "Make it a mandatory meeting. Next Wednesday. If anybody can't make it, I want them to talk to me directly about it."

"Okay. I'll get on it today."

"Can you contact the shipping department as well and find out if my boxes have arrived? I had some things sent from my old apartment, but I don't see them here."

"Got it."

Gretchen stopped unpacking and blinked at her. "Do you need to get a pad or something to write on?"

"No." Kylie held her gaze. After a couple of seconds, she tapped her temple with a fingertip. "I've got it."

Gretchen looked skeptical, but nodded and continued with her task. "Okay."

❖

The morning passed so quickly for Gretchen that she began to wonder if maybe she'd fallen through a hole in the space-time continuum and lost several hours. Her office was looking livable and she could find almost everything she'd unpacked. Still awaiting her boxes from Poughkeepsie, she'd headed off to a meeting with J. Edward Emerson himself, along with several of the VPs and three other regional sales managers who'd flown in to welcome her aboard.

She was sure she'd shaken the hands of at least a dozen new people since she'd arrived that morning, and she hoped against hope that she could actually remember their names...not that it mattered. She would probably only see them once a year or so at the company stockholders' meeting. These meet-and-greet type things were a nice gesture, but she was more annoyed than anything else. There was a ton of work to be done and she felt like she was wasting time shaking hands with everybody and their brother.

Deciding to stop by her office before she met her immediate superior for lunch, she heard Kylie answering the phone and was impressed with the professionalism in her voice.

"Gretchen Kaiser's office, this is Kylie. May I help you?"

Though it was ridiculous to pass judgment after only a few hours, she had a good feeling about the competency of her EAA. *And I have my own personal eye candy*, she thought with a devilish grin.

Kylie was quite a traffic stopper with her all-American good looks. Her dark blond hair was cut simply, just skimming her shoulders, and her build was most definitely feminine, but held a hint of athleticism. Gretchen wondered absently if she played any sports, remembering the creamy expanse of muscled calf that peeked out from under the conservative skirt. *Treadmill*, she thought. *I'll bet she's on the treadmill every day*. Sighing, she made a mental note to stop by the gym she'd noticed near her apartment before the week was out.

She waved at Kylie and entered her office to grab her purse, noting with disappointment that her boxes from downstate had yet to arrive.

"Kylie, were you able to get ahold of shipping?" she tossed over her shoulder as she bent to open her bottom drawer. When she stood back up, Kylie was standing in front of her desk not two feet away.

"I've got a call in. They haven't seen them yet."

"Jesus." Gretchen pressed a hand to her chest, trying to recover from Kylie's silent appearance. "You scared me."

Kylie smiled. "Sorry. Jim always said I moved like a cat. Would you rather I stomp in?"

"It might save me a heart attack or two."

"Do you have your paperwork from when you shipped the stuff? I can trace it and find out where it is."

"Good idea." Gretchen pulled the papers from her bag, handing them to Kylie as she headed for the door. "Thanks."

"Lunch with Margo Wheeler now?"

"Yeah." Gretchen lowered her voice and asked, "Do they really call her Hell on Wheeler around here?"

Kylie laughed outright, surprised that Gretchen had heard the nickname already. "I'm afraid so."

"For good reason?"

"I'm afraid so."

Gretchen nodded. "You know, I am hoping to be able to actually *sit* at my desk before this week is over. Really. I swear."

"Such is the life of a big corporate executive. Do what you've got to do. I've got everything under control here."

Gretchen stopped in the doorway and turned to look at Kylie. She was surprised that she hadn't noticed how blue Kylie's eyes were. The thought that she and Kylie were both the same height as long as Gretchen had heels on zipped through her brain for no reason at all. *Note to self: always wear the heels.*

Aloud, she said, "That's good to know. You've got my cell number, right?"

"Got it. Enjoy lunch."

"I'll try."

❖

Okay, these people need to leave me the hell alone. Anytime soon would be good. Gretchen's head was so full, she was surprised it hadn't just exploded by now, leaving her brains in colorful splashes all over the walls of one of the posh conference rooms of Emerson, Inc. She considered herself a rock, able to withstand enormous amounts of pressure without cracking—she certainly hadn't got where she was by being a shrinking violet. But the stress and anxiety of the job change, the move, the new city, the new coworkers, and the seven hundred meetings she'd taken part in were conspiring to turn her into a raving lunatic.

A very large part of her wanted to shriek at all of upper management to get the hell out of her face so she could do her damn job already. She knew she needed to have time to sit at her desk and go over the files of her sales reps or she'd be woefully unprepared for her first meeting with her new subordinates. That was not the way to instill confidence and respect. Despite the fact that it was only Monday, she already knew a weekend of working from home was in her very near future. Not that that was anything new to her.

She was relieved to note that she'd just completed the last of her meet-and-greets of the day. "Thank God," she muttered.

It was after four, but she was now free to take a deep breath and sit at her desk for a while…hopefully undisturbed. There was so much to do. She touched Kylie on the shoulder as she passed; the EAA was on the phone and looked up at Gretchen with a smile and a small wave. She found herself feeling a twinge of jealousy that her assistant seemed fresh, energetic, and unfazed by the day.

With a heavy sigh, she dropped into her leather chair but resisted the urge to slide down into a comfortable slump. It was still business hours, her office had windows, and the last thing she wanted was for anybody in the company to think the hectic schedule had gotten to her on her first day. A quick glance around the room told her that her boxes still had not arrived. She growled under her breath. Having some of her personal office items would go a long way in helping her to settle in.

"Kylie?" she called. "Any news on my stuff?"

After a brief silence, the phone on her desk beeped. "You know," her EAA's voice dulcetly confided, "this thing on your desk is called a phone and it actually has an intercom that you can use to call me."

Gretchen laughed before she could catch herself. "Are you saying you don't like me hollering to you from in here?"

"I'm not saying that at all." The playful grin was apparent in Kylie's voice. "I'm just sharing information."

"I appreciate that. Any information to share on my boxes?"

"According to UPS, three boxes were delivered here on Thursday."

"Thursday? Then where the hell are they?"

"That's the big question. I've got a call in to the shipping department right now. They're looking."

"God damn it."

Gretchen rang off the intercom and rifled through her drawers until she came up with the Emerson Company Directory. She had experience dealing with more than one shipping department in more than one corporation and was inclined to believe that more often than not, they were staffed by idiots. She flipped through the directory until she found what she was looking for. *Shipping Manager: Michelle Ramsey.*

"Okay, Ms. Ramsey," she muttered as she dialed. "Where the hell is my shit?"

The phone was picked up after the second ring. "Shipping."

"Michelle Ramsey, please."

"Hang on. I'll see if she's still here." The phone was muffled and Gretchen could hear muted voices. Then it was picked up again.

"Ramsey." The woman's voice was strong, confident.

"Ms. Ramsey, this is Gretchen Kaiser up on the fourth floor." Gretchen kept her voice stern, making it very apparent who the boss in this conversation was. "I had some boxes shipped here from downstate and UPS says they were delivered on Thursday. It's Monday and I have yet to see them. Can you help me with that?"

"I believe your EAA has already called about them, am I right?" Michelle's tone was just as tight as Gretchen's.

"You are. Unfortunately, your department hasn't given her any answers and I'd like to get some. Now, please."

There was a slight pause. Then Michelle Ramsey spoke, her voice coated with artificial sweetener. "Well, Ms. Kaiser, I believe it was noted that your boxes were of a...*personal* nature. Therefore, they were set aside last week to get them out of the way, as we had a large shipment of *business* equipment delivered on the same day. Since shipments related to *business* are what my people are paid to handle, I had to prioritize. I'm sure you can understand."

Gretchen ground her teeth at the patronizing tone. She spoke slowly, as if dealing with a small child. "That was *three days* ago, Ms.

Ramsey. One day, I can deal with. Two days begins to piss me off. But three days teeters on the edge of incompetence. Do you think you could have one of your people get them up here before I retire?"

There was enough of a pause this time to let Gretchen know that Michelle Ramsey might also be grinding her teeth, and she felt a tingle of satisfaction at the knowledge. "I'm very sorry, but my people are off the clock at four."

Gretchen let out a slow, annoyed breath. "I see my department isn't the only one that needs cleaning up. I can be sure to mention that to Margo Wheeler during our next meeting."

There was another short silence. This time, it was blatant that Michelle wanted to come through the phone at her. Her voice was clipped and dripping with feigned cheerfulness. "Not to worry, Ms. Kaiser. I'd be happy to bring your boxes up myself."

"I'll expect to see them before I leave today." She hung up the phone without another word, shocked that the handset wasn't frozen over with ice. Turning to her computer and the usual overflow of e-mail, she muttered, "Fuck with me, will you? Bitch."

Nearly an hour went by before there was a hesitant rap on her door frame. The office had quieted considerably once five had come and gone, and the knock seemed offensively loud. Gretchen looked up to see Kylie in the doorway.

"Sorry to interrupt." She seemed a little uncomfortable. "Your boxes are here."

"It's about goddamn time." Gretchen stood up as the end of a box on a handcart was wheeled into view, followed by the other two boxes stacked on top of it, followed by Michelle Ramsey, who was pushing it all.

Oh, shit.

Gretchen was momentarily speechless and wondered if the shipping manager felt the same way.

Kylie looked from one woman to the other and back, obviously confused by the discomfort in the room and assuming it had to do with the shipment. "Um…Gretchen Kaiser, this is Mick Ramsey. She runs our shipping and receiving department. Mick, Gretchen is our new regional sales manager."

"Oh," Mick said hesitantly, smiling with recognition. "*You're* the new RSM."

Gretchen recovered quickly and cleared her throat. "Right there in the corner is fine." She kept her voice cool, determined to remain on top despite the fact that Mick's presence took up so much of the room.

She swallowed when she saw Mick's smile dim several watts and her green eyes harden. Pulling her own eyes away, Gretchen sat down and went back to working on her computer, effectively dismissing both Mick and Kylie. When she heard the wheels on the handcart squeak away down the hall, she let out a quietly relieved breath. Several minutes went by before a small cough called her attention away from her monitor. She snapped her head around to find Kylie still standing in her office.

Gretchen raised an aggravated eyebrow. "Yes?"

"Um…do you need anything else from me before I pack up for the night?"

Gretchen glanced at the clock in the corner of her computer monitor. It was going on six. "No. You go on home." She went back to reading her e-mail.

Kylie hesitated. "Are you all right?"

"I'm fine." She didn't look up from her work. "I'll see you in the morning."

"Okay. Have a good night."

Gretchen heard Kylie getting her things together, the sound of her footsteps clicking down the hall. She inhaled with effort, and exhaled slowly. *One day*, she thought. *I've been here for exactly one day and I've already had to wear my bitch hat. That's got to be a record.*

CHAPTER THREE

S o that's how it's going to be, huh? Goddamn fucking bitch."
Mick couldn't remember the last time she'd been so pissed off. Or so disappointed. The Gretchen she'd met at the Widow on Saturday and the Gretchen she'd met on the fourth floor half an hour ago certainly looked like the same person, but wow…if she didn't know better, she'd think the woman had a split personality.

"Goddamn fucking bitch," she muttered again as she maneuvered her SUV along the expressway. The late April weather held hints of spring, but the lawns were brown and the roads were dirty, perfectly suiting Mick's mood. "Who the hell does she think she is?"

She picked up her cell phone and pushed two buttons, speed-dialing the same number she called daily, sometimes half a dozen times.

Kylie picked up after half a ring. "Hey."

"What the fuck is the matter with your new boss, Ky?"

Kylie sighed. "I don't know what to tell you, Mick. I don't know her yet."

"Well, Jesus Christ. Could she be more of a bitch?"

"I guess she just wanted her stuff."

Mick bit back a snide comment, not wanting to transfer her anger at Gretchen onto her best friend. "Then she shouldn't have shipped her personal shit to work, God damn it."

"I know."

"My responsibility is the stuff that directly affects Emerson."

"I know."

"Gretchen Fucking Kaiser's office trinkets do not fall into that category."

"I know."

"She didn't have to be such a bitch about it."

"I know."

"It's hard for me to stay on a rampage when all you keep saying is 'I know.'"

"I know."

Mick didn't want to smile, but she couldn't help it. Kylie was always able to defuse her anger just by letting her vent. It was one of the best aspects of their friendship: how well they knew one another.

Mick sighed. "She just really pissed me off."

"How come?"

"What do you mean, 'how come?' You were there."

"Yeah, but you've had people be less than courteous with you before and you usually don't give a crap. Why did Gretchen get under your skin so badly? She really just told you where to put the boxes. I mean, she could have been friendlier, but I've seen you treated worse than that and it didn't faze you."

Mick hesitated, surprised by the quick spurt of indignation she felt at Kylie defending Gretchen. She hadn't planned on telling Kylie about Saturday night; she was a firm believer in not outing people who were obviously trying to stay in the closet, whether or not she agreed with them. But she was not about to sit by and let Kylie think she'd overreacted.

"I went to the Widow Saturday night."

"Yeah. So?"

"So did your boss."

"What?" The disbelief was clear in Kylie's voice.

"You heard me. Apparently, it was her birthday, so we bought her a lot of drinks. And she doesn't drink the cheap stuff."

"Gretchen was at the Black Widow?"

"That's what I said. Don't let the panty hose and heels fool you. She's as gay as I am. She was inches from picking up Christy when I left."

"Wow. I'm...wow."

Mick felt annoyance prickling the back of her neck, so she honked at a minivan that cut in front of her. "Fucking soccer moms," she grumbled.

"I work for a lesbian?" Kylie asked.

"Apparently." Mick rolled her eyes at the awe in Kylie's tone.

"I've never worked for a lesbian before."

"Yeah, well she's a bitchy lesbian, so maybe it's not such a good thing."

"Come on, Mick. It was her first day. She was probably stressed out. She doesn't know yet how conservative the company might be so she's decided to keep quiet about her sexual preferences, and then you come strolling in. You, a person who knows what her sexual preferences are. And you, a person who works for the same company she does. She probably panicked, that's all."

"What the hell for?"

"Some people don't like their sexuality to be common knowledge. Not everybody wants it broadcast all over the place. Some people keep that stuff private."

"Which is just ridiculous."

Kylie tried to keep her sigh silent, but was sure Mick picked up on it. They'd had this same discussion countless times.

"It's ridiculous to you." Kylie sounded a little defensive. "But not everybody is as comfortable in their own skin as you are."

Kylie herself wasn't completely out at work. Mick didn't consider her closeted, but she wasn't terribly free with the information, as Mick was. She often told Mick she wished she had half the courage Mick did when it came to the subject.

"Maybe so. I still don't like her."

Kylie let out a frustrated breath, a sign that she knew she wasn't changing Mick's mind anytime soon. "Okay."

Mick mentally gave herself a point and decided to change the subject. They'd talk about it another day, she knew. "What's for dinner?"

If Kylie was startled by the shifting of gears, she didn't sound it. "I think my mom's making stew tonight. I'm going to go over there for a bit. Want to come?"

Mick knew the truth. Kylie didn't want to stay home much these days…not since she'd lost Rip, her beloved Australian Shepherd. He'd been gone for nearly a month, but Kylie still struggled. Mick wished there was something she could do for her friend, and truthfully, she wanted nothing more than to join Kylie at her mother's for dinner, but she was still smarting over the events of the afternoon.

"Nah. I need to get to the gym."

"Oh, come on. Your muscles can take one day off, can't they?"

"Yeah, they can, but there's a new aerobics instructor I've been meaning to chat up."

"And by 'chat up,' you mean 'feel up.'"

"That, too."

"You're a pig." Kylie laughed.

"Tell that gorgeous mother of yours I said hello."

"I will. She'll be sorry she missed you."

"Hey, when do you want to do your kitchen floor?"

"Maybe next weekend. Let me see what I've got going on."

"Let me know. I'll catch you later, Ky."

They disconnected just as Mick pulled into her own driveway. She grabbed the mail out of the mailbox and headed straight to the refrigerator. Popping open a beer, she sifted through the pile of junk and bills, willing her anger to relinquish its hold on her psyche. She flopped onto the couch, snatched up the remote, and tuned the TV to a rerun of *Friends*, forcing thoughts of Gretchen Kaiser and her condescending expression out of her mind.

Instead, she thought about Kylie. Mick was already looking forward to next weekend.

❖

Gretchen is a lesbian.

Kylie shook her head, smiling, not sure why she had such a hard time absorbing the fact. Maybe it was simply the way it would have changed how she'd looked at Gretchen in the bathroom that morning. It was one thing to look at an attractive woman and appreciate her appearance while assuming she was straight. It was quite another to look at her and *know* she might somehow be attainable. Not that Kylie would ever make a move like that…and certainly not on her boss. She'd never picked up a stranger based solely on her looks, but she knew it was done—Mick did it all the time.

Kylie's mind tossed her a quick visual. Her, pushing Gretchen against the wall of the bathroom, pressing their lips together in a blistering kiss while plunging her hands beneath the black suit jacket, searching for treasures inside and trying her best to rumple that calm, cool exterior.

"Jesus, O'Brien, cut it out," she mumbled to herself as she pulled into her parents' driveway. Shaking her head, she strolled into the garage and reached for the door to the kitchen. There, she paused and whined softly, "I need to get laid."

The O'Brien kitchen smelled divine, as usual. Freshly baking rolls wafted the scents of home through the air and Kylie breathed deeply the aroma of her childhood. The kitchen was a cheery yellow even in the approaching twilight. Knickknacks and plants took up every open space. She often marveled at how the room seemed smaller now than it had when she was a kid; funny how that happened.

"Mom?" she called as she stopped and lifted the lid off the enormous pot simmering on the stove. Using the giant spoon dripping onto the spoon rest, she scooped up a small amount of the stew and blew on it. She tasted a small dab, letting the flavors of beef and vegetables coat her tongue. She closed her eyes, loving the memories such tastes and smells could generate for her.

"What do you think?" Caroline O'Brien bustled into the room just as she bustled everywhere, a dishtowel draped over her right shoulder. Her hair had once been a lush blond, but was now more of a brassy blond from a bottle since she refused to go gray. It curled gently just over her shoulders, skimming the neckline of her light blue sweater. She still somehow looked shapely in jeans, and her ever-present slip-ons were starting to look worn.

Kylie made a mental note to get her a new pair for Mother's Day. Caroline was smaller than Kylie, but it was easy to tell how attractive she'd been in her twenties. She still was, even in her sixties. The two of them shared the same startlingly blue eyes; Kylie was the only child who'd inherited them.

"Maybe a touch more salt." Kylie removed her jacket and tossed it over a chair.

Caroline smacked her daughter playfully with the towel. "You always say that. And hang that jacket in the closet, please."

"Everything needs more salt, Mom." Kylie did as she was told, feeling twelve again.

Caroline shook some more salt into the pan. "If your father says this is too salty, I'm blaming you."

"Yeah, but I can just use my little-girl voice and call him Daddy and he'll let me off the hook."

"It's always worked for you in the past."

The playful banter was something Kylie cherished about her relationship with her mother. It hadn't come easily. As the youngest of four children, Kylie didn't get as much attention as the older siblings... there were just too many chores to be done and things to handle. She had learned to take whatever time she could get from her mother. But when she'd finally accepted her own sexuality, as a junior in college, she worried immensely about telling her parents. She was sure it would be the final hammer blow on the wedge that seemed to keep her from being friends with her mother. Instead, the admission had brought them together.

"I love you no matter what, Kylie Jane," Caroline had said with tears in her eyes. *"And I love you even more for trusting me enough to tell me."*

It had been the beginning of their adult relationship.

"When are we going out to dinner again?" Caroline asked. They had a standing monthly dinner date, just the two of them, but they'd missed last month's. "I need some adult time soon."

"You need a break from being Grandma?"

"I do." Caroline stirred the stew absently. "I love my grandkids and I don't mind babysitting at all, but there are days I just want to have a glass of wine at a nice restaurant and talk to adults. Or at least people without headphones on." She glared at Kylie with a mock-threatening expression. "And if you breathe a word of that to your sister or brother, I'll beat you with this spoon."

Kylie laughed. "It'll be our little secret. And we'll do dinner next week. I'm not sure how many free evenings I'll have this week."

"Oh, that's right. I forgot. How's the new boss?"

Kylie began setting the kitchen table for three. "I'm not really sure yet. She seems to know her stuff."

"That's a plus. Is she nice?"

"Hard to say. She was nice to me, but she wasn't in the office much—she had a bunch of meetings with upper management to introduce herself around, so I only got a small taste. I'm just going to have to give her some time before I have a solid opinion."

"Well, it's always hard after you've had a boss you liked. But I'm sure things will settle down before you know it."

"Yeah, you're probably right. She seems ready to crack down on those who aren't pulling their weight, though, so I know some of the salespeople are going to hate her. But that's what a sales manager does, right? Manages?" Kylie retrieved silverware from the drawer. "She and Mick had a little problem."

"About what?" Caroline glanced up from the bowls she was filling.

Kylie smiled. Her mother had a soft spot for Mick and treated her like one of her own children. It had been that way since high school. Mick's home life had been less than cozy and she'd spent a lot of time in the O'Brien household, always loving and respectful of Kylie's parents. To this day, Mick still thought of them like they were her true mother and father.

"It was just a shipping miscommunication, but they've sort of gotten off on the wrong foot." For some reason, Kylie felt the need to defend Gretchen, despite the coolness she'd displayed when Kylie left for the day. She knew if she told the story of the boxes in Mick's words, her mother would immediately side with Mick and be wary of Gretchen, and somehow that bothered her. "I'm sure they'll clear it up, though."

They worked quietly for several minutes before Caroline spoke again. "Can you believe it's almost May already?" She was staring out the kitchen window at the beginnings of green in her back yard, no doubt imagining which flowers would go where in the next month.

"Incredible." Kylie put the basket of rolls on the table and got the milk out of the fridge. "Almost time for the annual O'Brien Memorial Day cookout."

Caroline looked shocked. "My God, you're right."

"Mom. It's over a month away. Don't panic yet."

Caroline was already rifling through the junk drawer for a pad of paper. "I can at least start making my list," she muttered, more to herself than to Kylie.

Kylie rolled her eyes, chuckling as she poured the drinks. "Relax, Mom. Everything will come together beautifully. It always does." She kissed her mother on the cheek while directing her toward the table. "Sit. I'll get Dad."

Chapter Four

K ylie! Kylie, come sit with us."
Damn it. Kylie closed her eyes when she heard the voice shouted from behind her. It was Jason Bergman; she'd recognize his baritone anywhere. She also knew what was coming. She'd known it fifteen minutes into the morning-long sales meeting.

She continued through the cafeteria line, put a chicken salad and a Coke on her tray, paid at the register, then turned to locate Jason. Her stomach flip-flopped when she found him, along with the six other sales reps sitting at his table. Behind them was a second table of eight. On the other side, another. Every set of eyes was fixed expectantly on her and Kylie just knew the entire team had been awaiting her arrival so they could pounce.

"Here we go," she mumbled, heading toward them.

The sales reps were dressed in their business best…suits and ties for the men, skirts and jackets or dresses for the women, though Sarah Stevenson was wearing a navy blue pantsuit that looked expensively fantastic on her. The group appeared successful, but according to Gretchen that wasn't what their numbers were reflecting.

"What the hell, Kylie?" Jason spoke up for the gang the second Kylie sat down, leaning forward slightly to emphasize his words. "Where the hell did the Cruella De Vil type come from? And who shit in her corn flakes?"

Kylie popped open her Coke while trying to figure out how to handle this situation. The sales reps relied on her. She was their point of contact and they trusted her to get them what they needed. Gretchen had been extremely hard on them, criticizing their low sales figures and browbeating them about improvements for nearly four hours.

"I'm not sure what to tell you, Jay. She's tough."

"Tough?" Sarah piped in, popping a potato chip into her mouth. "She's nasty."

Kylie rubbed at her forehead, feeling the beginnings of a headache coming on. "I think she's just trying to ruffle your feathers to help increase your sales."

Jeff Carson was to Kylie's immediate left and he snorted at her comment. "Oh, she did some ruffling, all right. Telling me my profit margins were a joke in front of the entire region certainly ruffled me. Jesus. Tactless much?"

"And didn't she tell Roxy to get her ass out of her chair once in a while?" Jason clarified to emphatic nods and murmurs.

Kylie winced inwardly. That had been a particularly bad one. Not that Gretchen hadn't been right. Roxy was far too comfortable with e-mail and didn't visit her clients nearly as often as she should, and her numbers supported those facts. But Roxy was sweet and kind and soft-spoken, and Gretchen had made an example of the poor girl. It hadn't been pretty.

"I think she's still in the bathroom fixing her mascara." Sarah shook her head. "Jim would never have treated us like this, Kylie. You know that."

Kylie nodded. It was the truth.

"We're not children," Jason stated matter-of-factly. "We don't need to be scolded like that, and certainly not in front of an entire room of reps. I didn't appreciate being told that my numbers suck."

Kylie pressed her lips together tightly. Those had been Gretchen's exact words, and she was right. Jason was the most demanding of the reps, calling Kylie two or three times a day needing one thing or another, so she'd felt a small tingle of satisfaction over Gretchen shredding him the way she had. Now, she wanted to grin at his indignation. She managed to keep a straight face.

"Can't you do something?" Jeff asked.

And there it was, the request she'd known had been coming. These reps depended on her for everything. She was their most solid link to the company; she was like their mother. Of course they'd ask for her help.

She chose her words carefully. "I'm not sure what I can do, guys. She's the boss."

"You need to tell her that we're the top-selling region on the East Coast," Jason said, determination and anger coloring his gaze. "Doesn't she know that? We make a lot of money for this company. Tell her *that*."

Jason was right, but it didn't make him sound any less obnoxious. Kylie kept her eyes on her uneaten food.

"Can't you just talk to her?" Sarah's voice was softer, less demanding. Sarah's blond hair, light blue eyes, and knockout figure served her well in the sales field. They also served her well with Kylie. This time was no exception, as she held Kylie's gaze and sweetly urged, "Please. Just ask her to ease up a bit."

Kylie couldn't help but relent. "I'll try," she answered with a sigh, and murmurs of relief could be heard coming from all three tables. Kylie had forgotten that the occupants of the other two were probably tuned in to the conversation. "But no promises. Remember, she's new to me, too, and I have to see her every day. You guys don't."

"Sucks to be you," somebody commented and Kylie pretended not to hear.

"But you'll talk to her," Jason confirmed.

"I'll talk to her." Kylie looked at her chicken salad, suddenly finding she had no appetite. She sipped her Coke and noted with worry that all three tables were extremely quiet, a very unusual thing for a group of salespeople who liked nothing better than to chatter on endlessly.

Gretchen had certainly done a number on them.

❖

It was nearly six thirty when Kylie glanced at the doghouse-shaped clock on her desk. "Jesus," she muttered. She hadn't noticed the office quieting down or the phones becoming silent.

In the distance, she could hear a vacuum cleaner running—the cleaning staff tidying the conference room. She blinked and rubbed at her tired eyes, thinking not for the first time that she might need to get glasses as a result of all the time she spent staring at the computer monitor. Glancing over her shoulder, through the hallway windows into Gretchen's office, she could see Gretchen staring at *her* computer.

Kylie wasn't surprised. They definitely seemed to be of like minds when it came to working hours. She was already familiar with the routines of her new boss after only a week and a half working with her, and she was beginning to wonder if Gretchen ever did anything besides work. The majority of the time, she was in her office when Kylie arrived in the morning and still in her office when she went home at night. Taking in the dark hair, dark eyes, and alabaster skin seemingly untouched by the sun, Kylie smirked. *Maybe she's a vampire.*

She'd spent much of the afternoon trying to decide when the best time would be to talk to Gretchen about the sales reps. They had yet to go over yesterday's meeting and Kylie had fielded about a dozen phone calls from Jason Bergman alone, angling to hear how Gretchen had responded to the message Kylie was supposed to pass along. Kylie had some choice words on her tongue for the man, but managed to keep them safely locked in her brain for the time being. Pissing off their top sales rep probably wasn't a smart career move. Jason might be arrogant and self-centered, but he also took care of some very large accounts; that fact gave him power.

Talking to Gretchen about the reps' opinion of her methods wasn't a conversation Kylie was looking forward to, but only because she didn't know Gretchen well yet. She and Jim used to have such discussions quite often. Jim had relied on her to keep him abreast of numbers, new clients, potential clients, and profits. They'd had many talks over lunch about which reps brought in the most money, who needed to work a bit harder, and so on. Talking to Gretchen about such things should be no big deal. It was part of Kylie's job, after all. And once they got into the subject, Kylie's plan was to slip in a comment or two about maybe going a little easier on the crew in the future. No big deal.

She jumped when she heard Gretchen's voice cut through the quiet of the office. "Kylie, can I talk to you for a minute, please?"

"Be right there." Kylie closed the open application on her desktop and grabbed a pad and a pen. She'd realized that, though she didn't really need to jot notes during their meetings, it made Gretchen feel better if she pretended. She headed in.

Kylie had noticed, over the past few days, that Gretchen's office had begun to fill up. The bookshelves were lined with sales report binders and several books on sales managing and sales in general. There were also several awards from the various companies she'd worked for. Kylie had snuck a peek one day last week while Gretchen was out.

One trophy and three crystal awards were engraved with *Sales Rep of the Year*. Three plaques reported *Highest Percentage over Quota*. Five different pieces read *District Sales Manager of the Year*. The twelve decorations were from three companies. The woman apparently knew her stuff when it came to sales. It seemed that Gretchen was a phenomenal success wherever she happened to be working. Kylie found herself hugely impressed and unexpectedly proud to be working for someone who was such an asset to any company.

One odd discovery Kylie had made during her covert perusal of her boss's décor had been the two framed photos on Gretchen's desk. They seemed to be the only personal items in the entire room and both faced Gretchen's chair, as if they were not meant for public consumption. Kylie had had to walk around behind the desk to see them.

One was an older picture of a family of four: a man and a woman in their fifties or sixties, the man's dark eyes and chiseled jaw line telling Kylie he could be none other than Gretchen's father, along with a tightly smiling Gretchen and a younger man Kylie assumed was her brother. In the other picture a much more relaxed version of Gretchen was with a smiling, handsome man of about fifty. Both were wearing sombreros and holding up large margaritas in salute toward the camera. Gretchen's cheeks were rosy and there was a sparkle in her eyes; she looked like she was laughing out loud. Kylie was struck by the contrast between the two photos. Gretchen could have been two different people, one the boss Kylie saw every day, and the other a more playful and vibrant woman. Kylie liked that there might actually be more to her new boss than seriousness and concentration.

Yet again rehearsing what she was planning to say about the sales reps, she took a seat in one of the maroon fabric-covered chairs in front of Gretchen's enormous mahogany desk, perched her pad on her knee, and waited for Gretchen to finish typing whatever it was she was working on. Charts, graphs, and computer reports were strewn all over the desk's surface. A long-cold mug of coffee sat on a leather coaster near the keyboard.

Gretchen's brow furrowed with concentration as she switched from her computer keyboard to a large adding machine, then back, her lips pursing and un-pursing as she thought about her task. Kylie watched Gretchen's hands as she typed, admiring them. They were small and feminine, but looked strong, like Gretchen could go from typing or applying make-up to climbing a ladder or swinging a hammer without missing a beat. She'd taken off her black suit jacket and tossed it over the back of her chair, the red short-sleeved shell giving Kylie her first view of Gretchen's bare arms. Her smooth, porcelain skin looked impossibly soft, and Kylie was embarrassed to realize she wanted to touch it, to test its softness with her fingertips. She swallowed and quickly looked down at her pad as Gretchen finished what she was doing.

"So. I noticed you had lunch with the reps yesterday." Gretchen leaned her forearms on the desk and focused serious eyes on Kylie.

Kylie nodded, wondering when Gretchen had seen the group of them. "They had a few tables in the cafeteria and asked me to join them."

"I don't suppose they were happy about the meeting."

"Um, no."

"And how many calls have you gotten from them today?"

At that, Kylie chuckled. "A few."

"They're going to try to get you 'on their side,' you know." She made quotation marks in the air with her fingers. "They think I'm the Snow Queen or something."

Kylie pressed her lips together and nodded again. *Actually, it was Cruella De Vil.* The woman obviously knew what kind of reputation she conveyed. Kylie made no comment.

Gretchen laced her fingers together and leaned her chin on them, studying Kylie for several long seconds. Arching one eyebrow, she stated simply, "You think I was too hard on them."

A dozen responses leapt into Kylie's mind and she opened her mouth to speak in her own defense. Something in Gretchen's gaze wouldn't allow her to settle on anything but the truth, however. She let out a breath. "Yeah. I do."

"How so?"

"What do you mean?"

"How was I too hard on them?"

Kylie squirmed slightly in her chair, feeling like a deer caught in the headlights. "I...maybe..." She had no idea how to phrase what she wanted to say without sounding completely out of line, and she felt some resentment begin to bubble at being put on the spot. She stammered instead, "Um..."

Gretchen sighed. "Just spit it out. It's not rocket science. What would you have done differently?"

"I think…" Kylie cleared her throat. "I think you could have been a little nicer."

Gretchen seemed to absorb the statement and nodded slowly. "A little nicer."

"Yes."

"Interesting." Gretchen continued to nod, but her gaze hardened. "First of all, I'm not here to be nice. If a few blunt words are all it takes to make Roxy cry, she needs to grow some thicker skin." Gretchen sat back in her chair and folded her arms. "Second, their numbers are way down and they all need to get their shit together. This isn't high school. It's the real world and they need to start acting like grown-ups."

Kylie felt herself becoming defensive and didn't like it. After all, she'd worked with these people a lot longer than Gretchen had. "You don't even know them. They're the best sales team on the east side of the country, Gretchen. They're good salespeople."

She knew she might have crossed a line when she saw Gretchen's eyes flash. "Are they?" Gretchen asked. "Have you seen this report?" She tossed one of the computer printouts in Kylie's direction.

Kylie tried to backpedal a bit. "Look, I don't mean to step on your toes or anything. I'm just not sure I agree with how you handled things yesterday. This group is just used to…" She grasped for the right words.

"Jim. They're used to Jim."

"Yeah."

"He babied them, Kylie. He gave them no discipline, no goals."

Kylie felt her temperature rising at the slight against her old boss and fought to keep it down. Gretchen obviously didn't understand the point. "No. No, he didn't baby them. But he was gentler. They liked him. He was *nicer*." That last word sounded snide and it slipped out before she could catch it.

If Gretchen was fazed, she hid it well. "Well, I'm not Jim."

"I know that."

"Nice only goes so far in the corporate world." Gretchen pointed at the report again, which Kylie had yet to glimpse at. "Look at the bottom line, Kylie. This region is down nearly thirty-five percent from last year. And twenty percent from the year before."

Kylie blinked at the numbers. Thirty-five percent? That didn't sound right. Wouldn't Jim have told her if they were that far off?

"You haven't even seen that report, have you?" Gretchen asked as if reading Kylie's mind. Her voice registered a note of triumph. Apparently she'd suspected that Kylie wasn't privy to all the information. "Kylie." Her deep voice reverberated in the pit of Kylie's stomach, forcing her eyes up. Gretchen spoke carefully, but with granite resolve. "It was time for Jim to retire." She waited a couple minutes, let Kylie absorb the meaning of that statement, and then continued. "Those numbers? They're why I was hired…to get them back up. And they're why he was pushed out early."

Jim took a forced retirement? Kylie didn't want to believe that she'd been so completely out of the loop with a man she admired so much. She looked up into Gretchen's rich brown eyes and hoped to see them soften with understanding. They didn't. If anything, they seemed colder.

"I can't have my EAA second-guessing me. It's counterproductive and makes my job harder."

Kylie nodded, her face warming.

"Not to mention, it pisses me off."

"I'm sorry." Kylie's voice was tiny and she dropped her eyes. "It won't happen again."

"I'm aware that the reps don't like the way I spoke to them yesterday, but you know what?" Gretchen dipped her head so she could catch Kylie's eye again and bring her gaze back up. "I don't care. My job is to increase the bottom line. I'm not here to be their friend or yours. I don't really care if any of you like me. That's not my concern. Do you think Margo Wheeler cares whether Jason Bergman thinks I'm a bitch?"

Kylie shook her head.

"No. She cares what that number at the bottom of that report says. If it's too low, she hears about it. And you know what they say about shit rolling downhill. The next one down from her is me, and I happen to have a nice wardrobe. I don't like the idea of getting crap all over it."

Gretchen inhaled and let out her breath slowly, tilting her head to the side as she regarded Kylie. "Kylie, I think you're a great EAA. I'm really glad that I ended up with you as my assistant. You've made things easier already and I've been here less than two weeks. I know Jason can be a squeaky wheel, as can most salespeople, but you can't let him browbeat you. And, God damn it, if he's got an issue with me, you tell him to be a man and bring it to *me*. He may not like my methods.

You may not like my methods. But his opinion doesn't matter to me and frankly, neither does yours. My job is to increase the sales of this region. That's why I'm here and that's what I'm going to do. I'd rather have your help than have you working against me, but it's your choice." She paused for effect. "Am I making myself clear?"

Kylie swallowed, knowing her face was flaming hot and hating it. She nodded, feeling small.

"Good." Gretchen sat back again and waved Kylie off like a fly, ending the discussion. "Go home. Eat something and get some rest. We've got a lot to do tomorrow."

Kylie stood, clutching her pad to her chest, and beelined to her cubicle without looking back. She didn't want Gretchen to see the tears that, much to her dismay, had filled her eyes. Painfully embarrassed, she packed up in record time and walked down the hall and out the employee entrance, wanting only to get to her car as quickly as possible. She was determined not to cry and annoyed that it was even a possibility. All she wanted was to get home and hug Rip. He had always understood when she was frustrated, his loving blue eyes reflecting his unconditional love for her.

At the realization that he wouldn't be waiting, she stopped dead in her tracks in the middle of the nearly empty parking lot. Only then did a tear spill over and roll silently down her cheek.

CHAPTER FIVE

Gretchen sipped her Pinot Grigio and stared out the window of the restaurant at the people walking up and down Park Avenue. It certainly wasn't Manhattan, but as smaller cities went, it was nice. The population seemed fairly diverse. A young, obviously gay couple was followed a few feet back by a man and woman in their sixties, holding hands. Many people were walking dogs, anxious to get out into the much-awaited spring weather. Gretchen enjoyed the simple act of people-watching, sipping her wine in complete relaxation. It was a state she didn't reach often.

Activity on the street was beginning to pick up with the promise of summer. Just in the three weeks she'd lived in Rochester, Gretchen had already seen it. The number of people seemed a little higher; the shops seemed a little brighter and seemed to stay open a little later. It even smelled like summer was coming.

Taking note of the small outdoor tables, Gretchen decided that once May's evening chill left the air, she'd sit outside and dine. She glanced at her watch and noted with a smile that Pete was late, as usual. It had grated on her nerves when they were married, but now she just chalked it up as a Pete-ism and shrugged her indifference with an *oh, well, that's Pete* resignation. If you didn't expect to have to wait for Pete, you didn't know him very well.

They were meeting at six thirty. At precisely six fifty, Pete strolled through the front door. Gretchen waved at him. He exchanged smiling words with the hostess, then crossed the room and met Gretchen at her table, giving her a warm, tight hug as she stood to greet him. As her face brushed his shirt, the spicy aroma of his cologne hit her senses and she was swept momentarily into her past, remembering when their bathroom smelled of that same scent and how much she'd adored it. She'd purchased it for him every Christmas for the six years they were together.

"Right on time, as always," she teased.

"I just wanted you to be sure to get a glass of wine in you before I got here," he teased back as they sat. "God, it's good to see you. What's it been? Last summer? I can't believe you're here."

"Last summer at your cottage," Gretchen replied, feeling more content than she had in several days. She smiled, hoping to convey the warmth in her heart. "It's good to see you, too."

"I'm so happy that you moved up here. We're practically neighbors now." His blue eyes twinkled with excitement, making him appear much younger than his fifty years despite the gray at his temples.

"How's Allyson?" Gretchen asked, making eye contact with the waiter in order to get Pete a drink. He zipped over quickly and took the request.

"She's wonderful. She sends her love and says to find out when you can come over for dinner."

Gretchen laughed at the generosity of Pete's wife. "I've been here barely three weeks and I've already got a dinner invitation."

Pete narrowed his eyes at her in a mock threat. "Don't make her call you about it. Check your schedule and give her a date. She really wants to see you. She was annoyed that she couldn't make it tonight. I keep telling her you're fine, but you know how she is. She needs to see you with her own eyes."

Gretchen inclined her head, conceding his point as the waiter arrived to set down Pete's glass and take their orders. Much as she liked to be witty and snide, she considered Allyson off-limits. She was just too sweet and caring, and she treated Gretchen like a big sister. Gretchen was well aware of how lucky she was to have two caring friends like Pete and Allyson. Most people had trouble believing that she'd actually been married to Pete. They'd parted more than twenty years ago, but so much of their time together was burned lovingly into her brain that it sometimes seemed to have happened last week.

They'd met in college; he was a senior when she was a freshman. He graduated, but they continued as a couple all through Gretchen's education and married as soon as she graduated. He devotedly and stupidly overlooked several flings she'd had with women during her dorm-living years, interpreting these as part of a collegiate phase and insisting that marriage was the best way to cure such things. Theirs lasted for three years before he finally sat Gretchen down and told her she needed to face the fact that she was a lesbian.

She knew he was right, and that she was keeping him a prisoner by staying married to him. Their divorce was painful and they took over a year to lick their wounds, then they bumped into each other at a conference, had a drink, and had been best friends ever since. When Pete married Allyson the following year, Gretchen stood up as his "best man" in the wedding.

"So, where's your place?" Pete asked, sipping his Merlot.

"About two blocks from here and around the corner. It's great. Very roomy as apartments go, and I have my own tiny little balcony." Gretchen smiled at the realization of how much she liked her new abode.

"You should think about buying a house, you know. The market's hot and you can find a nice one in the city for the same size mortgage payment as your rent." He smirked as Gretchen sighed over their familiar conversation. "Or, hell. You make a nice wad of cash. Go out to the suburbs and buy something big."

"For who? Me and my plants? I don't need big."

Pete held his hands up, palms forward, feigning surrender. "Wouldn't want you to actually settle down anywhere."

"What? Pete, I haven't even been here a month. You want me to settle down already?"

"Well, I'd prefer you settle down *with* somebody, but I'll give you some time on that one."

Gretchen growled at him as the waiter arrived with their dinners, saving Pete from a sarcastic retort. He shook his head over the huge slab of beef on her plate.

"I've never seen any other woman devour red meat like a caveman the way you do. You'd think I'd be used to it by now." He laughed, then changed the subject completely. "How goes the job?"

Gretchen nodded, popping a piece of steak into her mouth. She closed her eyes for a second, savoring the taste of the seasonings and juices mingling on her tongue. "It's going well," she responded eventually. "I've had to do some ass-kicking—my sales force is in a bit of a slump—but overall, I really like the company. The benefits are great, upper management has been easy enough to deal with." She shrugged. "So far, so good."

"And you've got enough help?"

At Gretchen's last job, her support staff left much to be desired, and she'd often bent Pete's ear on the subject. "My help is great, this time." She filled Pete in on Kylie and what a competent, helpful assistant she'd been. "We did have a bit of a tiff last week, though I'm sure it'll be fine." Her tone was less confident than she'd intended and Pete instantly picked up on it.

"What happened?"

"She disagreed with my methods and made me aware that I'm being too hard on my sales staff—you know, the underperformers I mentioned."

Pete grimaced. "Oh, poor Kylie. I guess she's clear now about that being a big no-no. Poor girl."

"It was no big deal. I laid it out for her and she got it."

"What did you say? You didn't make her cry, did you?"

Gretchen gave him an indignant stare. "No, I didn't make her cry."

"You say that like it's never happened." Pete winked at her.

"Shut up." Gretchen sipped her wine. "I simply told her that salespeople don't like being told they're not doing well, and that it was natural for our team to try to get her to side with them against me. I said I wasn't there to make friends, and her opinion of my methods didn't matter, and that I needed her working with me and not against—" At Pete's aghast expression, she stopped and demanded, "What?"

"You told her that her opinion didn't matter?"

"It doesn't."

"But you *told* her that? To her face? Jesus, Gretch, way to make her feel valuable."

Anybody else would have gotten a sarcastic, angry retort. Pete was different...because he knew her so well and he was usually right.

Gretchen pushed her remaining vegetables around with her fork. "Too harsh?"

"I'd say yes, but that's just me. She didn't cry, so that's a plus."

"No. She just packed her stuff up and left. It was late."

"Uh-huh. When was this?"

"Thursday night."

"And how was she yesterday?"

Gretchen thought back to the previous day and her interactions with Kylie. Work had gone smoothly. Things had gotten done with no problems. Kylie's friendly, smiling face appeared in her mind, causing the corners of her own mouth to turn up slightly until it occurred to her that Kylie had barely smiled in her presence at all yesterday. She'd been very business-like. Very distant and cool. Very much like Gretchen.

"Crap," she muttered.

After several long seconds, Pete commented, "Interesting."

Gretchen's eyes snapped to his face. "What do you mean, 'interesting'?"

Pete pressed his lips together, obviously trying to decide how far to push her. "I mean, it's interesting that it's bothering you a little bit."

"What are you talking about?"

"You like her."

"What the hell is that supposed to mean?"

"Jesus, Gretch, relax. It's not a crime to like somebody. I'm just saying you seem to give a shit about what this woman thinks of you. That's unusual for the Gretchen Kaiser I've known for more than twenty years. That's all."

"She's nice," Gretchen said, shrugging.

"And you don't want her to think you're a complete bitch."

Gretchen sneered at Pete's feeble attempt to hide a grin. "Well, she already does, so it's kind of a moot point now."

"Uh-huh." There was a glimmer in Pete's blue eyes, but he let the subject drop.

❖

So far, Monday had been complete and utter chaos. The phone rang incessantly. Five times, it was Jason calling to pump Kylie for information. By the third call, she wanted to throttle him. Margo Wheeler was chomping at the bit to see Gretchen, who kept putting her off. With the new fiscal year beginning on the first of June, Wheeler needed budgets and sales projections in place. The tone of her voice said she was getting a little nervous. The way Gretchen dodged Wheeler told Kylie she was getting a little nervous, too.

Kylie avoided any attempt to be personal with Gretchen. After her dressing down on Thursday, she had sulked, cried, gotten angry, and then hardened her resolve. It was fine. If Gretchen didn't give a shit what she thought, Kylie didn't give a shit about knowing anything there was to know about Gretchen outside of work. So there.

But it was hard. Kylie was naturally inquisitive and genuinely friendly. She liked to talk to people, to learn about them, to debate with them and have in-depth discussions. She and Jim Sheridan used to talk well into the evening about politics and entertainment, and religion and philosophy. Often, Jim's wife would call his cell and only then would either of them look at the clock and realize they'd missed dinner. She would refer to Jim as a father figure if she didn't feel that was an insult to her own dad. So she thought of him as a favorite uncle instead.

She missed him.

That first day, when Gretchen left the coffee on Kylie's desk, Kylie was sure they'd be great friends. Gretchen had put up a wall, though. She apparently didn't want such a relationship with her EAA and she'd made that perfectly clear last week. *His opinion doesn't matter to me and, frankly, neither does yours…*

Kylie was annoyed by how much that sentence had stung her. After all, she barely knew Gretchen. Why should she care about what Gretchen thought of her? What did it matter? She sighed in frustration, looking at the clock and noting that it was going on seven already. The truth was, Gretchen's opinion did matter and she had no idea why. The thought that Gretchen might not like her, didn't think of her as a friend or even as a valued employee with good business sense, bothered the hell out of her.

Dismayed to feel the beginnings of emotion well up behind her eyes, she muttered, "Goddamn PMS," and pressed her fingers into her eyelids.

After a couple of sniffs, she took a deep breath, raked her fingers through her hair roughly, and squeezed her shoulders, hoping to work out some of the tension. She wanted to go home, have a glass of wine to allay the oncoming cramps, and be a pile on the couch. She glanced at the framed photos of Rip on her desk and smiled wistfully.

A softly clearing throat made her whip around in surprise. Gretchen stood in the cubicle opening. She didn't look the least bit stressed and

Kylie suspected that this kind of pace was what she lived for. Her black slacks hugged her hips intimately and the pink blouse was open at the throat, inviting the tiniest peek at a collarbone. Almost-black curls framed a face that showed a crooked and uncertain semi-smile.

"Hey," Gretchen said, and even that one word rumbled so low that Kylie felt it in the pit of her stomach.

"Hi."

"Busy day, huh?"

"Insane." Kylie worked hard to keep her business face in place, despite the fact that she wanted to ask Gretchen how she was holding up, how she liked Rochester, how she liked Emerson. But she knew Gretchen didn't want that, so she bit her bottom lip and remained silent while Gretchen shifted from one black pump to the other.

"Um…" Gretchen had a small, white paper bag in her hand. She held it out to Kylie. "I went out to dinner on Saturday and I had steak. I thought…" Her eyes pointed to the pictures of Rip on Kylie's desk. "I thought you might want the bone for your dog, so I saved it for you." She seemed embarrassed and looked out over the top of the cubicle while she waited for Kylie to take the bag.

If Kylie hadn't been premenstrual, she would have been able to accept the bag for what it was: a peace offering from a woman who rarely gave them. Instead, her eyes filled with tears. A horrified look appeared on Gretchen's face as big, fat drops rolled down Kylie's cheeks and she covered her mouth with her hand.

"Oh, my God," Gretchen said, her voice laced with confusion. "Oh, God, Kylie, what's wrong? I'm sorry. What did I say?"

Kylie made a snorting sound that could have been a sob or a laugh. When she glanced up at Gretchen, the poor woman looked like she was at a complete loss, an expression she never expected to see on the face of Gretchen Kaiser a.k.a. Cruella De Vil. Kylie's tears were free-flowing. She sniffed and grabbed Gretchen's wrist, worried that the panicked woman would flee in terror within the next few seconds, before she had a chance to explain herself. With her free hand, she snatched a tissue from the box on her desk and wiped her nose, then her eyes.

After a few minutes, when she felt like she could speak, she realized absently that she was still holding Gretchen's wrist. The skin was soft and warm in her hand…not at all cold and brittle like many might suspect. It was with regret that she let go and with great relief that she noted Gretchen didn't leave. She looked up into Gretchen's eyes, as dark as rich coffee, and saw worry there. Concern.

Surprised by the depth of emotion in them, she pointed to the picture on her desk and said softly, "That's Rip. I lost him four weeks ago. He was fifteen. I've had him since I was twenty-two. He was very old and weak and sick and I finally had to put him down. It was the hardest thing I've ever done." Her eyes welled once more and she cleared her throat to keep it from closing up.

"Oh, Kylie. I'm so sorry." Gretchen's voice was tender. She looked at the bag in her hand and embarrassment clearly registered on her face. "I'm so sorry. God, I'm an idiot."

"No," Kylie assured her. "No, not at all. I think it was sweet. It was a really nice gesture."

"Well, still. I'm really sorry. I feel terrible."

Kylie couldn't help herself; she laid her hand on Gretchen's bare wrist once more. "Really. It's okay. You had no way of knowing. Thank you for thinking of me."

"You're welcome." Gretchen licked her lips and glanced around the empty office. "You should go home. It's late."

"Tomorrow is another day, right?"

"Yes, it is. I'll see you in the morning."

"Okay."

Kylie watched Gretchen walk back to her office and toss the doggie bag into the wastebasket. She blew her nose a final time, gazed lovingly at the picture of Rip lying on his back, paws up in the air, hamming it up for the camera, and sighed.

❖

"So, she threw you a bone, huh?"

Kylie couldn't help but laugh at Mick's analogy. "Yeah, I guess she did. It was a nice thing to do."

"Whatever."

Kylie rolled onto her side on the couch and switched the phone to the other ear. Absently, she hit the channel change button on her remote, surfing through shows as she talked. She recalled Gretchen's face, the horror at having made her cry, the worry in her eyes. Her empathy revealed a side of her that filled Kylie with pleasant surprise.

Stopping on a rerun of *The Simpsons*, she said, "You could give her a chance, Mick."

"She had her chance with me," Mick spat. "She treated me like a peon. I don't need that from somebody who doesn't even know me."

"I know, but like I said before, it was her first day. There were extenuating circumstances."

"Whatever," Mick said again. "You seem to have given her enough chances."

Kylie made a face at the accusatory tone. "What the hell is that supposed to mean?"

"Nothing. I just don't like her. I don't like the way she treats people at work. I don't like that she's closeted. I just don't like her."

"We've been through this before. You don't know that she's closeted."

"She's certainly not out and proud."

"Like you."

"Damn right."

Kylie frowned. "She does have that picture, though..." she said, more to herself than aloud.

Mick heard her. "What picture?"

Rolling her eyes at giving more ammo to Mick, Kylie reluctantly elaborated. "She's got a picture on her desk of her and some guy at a Mexican place or in Mexico or something. They look pretty comfortable with each other."

Mick snorted. "See? She's even got a beard for appearances at work."

"You don't know that. Jesus. It could be anybody. Why are you so quick to crucify her?"

"Why are you so quick to defend her? Have you told her *you're* gay?"

"No. Why would I tell her that?"

"Why wouldn't you?"

"It's not exactly a standard topic of conversation at work for me and my new boss that I've barely known a month."

"You could work it in."

"'Work it in'? Yeah, okay. 'Hi, Gretchen. Here are the sales reports from Syracuse you asked for. By the way, I'm a lesbian.' God, what is your problem, Mick?" Kylie blew out a frustrated breath. After a few long seconds, she softened her words by adding, "Are you PMSing? Because I am."

A beat passed, then Mick chuckled and Kylie could almost hear her letting the anger dissipate. She sent up a silent thanks; she hated arguing with Mick, especially when she wasn't sure what they were arguing about.

"Having a glass of wine?" Mick asked.

"You know it. Having a beer?"

"You bet your ass."

They were quiet, only the sounds of their respective TVs audible over the line for many long minutes. Kylie wished there was something she could say to change Mick's opinion of Gretchen, wished she could get her best friend to give her boss another chance, but then wondered why it mattered so much to her. She was too tired to analyze it all.

With a sigh, she said instead, "I miss Rip."

"I know you do, sweetheart." Mick's voice was gentle. "Me, too."

CHAPTER SIX

The first of June was approaching rapidly. Gretchen was not in panic mode yet, but if she couldn't figure out Jim's system of sales numbers within the next day or two, she was afraid she soon might be. The mode was not one with which she was familiar and she certainly had no intention of starting now if she could possibly help it. She shook her head in bewilderment, clicking here and there on the computer, wondering how the hell his records were organized. The guy's files were all over the place.

Not one to ask for help, Gretchen weighed the pros and cons of finding out if Kylie had any idea how to locate the bottom-line totals she was searching for. She had numbers for the individual sales reps but couldn't seem to come up with any for office supplies, travel expenses, shipping, or any of the other items she would need if she wanted Margo Wheeler to approve next year's budget. She certainly didn't want Kylie to think she was having any trouble, but she was down to the wire, plus, chances were, Kylie knew a thing or two about Jim's filing logic…or lack thereof.

Ready to succumb to the inevitable, Gretchen swiveled her chair around to peek out the window in Kylie's direction. Much to her dismay, her view was obstructed by a large woman in khaki pants, a burgundy polo shirt, and work boots. She was holding a box and talking to Kylie. Mick Ramsey.

"Terrific." Gretchen glowered at the intimidating figure. "Just what I need to top off a banner day."

Inhaling deeply to steel herself against a possible ice storm, she headed out to the hall and approached Kylie's desk. Kylie's bright blue eyes ping-ponged from her surly friend to Gretchen.

"Hi," she said to Gretchen, and her smile seemed genuine.

Gretchen nodded once in Mick's general direction. "Ms. Ramsey."

"Ms. Kaiser," Mick responded in kind. No eye contact was forthcoming from her either.

Gretchen turned her attention to Kylie. "I need your help." Even as she pushed the words out, she wondered if Kylie had any idea how hard they were for her to formulate.

"Sure." Kylie stood.

Mick backed up a step or two to allow Kylie to exit her cubicle, and said quickly, "So, this weekend, right?" Gretchen noticed that her eyes never left Kylie's face.

Kylie looked blank.

"The Black Widow," Mick clarified. "You're coming out to meet us, right?"

Kylie's eyes flashed in what Gretchen could only describe as disbelief.

Mick backed down the hall, talking hurriedly. "I think that cute little redheaded chick that bought you all those drinks last time is going to be there, too." Winking, she added, "You know she wants you." Then she turned and practically fled, leaving Kylie to stand in the middle of the hallway, blinking, her face a bright red.

Gretchen could feel the embarrassment emanating like heat from Kylie and suspected that a minor power play had just taken place between the two women. *Wasn't that interesting?* she thought to herself.

Attempting to ease Kylie's apparent shame, she said, "Wow. Has she got a thing for you or what?"

Kylie gave a tiny gasp and stared at the floor, probably expecting it to open and swallow her.

"I can't figure out these damn reports of Jim's," Gretchen continued casually and headed into her office. "Can you show me where this stuff is hiding?"

She glanced back at Kylie, hoping she'd made light of the situation sufficiently to relieve any awkwardness. But Kylie looked shell-shocked and seemed unable to make eye contact. Slowly, she trailed into the office.

Gretchen sat at her desk and pointed to some items on her computer monitor. "What is this?" she asked. "And why can't I find the expense reports? Shouldn't they be here?"

Kylie stood behind the chair, one hand on the back of it, and reached over Gretchen's shoulder to take the mouse. A gentle scent tickled Gretchen's senses, and she was shocked to find herself trying to identify Kylie's perfume. They'd never been this close before and she had to fight to keep from squirming. She gazed down at Kylie's hand on the mouse, finger clicking. The skin on her forearm was covered with a soft-looking layer of blond, downy hairs, and several freckles marked a path to the bend of her elbow. Only when Kylie spoke did Gretchen begin paying attention to what was happening on the screen.

"Jim liked to hide his files here." Kylie moved the curser down a list of headings. "I have no idea why. He was sort of funny like that. I can help you find the rest of the stuff. I know where most of it is. He wasn't terribly organized."

"Maybe we can work out a system together that we can both follow easily?"

"Sure." Kylie backed away slightly from Gretchen's chair, her expression still just shy of mortified.

Her consternation was distracting and Gretchen sighed. "Kylie, relax. I'm not really sure what that was all about out there, but I don't care. I suspect Ms. Ramsey informed you that she and I met at the Black Widow the weekend before I started working here. So, you can see how your sexuality is no big deal to me."

"Okay." A small sliver of relief tried to push its way onto Kylie's face. She blinked and looked directly at Gretchen. "Can I ask you something?"

"Sure."

"Who's the guy in the picture?" Kylie pointed to the frame on the desk in front of her.

"Him?" Gretchen held up the picture in question. "This is Pete. He's my ex-husband and my best friend." As she set the picture back down, she smiled. "Actually, he's my best friend first and ex-husband second. That was a long, long time ago."

"You were married?"

"A long, long time ago," Gretchen repeated, still grinning. Glancing up, she said, "You look surprised. Why? Didn't you have a boyfriend in high school or college?"

Kylie nodded cautiously, and Gretchen could see she was

disconcerted by the somewhat intimate turn the conversation had taken. Though she certainly hadn't planned to lay out her life story, she felt safe confiding in Kylie, and continued.

"I was not only a late bloomer, but it took me well into my twenties to accept who I was. Who I am."

"And who are you?" Kylie seemed more at ease all of a sudden and Gretchen suspected this was her kind of conversation...personal and genuine. She was more surprised to realize that she was enjoying it herself. She normally made it a habit to avoid such discussions.

"A big ol' dyke, that's who."

Kylie laughed openly, her eyes twinkling as if Gretchen had bestowed a great secret upon her and trusted her to keep it. The funny thing was, though her sexuality wasn't exactly confidential, Gretchen did trust Kylie to be careful with the information. There was no fear at all, no doubt in her mind that Kylie would respect her privacy. She didn't think, for a second, that Kylie would be off at the Black Widow that weekend telling all her friends that her boss was a big fat lesbian.

Why do I trust you? she wanted to ask. Instead, she said, "Feel better?"

"Knowing our sales region at Emerson is being run by two lesbians? Absolutely."

Kylie's glowing smile made Gretchen inexplicably happy. "Good," she said. "Now show me how to generate these reports before Wheeler comes down here looking for my head on a silver platter."

❖

The phone was ringing as Gretchen slid her key into the deadbolt on her door. She hurried in, dropped everything on the floor in the foyer, and made a dive for the handset.

"Hey, big sis. How's life in the little city?"

Gretchen's entire body relaxed, as it always did when she heard the warm tones of her younger brother's voice. "It's good. It's really good. What's going on? To what do I owe this phone call?"

"I can't just call to talk to my sister once in a while?" She could hear the smile in J.J.'s voice, could picture his rugged face in her mind. He was probably unshaven and his dark, curly hair was probably too long. Both facts would make him seem much younger than his forty years, and still a chick magnet.

"Sure you can. You never do, though."

"Oh, now that hurts me."

Gretchen laughed, deciding to ease up. "How's Jenna? And the kids?"

They chatted about J.J.'s son and daughters, and about other members of the small Kaiser family. Gretchen poured herself a glass of wine and plopped onto her buttery-soft leather couch, propping her stockinged feet up on the oak coffee table as she listened to her brother describe the latest school projects, dance recitals, and soccer games. She hadn't felt so peaceful since she'd arrived in Rochester, and part of her wished he'd just talk all night.

"So, how's work?" J.J. asked her after exhausting his supply of new information. "How are they treating you at Emerson?"

Her brother didn't have the same business mind or experiences in the corporate world as Gretchen did—he was a school guidance counselor at their old alma mater—but he was a good listener and often came up with valuable suggestions or solutions to issues that she just hadn't seen. So she filled him in on her job—how she was not exactly a favorite among the sales reps, and Jim's record-keeping was disastrous. She also talked about Kylie's competence and value as an employee.

"They have no idea what they got when they hired you," J.J. said. "You're going to whip that sales force into shape in no time."

Gretchen smiled at the show of faith. "I hope so."

"How about personal stuff? Have you gone out yet? Met any new people? Any hot babes live in your building?"

"Jesus, J." Gretchen couldn't help but laugh, not only at her brother's talent for changing the subject in a split second, but also at his ability to get right to the heart of the matter he really wanted to address. "I haven't noticed any hot...er... babes in my building, no. I have met a couple of lesbians, though. Two of them right in my new place of work, as a matter of fact."

"Really?"

"If you can believe it, my assistant's gay."

"This Kylie you mentioned?"

"That's the one."

"Is she good-looking?"

"Extremely." Gretchen grinned at how true the statement was.

"I say go for it."

"Yeah, right. I'm her boss, J."

"I notice you didn't say she's not your type, or 'No way, she doesn't interest me.'"

Gretchen let her silence speak for itself.

"Oh, come on, Gretch." Her brother lowered his voice, conspiring playfully. "A little clandestine interoffice affair? Might be just what you need. Rock your buttoned-up little world a bit."

"Excuse me, but I am *not* buttoned-up. And my world doesn't need any rocking, thank you very much. I certainly don't need to get involved with anybody at work."

"Okay, okay. Just a suggestion."

Gretchen changed the subject. "How's Dad?"

"He's good. Busy. You know him—golf, board meetings, and poker. You should give him a call."

"He *could* call me." The retort was out before Gretchen could catch it, her bitterness coating the words like a powder. "I've been here for almost a month."

"I know."

Gretchen's relationship with her father was an old sore spot, and J.J. had been the buffer for years. He was used to it and knew where conversations like this one were going.

"I don't know why I give a damn," Gretchen said.

"Because you love him and you're a good person," J.J. said. "You know, he's really proud of you. Just last week, he was telling his poker buddies about your big, fancy new job and how Emerson chased after you and offered you gobs of money to come and work for them...what a big decision it was for you. He always tells people that stuff."

"Would it kill him to tell me once in a while?" Gretchen could hear the hurt and anger in her voice. The discussion was ancient, and the thought of going around and around the same old track one more time made her tired. "I'll never understand it, J."

"Maybe you're not supposed to understand it. Maybe it just *is*."

After a beat, Gretchen said, "What is that, your version of dime-store therapy?"

J.J. laughed heartily, a sound Gretchen had always loved. "Hey, my therapy is worth *way* more than a dime, missy."

"If you say so."

"Before I let you go, Lex wants to say hi."

Gretchen rolled her eyes and grimaced. Lex was her two-year-old niece. She was not at all adept at talking on the phone and attempts at conversations were usually exercises in futility, but the fact that she wanted to talk to "Aunt Getch" warmed Gretchen's heart in inexplicable ways.

Gretchen uh-huh'ed and oh-my'ed her way through three minutes that felt like twenty of indecipherable conversation with the little sweetheart before J.J. mercifully took the phone back.

"Did you get all that?" he asked with a chuckle.

"I don't think I got any of it," she responded gleefully. "But she certainly went on and on, just like a little boy I used to know way back when."

"She's learning new words all the time. She said 'fuck' the other day. Jenna almost killed me."

Gretchen burst out laughing, remembering the first time she taught her little brother to swear.

"All right, big sis. I've had enough of you." It was his standard closing line and it always filled her with love for him. "When are you coming home for a visit?"

"I actually have a couple of old boxes to pick up from Dad's basement, so I do need to make a road trip."

"And you want to see your nieces and nephew."

"And I want to see my nieces and nephew. I've got budget numbers due next week and then I'm going to need to sleep for days. Maybe the second or third weekend in June?"

"Let us know. Jenna will be thrilled."

They signed off and Gretchen hung up, a smile still clinging to her lips. Her brother was a good man, the glue that had held their family together after their mother died ten years earlier. If it had been left to Gretchen, she would have seen her father almost never. The fact made her feel ashamed.

Refilling her wineglass, she picked up her briefcase and headed for the bedroom, stopping at an end table to look at the wedding picture of her parents. They seemed so happy. Her father was regal and handsome in his tux, his dark hair slicked back away from his forehead, his perfect posture making the suit look like it had been invented just for him. Her mother was devastating in her off-the-shoulder white gown, her black ringlets the only physical attribute Gretchen had inherited from her. Her smiling green eyes and olive-toned skin had been passed on to J.J. Gretchen's dark, charcoal eyes—right down to the shape of them, the thickness of her lashes, and the arch of her brows—were replicas of John Kaiser's, as was her pale, alabaster skin and the ability to seem taller than she was just by the way she carried herself.

She hadn't been what she'd call close to her mother, but she loved and missed her very much. Emma Kaiser had been a kind and gentle woman, a housewife who baked cookies and looked out for all the children on their street. She and Gretchen didn't have a lot in common, but Gretchen admired her strength and generosity. Even ten years after breast cancer had claimed her life, Gretchen found herself itching to talk to her, sometimes going so far as to actually pick up the phone and punch in the first number before realizing that telephone lines wouldn't reach her where she was. The feeling knocked Gretchen back on her heels every time.

Running her fingertips over the picture, she sighed. Mother's Day had come and gone and she hadn't even thought about it. Guilt settled over her like a fog. She'd have to make sure to visit the cemetery next time she went home and leave some flowers.

❖

"Thanks, Frank," Kylie said with a smile as she passed through the employee entrance Frank held open. Her arms were loaded with bags smelling of smoked pork and cornbread.

"Working awfully late tonight, Ms. O'Brien." Frank walked ahead of her and pushed the call button for the elevator. He was a retired policeman who now spent three nights a week working security for Emerson. His balding head and rotund build reminded Kylie of a younger version of her late grandfather.

Kylie shrugged her shoulder to reposition the duffel bag hanging from it. "Somebody's got to keep this place running, you know."

"True enough," he smiled, reaching into the elevator and punching her floor. "You give a holler if you and Ms. Kaiser need anything, all right?"

"Thanks, Frank," she said again as the doors slid closed.

She had to admit how much better she felt being out of her work clothes. Eight hours in panty hose and heels was her limit; any longer than that and she started to get cranky. It was amazing to her that she felt almost revitalized simply by changing into her sweats. Certainly not even close to proper Emerson business attire, but once it was past eight o'clock at night, nobody cared.

The office was a little spooky at this hour. Not only did the absence of the usual hustle and bustle make the silence seem creepy, but the lack of most of the lighting made things seem even eerier. She could see Gretchen's office light throwing a rectangular yellow square onto the tile down the hall and she picked up her pace, mentally laughing at herself for acting like an eight-year-old who's watched one too many horror movies.

"I smell food." Gretchen's voice reverberated through the hall, causing Kylie to flinch, and then chuckle at her own reaction.

"I come bearing gifts," Kylie said as she entered the office.

Papers were strewn everywhere. Gretchen sat at her desk, squinting at the computer monitor, which showed endless lists of numbers. A laptop in sleep mode was perched on the small round table in the corner meeting area that would be Kylie's workspace for the night. They'd decided it was easier to be in the same room.

"Well, don't you look comfortable," Gretchen commented with a wry grin. "I'm jealous."

"Don't be." Kylie set down her armload of stuff on the floor and cleared off the table. Swinging the duffel off her shoulder, she sat it on the table and unzipped it. "I brought you some, too, just in case."

"You did?"

Kylie pulled out another pair of navy blue sweats, a gray University of Rochester sweatshirt, and a cozy-looking pair of white socks. Handing them over the desk to Gretchen, she felt herself flush a bit at the look of touched surprise on Gretchen's face.

"That was really thoughtful." Gretchen sounded almost at a loss.

"I don't know about you, but I work a lot better when I'm comfortable," Kylie said lightly, wanting to convey that it was no big deal despite the fact that she'd spent way too much time trying to decide on just the right selection to bring. "The sweats will probably be a little big, but nobody's going to see you but me. I didn't want to scare you with my stained and torn Lazy Ass Around the House sweats, so I brought you the Allowed Out in Public sweats. Big difference, you know."

Gretchen blinked several times as she took the pile from Kylie's outstretched hand. "Thank you."

"You're welcome. Go get changed." She turned to the bags of food and began laying out their dinner.

"Yes, ma'am." There was a note of amusement in Gretchen's voice that Kylie decided she liked.

Kylie moved the laptop and then set the round table with two plates, plastic silverware, and napkins. She scooted around the corner and snatched two Diet Cokes from the vending machine in the kitchenette. She opened all the containers, not knowing what Gretchen liked best but hoping she'd done okay in her choices. The smell was mouthwatering…pulled pork with barbecue sauce, sweet potato fries, black beans and rice, and fresh cornbread. They might be working until after midnight, but they would not go hungry doing it.

Gretchen returned to the office carrying her suit on a hanger and stopped in her tracks in the doorway. "Holy shit."

Kylie smiled. "I've been slaving over a hot stove all day. Come and eat." She let her eyes wander over Gretchen's small frame. The sweatpants were indeed too big and the sleeves of the sweatshirt were pulled up to her elbows, but she looked adorable. Kylie decided to keep that comment to herself, suspecting that the word "adorable" was not among Gretchen's preferences as a personal description.

"God, this smells good," Gretchen sat down at the small table across from Kylie. "I didn't know how hungry I was until I smelled you coming down the hall."

"I order from this restaurant all the time. It's really close to my place."

"And you're where?"

"In the city. Near Culver and University."

Gretchen took her first bite of the pork and closed her eyes in delight. "Oh, my God. This is sinful."

Her rapturous expression made Kylie swallow and run her tongue over her bottom lip as she sat down. "You like it?" she asked, as if the answer wasn't clearly written on Gretchen's face.

"Oh, my God," Gretchen said again, scooping another forkful into her mouth.

Kylie reached across the table with a napkin. "You've got..." She gently wiped the corner of Gretchen's mouth. "A little sauce." She cleared her throat and focused on her own plate.

"Thanks."

Kylie could feel Gretchen's eyes on her. It took an effort not to look up. "So, where do you live?"

"I'm off of Park Avenue."

"Nice. You're not far from me at all. You have an apartment?"

"Yeah." Gretchen bit into her cornbread. "You?"

"I have a little house."

"You do?"

"Mm-hmm. Why do you sound surprised?"

Gretchen studied Kylie's face. "I don't know. I guess I just assumed you were single and...I didn't expect somebody single to have a house alone."

"Hmm. You assumed I was single." Kylie raised an eyebrow. "I'm not sure if I should be insulted by that."

Gretchen chuckled, and Kylie felt a perverse sense of pleasure at having made her laugh. She glanced down at Kylie's hands. "No rings."

"Ah. A safe assumption, then, I must admit."

"And a correct one?"

Kylie met Gretchen's coal-dark eyes and felt suddenly exposed, as if she were sitting at the table naked under the intent stare. She swallowed the food in her mouth, then responded, "Yes. A correct one."

Gretchen simply nodded and went back to her plate.

"And you?" Kylie probed.

"And me, what?"

"An eye for an eye, Ms. Kaiser." As Gretchen looked at her, Kylie cocked her head to the side and said, "I get the impression that personal discussions aren't your favorite things. But I spilled, so you have to admit that it's only fair you spill a little, too."

Gretchen pointed her fork at Kylie. "Were you on the debate team in school?"

Kylie laughed. "Yes. Now answer the question."

"Yes, Ms. O'Brien. I, too, am single."

Kylie inclined her head in a nod of thanks. A wave a satisfaction rolled over her at having gotten a straight answer to a personal question from her boss. *We're making progress.*

They ate in companionable silence for a while, Kylie stealing glances at Gretchen whenever she could. She refused to take the time to analyze why she enjoyed looking at her boss. The woman was damn attractive, especially dressed in Kylie's clothes. It didn't take much of a leap to picture Gretchen lounging on Kylie's couch on a Sunday morning, newspaper open in front of her, steaming cup of coffee on the table, all bare feet and tousled hair.

Shaking the unsettling but not unpleasant vision from her head, Kylie asked, "So, this budget stuff is due tomorrow and then the pressure is finally off, at least for a while. What will you do for the weekend?"

Memorial Day was looming, a long weekend for the company, and Kylie was looking forward to it.

"I'll absolutely be sleeping in on Saturday. I can hardly wait. This four or five hours of sleep a night business is catching up with me. After that, I'm not sure." She shrugged. "I still have some unpacking to do. Maybe catch a movie."

"I have an idea."

Gretchen raised her eyebrows expectantly.

"My parents throw a big Memorial Day cookout every year. More often than not, it rains, but I think the forecast is actually calling for decent weather. It's very informal, lots of people coming and going all day. You should come by. You can grab something to eat, get to know a few locals, see my smiling face, and if you're not having fun, you can leave at any time." The words had fallen from her mouth in a jumble and when she finished, she caught her bottom lip between her teeth, waiting.

Gretchen's expression softened. "It's very nice of you to invite me, Kylie. Thank you. Can I say 'maybe' and leave it at that?"

It was about the answer Kylie expected. She'd be shocked if Gretchen actually did show up. But she had put the invitation out there and she was proud of herself. "Of course. I'll leave you directions in the morning."

They finished eating, passing food back and forth, snagging bites off one another's plates as if they'd been sharing meals for years. Finishing up, Gretchen stretched her arms over her head and yawned loudly. Kylie caught herself eyeing the peek of pale white tummy that was exposed and quickly averted her gaze.

"What do you say?" Gretchen asked. "Ready to get back to it?"

"Ready as I'm going to be at nine thirty at night."

"That's the spirit. I'd like to be able to e-mail this proposal and have it sitting on Wheeler's computer when she comes in tomorrow morning. She doesn't think we'll be able to do it. Let's knock her right off her chair. Want to?"

Kylie grinned at the little-kid tone in Gretchen's voice. "Absolutely."

CHAPTER SEVEN

Gretchen Kaiser wasn't used to being nervous. She'd done her best to banish the feeling from her internal stock and, for the most part, it didn't show up often. But now, as she sat in her black BMW parked on the side of Sycamore Street, where she'd been lucky to find a spot at all, she surveyed the bumper-to-bumper cars parked along the same block and wondered what the hell she thought she was doing.

Mingling with her staff on a personal level was not a good idea, not in her book. It could create difficulties in the long run, so she'd always avoided it like the plague. But something about the expression on Kylie's face when she'd extended the invitation…something in those damn blue eyes of hers was so…warm and engaging, Gretchen felt she really didn't have a choice in the matter. And then Friday, when she'd left the directions, she just slid them onto Gretchen's desk, right on top of the resume she was reading. She didn't say a word; she just smiled and winked at Gretchen. Actually *winked*!

So here she sat. The cookout must be huge; she could hear the noise all the way down the street. She weighed her options as she glanced at the bottle of white wine sitting on her passenger seat. She could leave now and Kylie would never know she'd been here at all. That way, she wouldn't have to deal with the nervousness, the awkwardness, or the uncertainty that were all clouding her brain. She wouldn't meet any members of Kylie's family and she would not have to see Kylie in a casual setting, relaxed and probably smiling. That was certainly the best course of action. *Just leave right now. Go!*

"Shit," she sighed as she grabbed the bottle and opened the car door.

Checking her reflection in the car window, she redirected a stray lock of her dark hair and hoped she'd dressed appropriately. She'd tried to keep it simple: jeans, a light pink scoop-neck T-shirt with long sleeves in case it got chilly, and casual black shoes. Fussing with her hair once more, she blew out a breath and headed toward the noise coming from the back yard of number 77.

The day was beautiful, the temperature hovering in the high sixties to low seventies—an unusual occurrence for this time of year in Rochester, Gretchen had deduced from the weather reports. The O'Briens had indeed lucked out. The sky was clear and blue, and a gentle breeze wafted off nearby Lake Ontario, rustling the new leaves unfurling on the trees. Gretchen inhaled deeply, savoring the fresh air after so many consecutive days stuck inside.

Sycamore was a nice, residential street in the suburbs. Unlike many of the new developments, it boasted sidewalks, and Gretchen followed one at an easy pace. The houses were nicely spaced apart and the lawns were neatly tended. Many people had begun to plant their summer flowers. Gretchen noticed impatiens and petunias in various colors and remembered how her mother had loved to plant annuals.

An older woman on her hands and knees, gardening gloves brown with dirt, waved as Gretchen passed. "Beautiful day, isn't it?" she asked.

"Gorgeous," Gretchen replied, thinking for the first time in ages that it would be nice to live in a little house on such a street and plant flowers out front every spring.

The O'Brien house was large and sunny yellow with white shutters and trim. The garage's front and back doors stood open, and through them, Gretchen could see a throng of people milling around in the back yard. The precisely edged lawn was lush and green, a by-product of either chemical enhancement or a retired owner. Not a blade of grass was to be found on the smooth blackness of the driveway. The front shrubs looked like they'd been trimmed up recently. Three pots of rich red geraniums lined the simple concrete front steps. It was a house from the pages of a fairy tale: neat, warm, and inviting.

Crossing through the garage and entering the back yard was like walking into a giant frat party. The beat of a classic rock tune pounded from somewhere, and there had to be fifty people mingling, eating, and drinking. The atmosphere was welcoming, and the guests looked happy, chatting and laughing with one another.

Standing off to the side, Gretchen felt herself smile at the sight. She located Kylie easily; she was surprised by *how* easily, as if Kylie was wearing some kind of homing device so Gretchen could find her. She was standing by the grill near the center of the yard. Puffs of burger-scented smoke curled into the air around her, and she gave a musical laugh that carried across the yard. Next to her, an older gentleman wielded his spatula as he spoke to her. Gretchen knew instantly that he was Kylie's father, and the obvious bond between them gave her a poke of sadness. She would never share such an easy rapport with her own father.

Kylie's jeans hugged her hips gently, and Gretchen tried to prevent her eyes from lingering on her assistant's backside, to no avail. She took in the white T-shirt and the way the sun glinted off Kylie's blond hair and sucked in a deep breath. She'd admitted to herself quite some time ago that she found Kylie extremely attractive. She'd even allowed herself to entertain a fantasy or two about her. But observing her unawares across the yard made Gretchen's heart pound, and she wasn't terribly comfortable with that. As a matter of fact, it increased her level of nervousness tenfold.

Maybe this wasn't such a good idea, she thought with a grimace. If she turned and fled right now, she could actually escape without being seen. After all, nobody else here knew who she was and Kylie hadn't noticed her yet.

As if on cue, Kylie turned in Gretchen's direction, met her eyes, and her face lit up. She said something to the grill master, who also looked at Gretchen, and then she headed toward her. Gretchen shifted uncomfortably, muttering to herself about the impossibility of escape now.

"You made it." Kylie said as she drew close. Her voice was filled with enthusiastic delight.

"I did." Gretchen held out the bottle of wine.

"You didn't have to do that. Thank you."

Kylie accepted the bottle, and she and Gretchen stood looking at one another, grinning, for several seconds. They were eye to eye, and Gretchen sent up a silent thanks that her casual shoes had a bit of a heel and Kylie had chosen to wear sneakers.

"Quite a party." Gretchen stated the obvious.

Kylie seemed to draw a deep breath. "I'm really glad you're here. Come on. I want you to meet some people." Grasping Gretchen by the wrist, she pulled her into the crowd.

In the six weeks they'd worked together, Gretchen had never thought of Kylie as reserved or shy, or noticed any sign of timidity around others. But in her element, in a large group of people she knew well, she was even *more* friendly, outgoing, and sweet. Trailing along behind her like a little lost puppy, Gretchen enjoyed watching her interact with people. She charmed the older folks, the kids followed her as if she was the Pied Piper, even the couple of dogs pulled at their leashes, wanting to be scratched and kissed. Kylie obliged without a second thought.

They stopped at the line of coolers along the deck. "What can I get you?" Kylie asked, holding up the wine. "Should I open this bottle? Do you want a beer? Pop? Oh, wait. You're not from around here." She smirked. "It's probably soda to you, isn't it?"

Gretchen laughed. "Yeah, what the hell is 'pop,' anyway? A beer would be great, thanks."

"Labatt? Coors? Light? Dark?"

"So many choices. Got a light in there?"

Kylie shook the ice water from the bottle. "Watching your figure, are you?" She winked at Gretchen and then pulled her along toward the grill.

She just winked at me again. Gretchen shook her head with a disbelieving grin as she followed.

"Hey, Dad," Kylie said to the man diligently flipping burgers. "This is Gretchen Kaiser. Gretchen, my father, Matthew O'Brien."

Gretchen shook the hand he held out. His grip was firm, his hand large and callused. "Nice to meet you, Mr. O'Brien."

"Please. Matt. Mr. O'Brien makes me feel old. Nice to meet you, too."

Matt O'Brien was tall, probably six-one or six-two, and looked to be in his late sixties. What remained of his white hair circled his head like a donut. He gave the impression of a man who was in very good physical condition when he was younger; the only signs of his age were the balding head and the slightly protruding belly visible beneath the Kiss the Cook apron he had tied over it. When he smiled, the wrinkles at the corners of his brown eyes were very prominent, making Gretchen suspect that he smiled often. *Kylie's eyes will crinkle just like that when she's older.* The thought came out of nowhere and Gretchen blinked several times, trying to clear it from her head.

"Your yard is lovely," she said sincerely.

It was difficult to see it all through the crowd of people, but the back yard seemed to be as neat and well kept as the front, not huge, but large enough. A light-colored wooden deck off the back of the house sported flower boxes filled with the same red geraniums that decorated the front steps. A colorful swing set in one corner was completely covered with children. A small, barn-shaped aluminum shed stood in the other.

"Well, thank you. I can only take credit for the grass. My wife is the flower expert." Matt O'Brien took a swig from the beer bottle that was resting on the grill's counter space.

"Speaking of..." Kylie's eyes rested on an older woman approaching with a large, empty plate.

If Gretchen had known instantly that Matt was Kylie's father, the family resemblance was nothing compared with Kylie's likeness to her mother. The woman walking toward them was *exactly* what Gretchen pictured Kylie would look like at age sixty-five. She actually did a double take as Mrs. O'Brien handed the plate to her husband.

After Kylie made the introductions, Caroline O'Brien shook Gretchen's hand in the way older women tended to, more of a loose clasp than a firm pump. "It's so nice to meet you, Gretchen. Kylie has told me a lot about you."

Gretchen glanced at Kylie. "Should I be worried?"

Caroline chuckled. "Oh, no, no. She very much enjoys working for you."

"Well, she's a wonderful employee. I'm lucky to have her." She felt a thrill at the pink tint that suddenly colored Kylie's cheeks and took a swallow of her beer to hide her smile.

Caroline lifted the plate, now piled high with hamburgers of various sizes and doneness, and hurried back to the deck, where a table filled with food stood waiting for guests to indulge.

"Your mother's a very beautiful woman," Gretchen said quietly to Kylie.

Kylie's smile was filled with pride. "Yeah. I hear that a lot. Thanks."

"Hey, Short Round!" The greeting was followed by a slap to Kylie's behind. She tried to roll her eyes, but Gretchen could see that she was laughing instead. She elbowed the very tall, thin guy behind her, whose hair was exactly the same shade as hers.

"Shut up, Bean Pole," she sneered at him.

"Who's this?" he asked, holding his hand out to Gretchen. "Hot new girlfriend?"

Gretchen returned his firm grip in kind. "Hot new boss," she informed him.

"Oh, shit." He turned his suddenly pale face to Kylie and began to stammer. "Sorry, Ky. I…I wasn't…she's really…I should've…shit."

"It's okay. She's cool."

"Yeah? She's cool? Or *cool* cool?"

"She's *cool* cool."

"Ah, I see. Cool."

Turning to Gretchen, Kylie introduced the embarrassed male as her brother, Kevin.

After exchanging the requisite courtesies with him, Gretchen inquired, "Short Round?"

"Ugh." Kylie covered her eyes with her hand.

Kevin laughed. "Okay. Here's the deal. Our little Kylie was a late bloomer as far as height and stuff went. Rory and I got tall right away. I've been six-three since I was fifteen. Even Erin is, what? Five-ten?" He looked at Kylie, who nodded. "So, anyway, here we all are, teenagers, and we're all these string-bean-looking kids. All except Kylie. She's barely five-three and not exactly…bean-like." He laughed, but his eyes crinkled with great affection for his little sister.

"I just took my time," Kylie said in her own defense, her cheeks pink yet again. To Gretchen, she explained, "I lost fifteen pounds and grew three inches from my sophomore to senior years in high school." Turning to Kevin, she added, "So there," and stuck out her tongue.

"Topping off at a mere five-foot-six. Not short by any means, but certainly short for this family." He lowered his voice. "Mom would never tell us what the mailman looked like."

Kylie slapped at him. "Don't you have something better to do than harass me?"

"Can't think of a thing, Short Round," he answered playfully.

"Story of my life."

Watching the back-and-forth interplay between the siblings, Gretchen felt her heart swell. At times like these, she missed J.J. immensely.

"I could harass Gretchen," Kevin replied with a wink. "She seems to have the same vertical challenge as you. What are you, five-four?"

"Five-four and a half, thank you very much," Gretchen answered.

Kylie shoved him. "Get lost, Stilts. We don't need your kind here."

"Fine. I have more joy to spread, anyway. Nice to meet you, Gretchen. I'm sure we'll see each other again. Keep her in line, will you?"

Gretchen laughed. "I'll try."

"Ready for another beer?" Kylie asked.

Gretchen nodded, surprised at the good time she was having. "I think I am. Join me this time?"

"Okay, but I need to pace myself. I have zero alcohol tolerance."

Gretchen squinted at her. "Um...aren't you Irish?"

"Yeah." Kylie had the good sense to look embarrassed.

"Huh. Maybe it *was* the mailman..."

Kylie burst out laughing. "Shut up!"

They headed back to the coolers, Kylie getting stopped no less than three times by various neighbors to say hi. Introductions were made—Kylie was very good about that—and Gretchen shook hands and smiled politely, knowing she'd never remember all the names.

"Aunt Ky!" a small voice called from the direction of the swing set. "Come and play with us!"

Kylie smiled and waved. "Not now, sweetie. Later, okay?"

"Niece?" Gretchen asked.

Kylie nodded. "My sister's daughter. She's four and the baby of all the kids." Dropping her voice to a whisper, she reported, "Unplanned. Oops."

"Hate when that happens."

"You have nieces and nephews?"

"Two nieces and a nephew. They're ten, eight, and two."

"How many siblings?" Kylie asked.

"Just me and my brother."

"Is he older or younger than you?"

"He's younger by seven years."

"That's a lot. So, you guys didn't have much in common as kids, I take it?"

Gretchen laughed softly. "No. He was always getting in my way and wanted to hang out with me and my friends. I hated him and used to beat him up."

"And now?"

"He's one of my best friends."

Kylie smiled warmly. "That's great. You want to have kids?"

Gretchen snorted. "Oh, let's see…pregnant at forty-seven. I think I'm a little old for that, don't you?"

"But did you want to?"

Gretchen honestly thought about the question. "No. I didn't. Maybe I'm too selfish to have children. I like my independence, you know? I like that I can up and go whenever I want to. I like my quiet time. I like having money to spend on frivolous things." She glanced at Kylie, who was studying her face with those impossibly blue eyes. "What about you? Are you the motherly type? Because I think you totally are."

"I thought about it for a long time, but I feel very much like you do. I like my independence. Besides, being an aunt is really cool. When I hear the old biological clock ticking and I start to panic, I just go grab my little niece and take her out for the day. That usually cures me pretty quickly."

They both laughed, and Kylie waved to some new arrivals.

"You don't have to stand here with me, you know," Gretchen said softly. "I see a lot of people who look like they want to talk with you. I'm a big girl. I'm okay on my own."

Kylie studied her. "Actually, I'm good. At least until my mother comes looking for me. I'd like to hang right here with you. If you don't mind."

Gretchen held her gaze. "I don't mind." She sipped her beer.

❖

Mick grumbled as she parked her SUV over a block from the O'Briens' house. Her intention had been to arrive a good two hours earlier, but she'd slept in after her Saturday night out and Tina was becoming more and more difficult to shake loose in the morning. She was going to have to nip that situation in the bud very soon.

She hopped out of the truck after checking her hair in the rearview mirror and smoothing the sides back over her ears. Grabbing the twelve-pack of Killian's for Mr. O'Brien and the bouquet of daisies for the Mrs., she began whistling a happy tune and headed up the street, looking forward to seeing Kylie.

This was such a nice neighborhood, the residences way nicer than the piece of crap shed she'd grown up in. It was hard to believe a house of such dilapidation could be found only four blocks away. Mick had her alcoholic mother and absentee father to thank for that. The O'Briens had practically taken her in, not that her parents had noticed. She was sure she'd had more square meals served to her in her childhood by Caroline O'Brien than by her own mother. And she'd spent more school nights in Kylie's bedroom than in her own.

It used to make her sad. Then there were a few years where it made her furiously angry. Now, she was indifferent. Her mother was long dead and she had no idea where her father was. For all intents and purposes, the O'Briens were her parents and she treated them with the same respect she'd treat anybody who'd taken such good care of her.

"Hi, Mrs. Keeler," she called to a woman working on her front yard landscaping a few doors before the O'Briens'. "Looks great."

The older woman looked up. "Oh! Hi, there, Michelle. Good to see you."

"You coming to the party?" Mick gestured with the daisies in the direction of the O'Briens'.

"Soon, dear. I want to finish this up first."

"Do you need help?"

"Oh, no, you sweet girl. I've got it. Thank you, though."

"Okay, I'll see you there."

As she neared the house, a familiar figure approached from the other direction. Mick was staring, trying to pinpoint the identity of the newcomer, when the figure spoke, confirming her suspicions.

"Mick? Mick Ramsey? Is that you, you sexy thing?"

"Jorianna Elizabeth Victoria Mitchell? Are those really your lovely dulcet tones I'm hearing?"

"You're the only one who can call me that and survive," Jori scolded as they met on the sidewalk.

Mick set her packages down on the ground so she could wrap her arms around her old friend in a warm hug. "What the hell are you doing here? I can't believe you didn't call and tell me you were coming." She held Jori at arm's length and looked her over. "God, you look fantastic."

Jori had always been long, lean, and artistically in fashion. How they had ended up friends when they were such polar opposites was beyond Mick. The only thing she could chalk it up to was their shared sexual preference. They hadn't really become close until their junior year in high school. Mick had been sure of her lesbianism and Jori reasonably sure about hers, and Kylie had been fighting hers as hard as she could. The three of them had bonded, Mick and Jori more so as Kylie periodically went off to try dating a boy until she figured things out for herself.

Now, here they stood, close to forty and comfortable in their skins. Jori's straight, brown hair was shoulder-length, severe bangs cut across her forehead. Quirky, black-rimmed glasses perched on her slim nose. She was thin and leggy, wearing a stylishly casual black dress and chunky black shoes. Not quite right for the weather or a cookout, but just perfect for Jori Mitchell.

"Come on," Mick said, picking up her stuff. "I was about to head in."

Mick entered the house through the front door, rather than the garage. She wanted to greet Caroline O'Brien first and knew the chances of finding her in the kitchen were pretty damn good. Sure enough, through the screen of women milling around the room, she could see Caroline at the sink, rinsing the dirty hands of a small girl she held in front of her, a dish towel thrown over her shoulder. Mick snuck up behind her and nuzzled her neck.

"Hi there, Mrs. Gorgeous."

Caroline jumped, then laughed. She put the little girl down and wiped her hands with the towel before patting her playfully on her behind and directing, "Mommy's in the back yard with Papa. Go get her." She turned to Mick, plainly delighted. "Hello, Michelle. It's nice to see you, honey."

Mick set the beer down and held up the flowers. "For you."

"Oh, you don't have to bring me flowers so often." Caroline gathered her into a hug. "You have other things to spend your money on."

Mick ignored the all-too-familiar chastisement and nudged the twelve-pack with a toe. "I want this in the basement. It's for Mr. O'Brien, not the entire picnic." The American-made version of Irish beer was Matt O'Brien's favorite, but she knew he rarely bought it for himself.

"You are too good to us," Caroline said, then noticed the second figure standing in the doorway. Her eyes opened wide with recognition. "Jorianna!"

Looking over her shoulder as she was enveloped in a warm hug, Jori sneered at Mick's smug expression. "Okay. Two of you can get away with calling me that. But that's all."

"What brings you to town?" Caroline asked.

"A college friend of mine got married in Toronto yesterday."

"Yesterday?" Caroline sounded surprised.

"I know. Seriously. Who gets married over a holiday weekend? Anyway, I figured I was so close, I might as well drive the two hours and hang here for a while. Get some work done, maybe."

"You still have that lovely little place in the city?"

"My studio? Yup."

Mick snorted. What Jori referred to as a "studio" was actually a high-end loft apartment in the posh East Avenue area of downtown Rochester. In addition to a dark room and ample space for Jori to set up a photo shoot if she so desired, the loft boasted a one-bedroom apartment nearly as large as the O'Briens' entire house. She also had an apartment in New York City, where she spent the majority of her time.

Jori shot Mick a look. "I thought I'd stay around for a few weeks. And then I looked at the calendar and realized it was the weekend of your annual barbecue and thought I'd take a chance."

"Well, I'm so glad you did." Caroline patted her arm in a motherly fashion. "Kylie will be thrilled to see you."

At the mention of Kylie's name, Jori's face brightened. "Is she here?"

Caroline opened the refrigerator and pulled out a giant salad bowl. Pointing out the window with her chin, she replied, "She's out there with that new boss of hers. Very nice woman. Last time I saw them, they were talking to Matt near the grill."

Mick's stomach lurched when she realized who Caroline was talking about. *What the hell is she doing here?* She gave in to resentment for a few seconds, then made an immediate pact with herself to be as civil as possible out of respect for the O'Briens.

"Michelle, dear, can you take this out with you?" Caroline handed the enormous salad to her and stuck in a just-as-enormous set of plastic tongs.

"Sure." Mick gestured with her head for Jori to follow.

She spotted Kylie and *that woman* immediately. They each had a beer and were standing very close together, setting Mick's teeth on edge. They seemed to be enjoying one another's company immensely, as if they were the only two people there. Through the throng of people, Mick could see Kylie's dark blond head bobbing as she nodded, then laughed, at whatever it was Gretchen was saying to her. She plunked the salad down on the table and glared. It was unusual for Kylie not to be mingling, to be standing still in one place during her parents' picnic. *Maybe she feels bad leaving the bitch alone at a party where she doesn't know anybody. Why'd she even invite her, anyway?*

"Wow." Jori's voice summoned her from her reverie. "Who's that?"

"Who?" Mick asked, knowing exactly who.

"The hot little brunette talking to Kylie." A gleam appeared in Jori's eye and Mick fully expected her to go ahead and lick her lips. "She's...something."

"She's Kylie's boss."

"No way."

"Way."

"Yummy." Jori raised and lowered her eyebrows lasciviously and Mick couldn't help but laugh. Sexual enjoyment of women was another thing they had in common, as was their ability to find and size up exactly who they wanted, and nail her. In record time. Mick was very, *very* good. Jori was better. And she'd obviously focused in on Gretchen in about fifteen seconds flat.

Mick poked at the inside of her cheek with her tongue, her wheels turning, weighing her options. Her decision made, she offered, "She *is* family, you know." Not that sexual preference had ever mattered to Jori. She'd bedded as many straight women as lesbians, Mick was sure. Still, every advantage could help.

Jori's eyes lit up. "You don't say."

"She's tough, though."

"Yeah?"

"She's no pushover. I don't see her as the...submissive type. You might have a hard time."

"Well, you know how I love a challenge."

Mick held her gaze and smiled. "Come on, let's go say hi and you can meet the tasty morsel in person."

As they approached the two women, Mick almost laughed aloud at the completely opposite expressions on their faces. Kylie smiled at

Mick, and then her face lit up like a Christmas tree as she noticed Jori. Gretchen smiled automatically when Kylie did, but when she followed Kylie's gaze and saw Mick, that smile slid right off her face like a pat of butter on a steaming ear of corn.

"Jori! Oh, my God, what are you doing here?" Kylie's voice was a schoolgirl squeal and she threw both arms around Jori's neck.

Jori picked her up off the ground and swung her around before setting her down and going through the story again. All the while, she still held Kylie and the two friends looked adorable together. At least Mick thought so.

Gretchen seemed less impressed. Sipping her beer, she watched the interaction with a slightly peeved expression that bordered on bewilderment, as if she was trying to figure something out.

"It's so good to see you, Kylie Jane. You look...unbelievable." Jori's brown eyes shifted toward Gretchen and she smiled, holding out her hand. "Hi there. I don't believe we've met."

"God, I'm so rude," Kylie smacked herself in the forehead and introduced the two women, referring to Jori as her "dear, dear friend."

Jori took Gretchen's hand and shook it, not letting go right away. "So nice to meet you, Ms. Kaiser."

"Please. Call me Gretchen." Gretchen bit her bottom lip and seemed to hesitate. Then, as if finding her courage, she said, "Jori Mitchell. Why does that sound so familiar? And you *look* familiar, too."

"Jori's a famous photographer," Kylie piped in, her voice tinted with pride.

"I don't know about famous," Jori replied, waving her off.

"That's it!" Gretchen's face broke out in an enormous grin. "I have one of your pieces in my apartment."

"I don't believe it," Kylie said, laughing. "What a small world." Mick rolled her eyes.

"Which piece?" Jori asked, inching slightly closer to Gretchen.

"*Seaside Silhouette*. I saw it in a little gallery in Manhattan and I had to have it."

Mick knew the piece and had to internally commend Gretchen on her taste. It was a black-and-white photograph of two women walking on the beach at sunset, holding hands. It was very romantic and not what Jori would call "artsy" at all. Jori wasn't terribly fond of it, but it was her single best-selling piece of all time. *Lesbians want romance,* Mick had told her over and over. *Give it to them.*

"I think there was a small picture of you near the display," Gretchen was saying. "You'd had an exhibit there a few weeks earlier. That's why you looked so familiar to me. I just bought it this past winter."

Mick watched the master at work as Jori slowly reduced the distance between herself and Gretchen, nearly—but not quite—cutting both Kylie and Mick out of the circle. She and Gretchen were talking about New York City now, a subject Kylie and Mick knew little about, and Jori was laying on the charm. Kylie was watching with what appeared to be a shade of concern on her face.

"Hey," Mick said, trying to get Kylie's attention. "Rumor has it your late-night work sessions paid off. Wheeler was all smiles on Friday."

Kylie's gaze darted back and forth between Mick and the flirting pair. "That's good to hear. We worked hard to get her what she wanted."

Mick tried again. "Hey, who needs a drink?"

Everybody wanted one. "Ky, help me carry?"

Kylie looked torn for a split second before walking to the coolers with Mick. "Gretchen's drinking a light," she said as Mick pulled out four regular beers.

"Of course she is," Mick mumbled, exchanging one and handing the light beer to Kylie. "You two seem to be getting along pretty well," she commented, hoping the bitterness she felt wasn't as apparent in her tone as she suspected.

"We really are." Kylie added no more to the conversation as they headed back to the pair, her eyes never leaving Gretchen.

Mick stifled a growl of frustration. Gretchen smiled her thanks at Kylie as she took her beer, then turned back to the conversation she was still having with Jori about a particular gallery owner in Manhattan. Kylie blinked a couple times at them and then took a long swallow of her own beer.

Just as Mick was about to try engaging Kylie once more, Gretchen asked where the bathroom was and something almost like relief zipped across Kylie's face.

"I'll show you," she said, but as they began to walk away, Kylie's father called to her from the grill.

Kylie looked frustrated once again, but Mick saw her point toward the house, obviously giving Gretchen directions to the bathroom.

Gretchen handed her beer to Kylie and strolled off, while Kylie headed toward the grill.

"Wow," Jori said, taking a long pull from her bottle. "That Gretchen is one classy lady."

Mick snorted. "If you say so."

"You don't like her. How come?"

"Long story."

"Please. You mean the *same* story." She gave Mick a pointed look. "It's because Kylie likes her. You saw how close they were standing, didn't you?"

Mick looked indignant. "That's ridiculous."

"Ridiculous? Maybe. True? Definitely."

Mick glowered at her.

"Oh, please. You've wanted to keep the charming and beautiful Ms. O'Brien all to yourself since we were seventeen. It's old news."

"You don't know what you're talking about, Jorianna."

"Don't I?" Jori flicked her hair back over her shoulder and adjusted her glasses. "Come on, Mick. Don't I know you better than you know yourself? We're cut from the same cloth, babe. You're just like me. We go through women like tissues because none of them measure up to that one sparklingly perfect ideal. For me, it was Amy. For you, it's Kylie."

"Back off, Jori."

"Relax. It's good that we can at least admit these things. It means we're mentally stable, you know."

"I mean it." Mick felt her temper rising. She hated that Jori could so easily hold a mirror up in front of her face. She always could. "Back off right now."

Jori put her hands up in surrender. "Fine. I just call 'em like I see 'em. That's all I'm saying."

They both knew, from past experience, when to end this type of discussion. They'd revisit it again, Mick was sure. They always did. To her further annoyance, Kylie looked in their direction, and Jori motioned her over. Mick brought her bottle to her lips as she watched Kylie cross the yard, the T-shirt hugging her curves, the jeans looking custom tailored. Jori could have Gretchen as far as Mick was concerned; Gretchen certainly didn't deserve a second glance from somebody like Kylie. Kylie was in a class all by herself. Mick stared at her, willing

Kylie to feel her and make eye contact. Instead, she walked straight to Jori.

"What's up?" she inquired.

Lowering her voice, Jori asked, "Ky, would you mind if I asked Gretchen out?"

"Out? Like…on a date?"

Jori rolled her eyes. "Yes, Kylie Jane. That's generally what it means to ask somebody out."

Kylie hesitated a beat. "Why would I mind?"

Jori swigged from her beer, and then commented innocently, "No reason. I'm just making sure I wouldn't be…stepping on your toes or anything."

"Jori." Kylie put her hands on her hips. "She's my *boss*."

"Your very attractive boss."

"Yeah, well. She's my boss, just the same." Kylie's voice lacked the certainty Mick was sure she'd intended.

"Okay, then."

Gretchen emerged from the house, followed by Caroline. Both waved in the direction of the threesome.

"Kylie, honey," Caroline called. "Can you come in and help me for a minute?"

Kylie groaned. "Sure, Mom."

Aware of Jori watching for the smallest clue to support her pet theory, Mick tried not to show any reaction as Kylie passed Gretchen on the steps of the deck. They spoke briefly and Kylie handed Gretchen her beer, touching her arm for longer than was necessary. As they parted, she looked back at Gretchen once more. Mick knew Kylie well, and the emotion that zipped across her face before she headed into the house was definitely worry.

Mick's guilt poked at her, but she ignored it and instead turned to Jori and gave her a nudge. "You got the go-ahead. What are you waiting for?"

Mick noticed Kylie's brother across the yard mention something to the guy he was with and gesture in Gretchen's direction. If Mick had a gun pointed at her, she might be forced to admit that Gretchen painted quite a nice picture in her jeans and pink shirt, the expensive black shoes hitching her outfit up a notch from most of the people there. She looked comfortably in control. Mick hated her.

Within a couple seconds, Gretchen and Jori were deep in

conversation once again. Pleased, Mick grabbed another beer from the cooler and wandered over to the grill to talk with Matt and the two neighbors hanging with him. She sent surreptitious glances in the direction of the two women to reassure herself that things were going smoothly, but she needn't have worried. Jori had the situation well in hand, laughing and placing a hand on Gretchen's arm as they stood close and talked. Shifting her gaze up to the kitchen window, she noticed Kylie looking down at her boss and her friend, her concern apparent even from a distance.

Trust me, Ky, Mick thought, tamping down the unexpected feeling of remorse. *I'm doing you a big favor.*

CHAPTER EIGHT

Good afternoon, Gretchen Kaiser's office. This is Kylie. May I help you?"

"Hi, Kylie. This is Jessica Scott. Is Ms. Kaiser in?" The voice on the phone was female and pleasant enough, but Kylie's mood wasn't. She'd been annoyed for two days now and she hated feeling annoyed, especially when she couldn't put her finger on the reason.

"Hang on one second, Ms. Scott, and I'll check."

Kylie put the woman on hold. Looking over her shoulder, she saw Gretchen sitting at her desk, staring out the window, just as she'd been doing the last six times Kylie looked. She buzzed the intercom.

"Gretchen? There's a Jessica Scott on line one."

Gretchen didn't look at Kylie, but waved her hand as if shooing a fly. "She's a headhunter. Tell her I'm on my way into a meeting and send her to my voice-mail, would you?"

"Sure."

Frowning, Kylie did as she was told. Gretchen had taken no calls all morning. There had to be a dozen messages in her voice-mail. Kylie wondered what had happened between yesterday and today. After their Monday off, they'd come back on Tuesday and dove right in. Wheeler called Gretchen upstairs almost first thing, presumably to talk budget, and Kylie hadn't seen her again all day. Now Gretchen was staring endlessly off into space, just as she had since she'd arrived at work.

Concerned, Kylie finally got up and went to the doorway of her boss's office. She knocked lightly on the door frame and asked, uneasily, "Are you okay?"

Gretchen faced her. She didn't look angry or upset, just…inactive. "I'm fine."

"Everything's okay with Wheeler?"

"Wheeler is ecstatic."

"You're sure?"

Gretchen nodded. "Thanks."

They looked at one another for several long seconds. Finally, Kylie inclined her head and said, "Okay."

As she turned to leave, Gretchen said, "Kylie, wait. I didn't get much of a chance to talk to you yesterday. I wanted to thank you for inviting me to your cookout. I had a good time."

"You're welcome. I'm really glad you came. My mother says hello." Carefully, she added, "I'm sorry I missed you before you left."

"I'm sorry I left without saying good-bye." When Kylie shrugged, she explained, "Jori said your mom would keep you pretty busy for the rest of the night and you probably wouldn't even notice we were gone."

I noticed. Kylie continued to smile, though she felt it fail to reach her eyes. Once she'd realized Gretchen was gone, she'd tried to rationalize it. Gretchen didn't know anybody. Jori really didn't know a lot of people either. Of course they'd left. Why wouldn't they?

Trying to find the right words, she came up with, "She…treated you okay? Jori?"

Gretchen's smile got a little brighter. "Oh, yeah. She's great. I'm glad we met. She's a lot of fun."

"She is that." There was a hint of sarcasm in her response, and Kylie nearly grimaced when she heard it.

Gretchen studied her. "Kylie…are you…okay with this? My spending time with Jori? Because if you're not, if it makes you uncomfortable or something, just say so."

"What? No, no. It's fine. I'm fine. Really."

Gretchen continued to look at her and Kylie shifted under her gaze, feeling like she was completely exposed. How did a direct stare from Gretchen always seem to make her feel that way?

"Okay," Gretchen said, releasing her.

Kylie couldn't get back to her desk fast enough. "Spending time" with Jori? Did that mean she was planning to see her again? Maybe she already had. Kylie sat down and closed her eyes, trying to slow her racing mind. What she'd really wanted to do was to scream at Gretchen:

Run! Run as fast as you can from her! She'll charm you into bed, sleep with you a few times, then move on to the next. Don't get too attached. She'll only break your heart when she goes back to New York without you and never calls you again. I've seen it happen a million times.

Of course, Gretchen was a big girl and she certainly didn't need, or want, Kylie looking out for her.

Jori said your mom would keep you pretty busy for the rest of the night...

Oh, she was smooth, that Jori Mitchell. Maybe she could give Kylie some lessons. Kylie shook her head in a combination of awe and disgust. Her stomach was growling. Loudly. Making a quick decision, she called down to the mailroom and got Mick.

"Take me to lunch?" she coaxed.

"Tell me what you're wearing first," Mick ordered, dropping her voice as she always did when she play-flirted with Kylie. Kylie could almost see her waggling her eyebrows suggestively.

Smiling, she replied, "A dress today."

"Not the yellow print one that shows off your legs *and* your cleavage?"

Kylie laughed at the exuberance in her friend's voice. "The very same one."

"I'll be right there!" The phone hung up with a bang, causing Kylie to laugh out loud. Mick could always make her feel better. She always had.

❖

"So...Jori and Gretchen had a good time, from what I hear." Mick bit into her sandwich with a big grin. They sat outside at a local deli, the sun shining warmly down on them. The breeze was a little cool, but it was nice just to be in the fresh air.

Kylie's stomach flip-flopped and she sighed. This was not a subject she wanted to discuss, especially not with Mick. "Yeah, sounds like it. Hey, why didn't you bring Post Office Chick to the picnic with you?" She hoped the change in topic wasn't as obvious as it sounded to her own ears.

Apparently it was, because Mick studied her as she chewed. "What is it about her?"

"About who? Post Office Chick?"

"About Gretchen."

Kylie shifted uncomfortably, looked down, and began fiddling with her own sandwich. "What do you mean?"

"You know what I mean. If I didn't know better, I'd say you're jealous."

"Jealous? Of what?" Kylie's protest sounded too vehement to her own ears. She wanted to run as fast and as far from this conversation as she could.

"Of the fact that she left with Jori."

"I don't know what you're talking about."

She felt Mick's green eyes boring into her, but she refused to look up and kept eating, despite the fact that her stomach threatened to protest. What the hell was wrong with her?

"She's your boss, Ky. You get that, right? Nothing can happen. You'd get fired."

Kylie did look at Mick then, her eyes blazing a warning to end this discussion.

"I'm only saying this for your own good," Mick went on. "I've known you for more than twenty years and I can certainly tell what's going on in that head of yours. Why you insist on trying to hide it from me, I have no idea."

Kylie averted her gaze, denying Mick eye contact. It was the only weapon she had. *Pathetic*, she thought.

"The rumor mill has it that she got her last assistant fired when she was at Kaplan."

Kylie whipped around to glare at her best friend. "Maybe she was unhappy with her assistant's competence, Mick."

"Maybe she was fucking her assistant, Kylie," Mick shot back.

"Jesus Christ, I don't believe this."

Mick held up her hands in surrender. "Look, I'm not saying that's what happened. I'm just saying it's a possibility."

Kylie rolled her tongue around in her mouth, her anger building. "You know, you ask what it is about Gretchen for me. What about you? What's your deal with her? First, you're sure she's a big, lying closet case pretending to be straight. Now you think she was sleeping with her employees at her last job? Make up your mind, Mick."

Mick took another bite of her sandwich and offered no response.

They were both quiet for a long while. When Kylie had cooled down, she took a deep breath and said, "I would just prefer that Jori not suck her in and fuck her over like she does to every other woman she dates. I like Gretchen and I don't want that to happen to her. Okay? That's all."

Mick nodded and spoke just as softly. "And all I'm saying is, you don't know that Gretchen's not just like Jori."

It was true. Kylie hated to admit it, but there it was. What did she know about Gretchen, after all? *Not nearly enough*, a little voice whispered.

"I hate fighting with you," Mick said. "Can we just call a truce? Please?"

Kylie exhaled with quiet relief. "I don't want to fight with you either. Let's just agree to disagree, okay?"

"Deal."

They ate in silence for several minutes. Predictably, Mick couldn't sustain that.

"Hey, what do you have going this weekend? Want to do something?"

"Sure," Kylie answered absently. Hanging out with Mick was always a good time. "I need to yank that shrub out in front of my house. Maybe we could do that, and then I'll cook you dinner."

"And we can get a movie."

Kylie smiled. "Okay."

❖

When Kylie returned to work, Gretchen was up and out of her chair, pacing around her office and flipping through a binder. It was such a change from her earlier demeanor that Kylie stopped in her tracks and stared for several seconds before poking her head in the door.

"What's going on?" she asked.

When Gretchen looked up, she was smiling widely. Kylie noticed for the first time that Gretchen had high, chiseled cheekbones and gorgeous, perfectly straight teeth. Gretchen crossed her office to the doorway and astonished Kylie by lightly pinching her cheek.

"Ms. O'Brien, things are starting to look up. They're definitely starting to look up."

Gretchen's giddiness was contagious and, in seconds, Kylie was also smiling, her face still tingling where Gretchen had touched it. "Tell me."

"Sarah Stevenson has a huge appointment next week in Albany. I'm going to drive down there and see the client with her. And Jeff Carson's got one that's almost as big in his neck of the woods." Her smile lit up the office. "They're getting off their asses, Kylie. See? I told you. They're cranking it up. All they needed was a kick in the pants."

The phone rang before Kylie could respond and she picked up the extension in her cubicle.

"Gretchen Kaiser's office. This is Kylie. May I help you?"

"God, you've got a sexy phone voice."

Instead of being happy to hear the greeting from her old friend, Kylie felt her spirits deflate. "Hey, Jori. How're you doing? Still in town, huh?"

"For at least a few more weeks. Hey, we need to get together. You, me, and Mick. And maybe Gretchen would want to come. You think?"

I'd rather stick needles in my eyes. "Sure, sounds great."

"Cool. Is she there?"

"Yeah. Hang on." She buzzed Gretchen. "Jori's on the line."

"Oh, great," Gretchen replied. "Put her through."

As the call was transferred, Gretchen closed her door. Kylie deliberately turned away from Gretchen's windows. She didn't want to see her talking to Jori, all smiles and good news, and it bothered her that she felt that way. She was glad Gretchen had shut the door, yet at the same time, she was hurt. She didn't want to hear the conversation, but she felt excluded and resented it. She picked up the handset to her phone and rapped herself in the forehead with it.

"Jesus," she muttered. "What am I, twelve?"

❖

Saturday's weather was crappy. The temperature was chilly and it rained on and off all day long, creating a dampness in the air that sent Kylie looking for a sweatshirt.

"Don't like the weather in Rochester?" she mumbled, pulling the dark green shirt over her head. "Just hang out for a minute. It'll change."

The sound of tools against porcelain rang through the upstairs of her little house. She grabbed a Corona from the refrigerator, pushed a wedge of lime into the opening, then plugged it with her thumb and turned it upside down to move the lime down into the beer, just as Mick had taught her. Taking her own Diet Coke from the counter, she headed up to the source of the noise.

"Here you go," she said, holding the beer out to Mick, who was elbow-deep in the tank of her toilet. "A reward for all your hard work."

Mick took the bottle, her green eyes crinkling with gratitude. "There's nothing better than a beautiful woman bringing me a beer. Life is good."

After a quick swig, she went right back to work and Kylie pulled herself up onto the vanity to watch. She was always amazed that Mick just knew how to fix things. She just *knew*, like it was in her blood or something. Kylie was sure she could learn how to fix things, too, but Mick was always offering and it seemed to make her feel good when she could repair something for Kylie. So, more often than not, Kylie took her up on her offers.

Despite the chill in the air, sweat beaded across Mick's upper lip. Her red T-shirt was clinging to her and Kylie admired the muscular build of her torso, not for the first time. The veins in her forearms stood out prominently and she exuded pure strength. It was a quality of Mick's that often sent a bit of an erotic tingle up Kylie's spine; all that power tended to make her mouth go dry. She took a swig of her pop.

The ends of Mick's brown hair were also dampened with sweat and Kylie smiled fondly at the sprinkling of gray that was visible. Had they really known each other for over two decades? Were they really old enough to be getting gray hair?

Mick caught her gaze and narrowed her eyes playfully. "What are you grinning at?"

"Your gray."

"Forty's just around the corner, babe. For both of us."

"Hey, I think gray can be sexy."

"Says the blonde whose gray can barely be seen."

"That's because I don't have any," Kylie teased.

"Bullshit."

Kylie laughed. Mick was right. Kylie affectionately referred to her hair stylist as the Hair Goddess. She'd subtly introduced highlighting into Kylie's regular hair-maintenance routine so the encroaching gray was covered before anybody noticed. Except Mick.

"You know all my secrets. It's unfair."

Mick gave a final twist and sat back on her heels. "There. That ought to do it." She cranked the water back on and waited while the toilet filled. Once full, it stopped and sat silently. She and Kylie looked at each other.

"It's not running!" Kylie was happy but not surprised.

"No, it's not."

"I don't believe it."

"Told you I could fix it." She stood up and brushed her hands on her pants.

Kylie threw her arms around Mick's neck, standing on her toes to do so. "You're the best."

"Don't let it get around." Mick hugged her, humming a soft sound of pleasure that buzzed at Kylie's ear. Kylie began to ease her grip, but Mick held tightly for several more seconds before letting her go.

"You get yourself cleaned up and I'll go get dinner started," Kylie ordered. "Okay?"

"Sounds good."

In the doorway of the bathroom, Kylie turned back. "Hey, Mick?" Mick looked at her expectantly. "Thanks."

Mick's smile was filled with warmth. "For you? Anything."

❖

Later on, their stomachs were full of pork chops, potatoes, and green beans. Mick put a DVD into the player and Kylie brought two mugs of coffee into the living room.

Plopping down on the well-worn couch, she said, "Did you have enough to eat?"

"Good God. If I ate here every night, I'd weigh three hundred pounds." Mick had taken a quick shower and donned the clean T-shirt and jeans she'd brought in a duffel bag. She still had a few damp tendrils of hair around her ears and it made her seem younger than her thirty-seven years.

"Well, I made an extra pork chop, so I'll wrap it up for you and you can take it home and eat it tomorrow or take it for lunch next week."

"Great. Thanks." Mick gestured at the wicker basket filled with dog toys that Kylie hadn't had the heart to pack away. "You thinking about a puppy yet?"

Kylie sighed. "I don't know. Not yet. A little more time, I think."

She had just reached a point where she could enter her house after work and not burst into tears over the painful absence of Rip. She needed a few more weeks before she could entertain the idea of replacing him.

Mick nodded. "Let me know. I'll help you look."

They hunkered down into the cushions and started the movie, propping their feet on the coffee table as always, enjoying one another's presence. It was nice to be single but not feel alone, Kylie decided. It was comforting to have a friend like Mick—somebody who knew her well and was low maintenance—to have dinner with or watch a movie with, somebody she could have deep conversations with or sit with in total, easy silence. *Not that I wouldn't enjoy some company in my bed once in a while.* She grimaced. She'd been on her own for quite some time now, and she was starting to feel the empty space left in her heart slowly growing. Rip's loss certainly didn't help.

Mick interrupted Kylie's reverie by patting her own thigh without taking her eyes from the movie. Kylie obeyed the wordless command, shifting her body and putting her left foot in Mick's lap. Her attention never leaving the TV, Mick pulled off Kylie's sock and began a slow, firm massaging. Her large hands were so strong, her fingers adept at finding just the right places to press and rub, Kylie could barely keep from groaning out loud.

She suspected Mick actually liked massaging her, as she offered the treat quite regularly. Kylie had made a pact with herself, however, never to give voice to just how much *she* enjoyed it. She and Mick talked about a lot of things, from politics to money to sex, but she refused to let Mick in on the fact that her foot massages were highly erotic. Right now, Kylie could barely keep from squirming, but the fact that she was grinding her behind into the couch cushions was her own business entirely and no more than the by-product of too many nights alone.

Face it, the little voice hissed, *you haven't been laid in almost a year. Any contact will get your juices flowing.* Once again, she wished she was the kind of woman who could participate in casual sex—just have sex for the sake of having sex and getting off. It would certainly help scratch the seemingly constant itch she felt lately. If she'd been built that way, she knew for a fact she could take Mick by the hand and lead her to the bedroom. Or hell, jump her right here on the couch. Mick could do casual sex; she often did, and made sure to fill Kylie in on all the dirty, intimate details the next morning.

But Kylie had never been able to sleep with somebody she wasn't in love with, and though she loved Mick with all her heart, she didn't love her like *that*. She sighed. *Which is too bad for both of us.*

Mick's voice interrupted her again and she was surprised to see that the movie had been paused without her noticing. "Did you see the paper this morning?"

Kylie blinked, trying to orient herself and pull away from her previous train of thought. "Um, no. I didn't have a chance."

"Home Depot has garbage disposals on sale. Good prices. We should grab one and get it installed for you. Yank out that piece of crap you have now."

"Oh. Okay."

Mick hit the play button and the movie started up again. Kylie took a deep breath and flopped onto her side, dropping her other foot into Mick's lap and wondering what it would take for her to be able to throw caution to the wind and just go get herself laid, mate-for-life tendencies be damned. *Seriously, how hard could it be?*

Exactly half a second later, she was laughing internally at herself, feeling silly for even entertaining such a ridiculous thought.

CHAPTER NINE

H ow'd it go?" Kylie's excitement was genuine and her voice was a welcome melody in Gretchen's earpiece as she sped south along the New York State Thruway at seventy-five miles an hour, chatting on her cell phone.

"It was fantastic. Sarah really knows her shit. I just hung back and let her do her stuff, answered a few big picture questions here and there." She smiled at the memory. "Let me tell you something, Kylie. In sales, there's nothing quite like the feeling of knowing you've got the client in the bag."

"And she bagged him?"

"She totally bagged him."

"She's good." Kylie's voice was tinted with pride. "Jim always said she's our best rep. Jason has larger numbers, but Sarah's got a tougher territory."

"She definitely charmed them. It was impressive."

"And now you're headed downstate for the weekend?"

Gretchen sighed. "Yes, I am."

"You don't sound thrilled about it."

"I've just got other things I could be doing, you know? I've got boxes to unpack. I've got a bathroom to paint. I've got groceries to buy."

"Will you get to see your brother's family?"

Gretchen smiled at Kylie's ability not only to remember details, but to find the bright spot. "I will. *That*, I'm looking forward to."

"See? So, it won't be a wasted trip."

"You're right."

"I usually am. You should listen to me more often." Kylie's tone was light and Gretchen felt herself wanting to stay on the phone with her for the entire ride.

"What's new? Anything I need to know?"

"Not really. It's been pretty quiet today." Gretchen could make out the sound of Kylie shuffling some papers. "Let's see. Jessica Scott called again. Persistent little bugger, isn't she? She wanted to congratulate you on turning the budget around or something like that. She's in your voice-mail. Wheeler wants to meet with you next Wednesday so I put that on your calendar. Jori called late this morning. That's about it. I handled anything else that cropped up, so you should be all clear for the weekend."

"What are your plans next week? In the evenings?" It was out of her mouth before Gretchen even realized it.

"The evenings?" Kylie sounded properly confused by the head-spinning change in subject. "What do you mean?"

Gretchen chuckled. "I mean, I'd like to take you to dinner. I never thanked you for working late to help me get the budget together and I rarely thank you for doing such a great job and making me look so good. I'd like to take you to dinner. Someplace nice."

"You don't have to do that, Gretchen. Really. It's my job."

"You don't want to have dinner with me?" She managed to squeeze a playful note into her reply to mask the seriousness of the question.

Kylie was silent for several seconds before answering quietly, "I'd love to have dinner with you."

"Tuesday after work?"

"Tuesday would be great."

"Good."

They talked business for a few more minutes and though Gretchen didn't want to hang up, she had no excuse to continue the conversation other than a desire to keep Kylie talking. Ending the call, she snapped her phone shut with a sigh, her thoughts bouncing around her mind like the little silver balls in a pinball machine.

She thought about Kylie, sitting in her cubicle, answering the phone with just the right blend of competence and sugar. The clients loved her. The sales reps loved her. Gretchen had seen her for a short time that morning and found her black slacks and raspberry silk shell quite an eye-catching combination. As she'd briefed Gretchen before the trip, a lock of blond hair had fallen forward and Gretchen had to fight to keep from reaching out and tucking it back behind Kylie's ear.

Suddenly feeling stifled, she shook the vision from her head as she passed a semi on the thruway and slid the sunroof open to let in some air. Fantasizing was fine; she'd done it ever since she first realized she liked women and wasn't about to stop now. But thinking beyond the physical was a no-no and she had to consciously turn her thoughts elsewhere. She replayed the list of calls Kylie had recounted. *Jori called late this morning.*

Jori.

Gretchen growled, annoyed. The subject of Jori had already taken up enough of her thinking time. Jori was fun. They'd been having a terrific time on a very casual level. Jori was worldly, wealthy, sexy, creative...all things that Gretchen found attractive. She'd known within ten minutes of meeting her at the picnic that they'd end up in bed together, and they had—or on Gretchen's couch, anyway. Jori had been just the right combination of fun and serious, with no pretense whatsoever that their time together was anything more than nonchalant and for-the-moment. It was exactly what Gretchen looked for in her informal pairings and they'd never failed to satisfy her temporary needs. Until Jori.

Gretchen hissed out a frustrated little breath. Jori had done everything right, everything Gretchen had expected and wanted of her. She was sexy and attractive and a great kisser. Her moves were smooth, not too gentle, not too harsh. They'd battled a bit for control; Jori had even joked about two tops trying to top each other. Gretchen had won the first match, despite Jori's height and weight advantages. Jori had orgasmed loudly, her fingernails digging into Gretchen's shoulder. Then she immediately flipped Gretchen flat onto her back on the floor and plunged her fingers in without preamble. Gretchen had been wet and ready and had come quickly and rather quietly, but was surprised to feel no relief at all.

She had carried it off well and she was sure Jori wasn't looking deeply enough to suspect anything was wrong. They'd joked and laughed and dressed and Jori had taken off not long afterward, just like a good casual sex partner always does. Baffled by her body's lack of contentment, Gretchen had gone immediately into the bedroom to try taking care of things herself.

Two climaxes later, nothing had changed. She couldn't remember the last time an orgasm had left her feeling so utterly frustrated, and she'd spent every free moment of the next two days staring off into space trying to figure out what the hell was wrong with her.

Self-analysis not being one of her favorite pastimes, Gretchen blinked rapidly and shook her head, forcing herself back to the present. She would wait and call Jori later that night or further on into the weekend. In the meantime, her thoughts had taken another path. On impulse, she picked up the cell and dialed, grinning.

"Good afternoon, Gretchen Kaiser's office. This is Kylie, may I help you?"

"I forgot to tell you to have a nice weekend."

She could practically hear the smile on Kylie's face, picture her blue eyes twinkling the way they always seemed to when she was pleasantly surprised. "You're right. You did forget."

"Have a nice weekend, Kylie."

"You, too, Gretchen."

She flipped the phone shut and hummed happily for the rest of the drive to Poughkeepsie.

❖

The house hadn't changed. Gretchen didn't know why she thought it might. It had only been a couple months since she'd been there. She swung the BMW into the driveway and parked next to her father's Cadillac. After turning off the ignition, she sat for several long minutes, hating that she was dreading the visit so much.

"Let's just get it over with," she muttered as she popped the trunk and exited the car. Retrieving her bag, she inhaled deeply. It was funny how different towns and cities and even states could smell different from one another. Happy as she was finding herself to be in Rochester, she still missed Poughkeepsie.

Gretchen was struck with the same weird feeling each and every time she'd entered her parents' house since her mother's death. It felt, quite literally, like a slap. The second she entered the foyer, she was smacked by the absence of Emma Kaiser and physically flinched. It happened every single time, no matter how thoroughly she prepared for it.

Today was no different, and shaking off the discomfort, she set her bag down and called, "Dad?"

Her voice echoed through the quiet house and she cocked her head to listen for signs of life. Despite their lack of closeness, she knew her father well. Walking directly to the basement door, which stood ajar, she pulled it farther open and heard the sound of the television.

"Dad?" she called again.

"Down here." His tone was deep and gravel-like. Gretchen had no illusions about where she'd acquired her own low voice.

She plodded down the carpeted steps to her father's haven. He had refinished the area with her mother's help about twenty years ago. Emma had decided her husband's collection was getting out of hand and suggested they create a space just for him. It was his pride and joy. Baseball memorabilia was everywhere, hung on the paneled walls, decorating the corner bar area. He had cards and balls and bats and hats and even seats. A large poker table sat to one side, looking well-worn from seeing its regulars at least once a week.

John Kaiser sat in a big, black leather recliner watching the Yankee game on the big screen TV in front of him, a bottle of Heineken and a bowl of pretzels on the end table to his left. He looked over his shoulder briefly, and his dark eyes softened.

"Hey, sweetheart. Is it that time already?" He glanced at his watch.

Gretchen approached him and kissed him on the cheek, the scent of his Old Spice sending her back to her childhood. "It's almost five thirty."

"Guess I lost track of time." He picked up one of the four remote controls from the end table. "Let me just set this to record the rest of the game." His eyes were glued to the set and he gestured at it. "Look at this moron." He shook his head in disgust, punched a few buttons, and turned everything off.

"Looks like you're getting pretty good with the electronics," Gretchen said.

"J.J. fixed it up for me and gave me a lesson. That kid knows electronics, let me tell you." After three tries and some help from Gretchen, John pulled himself up out of his chair. "Thank you, darlin'. These old knees don't seem to want to work anymore."

Gretchen was surprised by how much older her father appeared since the last time she'd seen him. He was no spring chicken at seventy-five, but she had certainly never considered him elderly. His hair had thinned and was all white now; no trace of the rich darkness Gretchen had inherited was left. His crow's feet were permanently visible, even when he wasn't smiling, and his jowls seem to hang more than she remembered.

"Why are you so dressed up?" he asked, startling her out of her head as they slowly climbed the stairs.

She glanced down at the red suit and pumps she'd worn to the appointment with Sarah that morning. There had been no place to change and she suddenly found herself itching to get out of her work attire. "I came from work, Dad. I'll change before dinner."

"We're meeting your brother at six thirty. You'd better get a move on."

Satisfied that he was up the stairs safely, Gretchen took one last glance at his astonishingly small form. He'd never been a big man, but he seemed impossibly frail and little now. Swallowing, she grabbed her bag from the foyer and headed upstairs to change.

Her room was still the same as it had always been. Somehow, she always expected it to look completely different when she returned, having finally fallen victim to her father's desire to convert the room into something else. After she'd moved out, he had wanted to use it for his baseball stuff, but Gretchen's mother had talked him into finishing the basement instead, using the excuse that it was bigger and he could have his poker buddies down there until all hours if he wanted.

Tonight, she would sleep in her old bed. Something about that thought stirred up discomfort in her stomach and she seriously debated asking Jenna if she could bunk at her and J.J.'s house with the kids. But there were things in the basement storage area she needed to sort through; the earlier in the morning she could do that, the sooner she could head home.

Home. Funny that she was already thinking of Rochester as home.

Her room was a mellow lavender, and daylight streamed in through the three adjacent windows running across the front of the house. It was definitely the nicest bedroom, with its own little bathroom, just like a miniature version of her parents' master suite. The large double bed sat high off the ground, and she was sure her feet would still dangle if she sat on it. The gingham-checked purple and white comforter looked as soft and fluffy as it had the first day she'd spread it out. She'd bought it on her last shopping trip with her mother before she died. The throw pillows were arranged neatly and Gretchen realized belatedly that the bed probably hadn't been touched since her last visit.

Sighing, she dropped her bag and pulled the sheets off so she could toss them into the washing machine rather than trying to sleep in six inches of dust. As she worked, she glanced up at the shelves of trophies and awards that occupied a corner of the room. Science, gymnastics, dance, honor roll. They were all there. She'd been a good kid, a studious kid. Too studious, she thought now.

Gretchen hadn't focused on much that had to do with a social life when she was in school. Her close friends were few, but that hadn't mattered. She'd worked her ass off to win her father's approval. Whatever it took, she did it. She'd graduated in the top ten of her class from both high school and college and to this day, wasn't sure if he'd even noticed. The day J.J. had brought home his first ever B in math, they had gone out for ice cream. An old anger flared in her, and Gretchen made herself look elsewhere.

The television on the dresser was a fairly new addition. Her father had hooked it up for when the grandkids stayed over. A DVD player sat next to it, topped with a stack of Disney movies and cartoons. She smiled, thinking how she'd never had a TV in her room when she was a kid, never even thought about it. *Times certainly do change.*

After tossing the sheets into a pile, she opened her bag and changed into jeans and a pink sweater tank. *Cool enough for summer weather, warm enough for a restaurant with too much air-conditioning*, she thought, examining herself in the mirror. She pulled some of her dark hair back and fastened it with a gold clip so it was off her face, but still spilled around her shoulders. It was a good look for her, and the one rebellious lock that refused to stay clipped and instead hung down near her left eye like a corkscrew made her appear a bit younger. She hoped.

When the phone rang, she knew it would be Jenna calling to remind them when and where to meet. Her father's ability to remember his day's schedule seemed to be eluding him as he got older, but J.J. and Jenna were good about keeping him on track. Gretchen thanked her lucky stars for the zillionth time that her brother was nearby and willing to take care of John Kaiser as he aged. She certainly had no desire to do it.

Realizing the selfishness of the thought, she muttered, "I am so going to hell."

She gathered up the pile of bedding and headed down to put it in the washer before they left for dinner.

"What are you doing?" her father asked as she descended the stairs. He eyed the sheets suspiciously.

"I thought I'd wash these before I slept in them tonight." Gretchen tried to keep the irritation out of her voice, but her attempt wasn't all that successful.

"I just washed them this morning."

"You did?" She stopped in her tracks, shocked.

"Of course I did. You said you were staying over. What, did you think I'd expect you to sleep in dusty sheets?"

"Oh." She could think of no response. Nothing. It had never occurred to her to actually smell the bed linen or look closely and see if it was clean. She'd just assumed. She tried to picture her father not only washing the sheets, but making the bed back up and doing a good job of it. The image wouldn't come.

"Oh," she repeated feebly and took the sheets back upstairs.

❖

Gretchen jabbed a finger across the table at her brother. "You. Outside. Now."

She stood, threw her napkin down forcefully, and stormed out of the restaurant in a blaze of fury. With J.J. on her heels, she stomped far enough into the back end of the parking lot that she was sure her shouting wouldn't be heard inside.

There, she whirled on him. "Are you *fucking* kidding me with this?"

"Gretchen, calm down. Please." J.J. held his hands up in a placating gesture. "Just get a grip."

His voice was irrationally composed, as far as Gretchen was concerned. She paced around the darkened parking lot, fuming, fully expecting that she was giving off some kind of steam. A couple glanced warily at her as they passed by, heading toward their car.

"Calm down? Get a grip? Fuck you, J. Fuck you. I can't believe you didn't tell me about this. I *cannot* believe it. Bypass surgery? That's not just some simple, everyday procedure. He's not having his tonsils out. He's not getting an appendectomy. This is his *heart*. His *heart*, J."

"I know. I wanted to tell you. He asked me not to."

"How long have you known?"

J.J. pressed his lips together and ran his hand through his unruly head of hair.

"How long?" she repeated through clenched teeth.

"A couple weeks," he said, his voice laced with guilt.

Gretchen's mouth dropped open and a sound something like a strangled snort escaped. "A couple weeks." She looked up at the sky, not even registering the beauty of the blanket of stars. "A couple weeks." She pressed the heel of her hand into her right eye, trying to stave off the headache that was approaching as rapidly and powerfully as a freight train; she knew she had little chance. "Tell me, J. Why did nobody think this might be something I should know about? For Christ's sake, I'm the oldest, if nothing else."

"Dad was worried about you. He didn't want me to tell you until you were settled. You had the move and the new job and all that. He didn't want to add to your stress."

"That's crap. Dad has *never* worried about me." Gretchen's voice was filled with such venom it shocked even her.

J.J.'s face hardened. He took a step toward her and she flinched. He wasn't a tall man but his presence was large, just like their father's. They were the only two people who had ever been able to make her feel small. He pointed at her as he spoke, aggravation tinting his eyes.

"You know what, Gretch? You need to get past this shit. You got a raw deal from him growing up. I know that. We all know that—you never let us forget it. But times have changed. People change. You're a big girl now and this isn't about you. It's about him."

Gretchen narrowed her eyes and poked her finger back at him, unable to keep the anger at bay. She kept her voice low, barely audible, but it was filled with a combination of pain and resentment plain even to her. "You have *no* idea what it was like to be me and live in your shadow. *No idea.*"

J.J. seemed to suddenly let go of his tension. He took a deep breath and released it slowly. "I know." His voice was tender, his face touched by the anguish Gretchen couldn't hide. "I know. You worked your ass off to get him to notice you and you felt like he never did. I knew it then and I know it now."

Gretchen nodded, irritated at the prickle of tears she felt behind her eyes, annoyed that J.J. could get to her so easily.

"He sees you now, Gretch. He does."

She shook her head and shrugged, not believing him and not having the voice to say so.

"Maybe you should have a discussion with him. Did you ever think of that?"

She looked at him like he'd grown three heads.

"I know, I know." J.J. placed a warm hand on her shoulder. "He's not the easiest guy to have a serious conversation with. He'll never bring it up. You know that. But I bet if you did, he'd talk to you and maybe you could put this all to bed once and for all. None of us are getting any younger, you know? And this has eaten you alive since you were seven years old."

Gretchen swallowed the lump in her throat, mentally warning the tears not to fall. She took a deep breath, reclaiming her composure. Talk to him? Discuss the fact that she'd always been sure he didn't really love her all that much? She chuckled inside. It was an interesting idea. Silly, but interesting.

"When exactly is the surgery?" Her voice was back to normal, authoritative and commanding.

"A week from Tuesday."

Gretchen began flipping through her schedule in her head. J.J. waited her out.

"Okay. I think I can be here."

It wasn't at all what he'd expected her to say and his smile gave away that fact. "Yeah?"

She nodded.

"Good."

❖

Sleep was elusive. Gretchen was one of those people who had a hard time shutting off her mind, even when she was utterly exhausted. That night, she lay in bed with her eyes wide open, listening to the familiar sounds of her childhood home: a barking dog, distant traffic, a car driving by with its music too loud. Her mind was a jumble of thoughts, people, and conversations. She was sure if she'd been a cartoon, she'd have several faces floating over her head, spinning around in some weird pattern that was supposed to represent random thought.

Her father, her brother, Kylie, Jori, and Margo Wheeler spun in circles, forcing her to squeeze her eyes shut in order to close out the ridiculous battle for her attention. She glanced at the clock. It was going on three, which annoyed the crap out of her. With a sigh, she threw off the covers, deciding a glass of milk might help, and stood in the dark room in her panties and tank top. It was mid-June, but the nights were still a bit cool. She reached for her pajama pants and pulled them on before opening the door and padding into the hall in her bare feet.

She was surprised to see light under the door of her father's bedroom and could hear movement within. Stepping to the closed door, she cocked her head, listening, her hand poised to knock. The sounds coming from in the room were faint—a shuffling, a sigh. Making a decision, she tapped softly.

"Dad?" When there was no response, she tried again, a little harder. "Dad? Are you okay?" She thought she heard his voice, just above a whisper, but she was uncertain. "Dad. I'm coming in." Under her breath, she muttered, "I hope you're decent."

She turned the knob and pushed into her parents' bedroom.

Her father was trundling slowly from the bathroom, his feet dragging along the hardwood floor. His pajama bottoms looked two sizes too big and his bare chest was covered with white hair, the skin sagging off his torso. Gretchen had never seen him look so old and it stopped her in her tracks.

"Gretchen." He glanced at her as he continued to make his way to the bed. "What are you doing up?"

"Couldn't sleep. I thought I'd get a glass of milk and I heard you. What are *you* doing up?" She crossed the room uncertainly, wondering if she should help him in some way.

"Something at dinner didn't agree with me."

He held out his hand to her and she grabbed his arm, helping balance him as he got into bed. His skin felt strangely foreign to her; they'd never shared much physical contact. As she helped him settle into the queen-sized, four-poster oak bed, she was transported back in time for a minute to the Saturday mornings she'd spent watching cartoons in bed with her mother, her father being off at work or playing golf with his coworkers. The bed seemed much smaller to her now, but her father also looked much smaller in it.

Gretchen covered him with the blankets. "Do you want some water?"

Not waiting for an answer, she went into the bathroom and filled up a glass, setting it on the nightstand when she returned.

"I do wish your mother was here." He said it so quietly and with such wistfulness that Gretchen almost wondered if he'd said it at all.

"Me, too."

"This is the time in your life when you look back. You analyze. You reflect. You figure out if you should have done things differently. I wish she was here so she could help me with that part."

Gretchen was surprised to feel emotion close up her throat. Her father was the least vulnerable person she'd ever met in her life, but right at this moment there was no better word to describe him.

"Of course, we can't change the past," he continued.

"No, we can't."

He closed his eyes and sighed heavily. He was silent for so long Gretchen was sure he'd fallen asleep, but he spoke again just as she made a move toward the door.

"If I could go back, I'd have done things differently."

When she looked back at him, his dark eyes were frighteningly clear and boring into her. She fought the urge to run. Instead, she nodded once. "Good night, Dad."

CHAPTER TEN

K ylie glanced at the clock and was shocked to see it was a little after five. "My God, where did the day go?"

The endless lists of phone calls, reports to generate, and packages to get out to the salespeople had forced her day into a blur. She hadn't even remembered to eat lunch.

"Hey, Ky." Mick peeked into her cubicle, then blinked and smiled appreciatively. "Wow. Nice suit. You look great."

"Thanks." Kylie smoothed her hand over the arm of the deep green fabric, always pleased when Mick complimented her like that.

"Do you think you can bring your green bat tonight? I want to try hitting with it, pull myself out of this slump."

"Tonight?" Kylie fiddled with the pearl-like button on the sleeve of her jacket.

"Hello? It's Tuesday. The game? You're coming right?"

"Shit." Kylie dropped her head into her hands. "I forgot."

"What?" Mick's face registered her disappointment. "How could you forget? We play on Tuesdays. We play every Tuesday."

"I can't come tonight. I'm sorry."

"You have to come, Ky. You're my good-luck charm."

Kylie waved her off. "Oh, stop it. You'll play fine."

"Why can't you come?" Mick stood with her hands on her hips, making it clear she was going to harass Kylie a bit longer before letting her off the hook. "What plans could you possibly have that are more important than coming to my softball game? Hmm?"

As if scripted, Gretchen inched up next to Mick in the small cubicle opening. Her purse was hanging from her shoulder, her briefcase dangled from one hand. She jingled her keys with the other.

"Excuse me," she said politely. "I don't mean to interrupt." Her eyes settled on Kylie and her voice grew warmer. "I'll pick you up at six thirty, okay?"

"Okay."

Gretchen cast a satisfied smile at Mick. "Have a nice night."

Mick and Kylie were both silent as Gretchen disappeared down the hall, Mick's lips pressed together in a tight line. When Kylie finally met her gaze, Mick's eyes were accusing.

"What?" Kylie asked. "Why are you looking at me like that? She's taking me to dinner to thank me for my help."

"Uh-huh."

"What the hell is that supposed to mean?"

"Nothing, Ky." Mick exhaled forcefully. "I've got to go get ready for the game. Have a nice dinner."

"Thanks," Kylie said to Mick's retreating back. "Good luck tonight. Hit a home run."

She slumped down into her chair, sulking for several minutes before pulling herself together. She'd been looking forward to this evening all day long and she wasn't about to let Mick's weirdness about Gretchen spoil it for her. After shutting down the open applications on her computer and logging off, she neatened up her desk. She hated to arrive in the morning to a pile of chaos. With a small rush of anticipation, she grabbed her purse from the bottom drawer and fished out her keys. Clicking off the desk lamp, she couldn't keep the smile from her face.

What the hell am I going to wear?

❖

The doorbell rang at exactly six twenty-nine, but Kylie swore anyway. She glared at her reflection in the bathroom mirror, begging the butterflies in her stomach to swarm elsewhere. They didn't listen.

"Get a grip, O'Brien," she ordered, heading down the stairs in her bare feet. "You have no reason to be nervous. This is dinner with your boss, not a date."

She took a deep breath as she rested her hand on the doorknob, hoping to calm her fluttering nerves. When she pulled the door open, that breath was knocked completely from her lungs as she took in the sight before her.

Gretchen stood on her doorstep in casual black pants and a red, short-sleeved sweater. Not only was red a fabulous color on her, but because everything else about her was so dark—her pants, her hair, her eyes—the red stood out even more, demanding attention. Her hair was drawn back just enough to spill unruly curls in a cascade along her shoulders. One stray lock dangled down alongside her left eye and looked devastatingly sexy. She smiled at Kylie, her hands clutching her small purse in front of her.

"Wow. Gretchen. You look fantastic." The compliment was out and hanging in the air between them before Kylie had any prayer of catching it. Rather than disapproval, however, a very gentle pink tint colored Gretchen's high cheekbones.

"Thanks. You're not looking too shabby yourself." Her deep voice sent a chill up Kylie's spine, something Kylie was beginning to wonder if she'd ever get used to.

Stepping back, she invited, "Come on in."

As Gretchen stepped into the small entryway, Kylie noticed she was wearing slight heels, making them almost exactly the same height. She liked being able to look directly into Gretchen's eyes.

"This is an adorable place." Gretchen wandered into the living room, taking in the small space with its cozy furniture and copious framed photos. Her face registered an approval that made Kylie swell with pride. "You've even got a fireplace."

Kylie's eyes were drawn to Gretchen's hand as she ran her well-manicured fingertips over the brick mantle. "It was the biggest selling point for me. It's great in the winter."

Gretchen took in the leather club chair and ottoman angled near the fireplace, a tall floor lamp bent over them. "Looks like the perfect reading spot."

Kylie smiled. "Exactly. Although I usually move the chair back near the window at this time of year. I haven't had a chance."

Gretchen's focus moved on to the pictures decorating the mantle. "I remember most of these people from the cookout." She pointed to several photos of Kylie's family members. "Who's this?"

"That's Angie. My ex."

"You're obviously still friends." It was said with what seemed to be a knowing smile.

"Yes, we are, smart-ass. And yes, I'm friends with all my exes, before you feel the need to ask."

"And just how many exes do you have?" If Gretchen felt the question was inappropriate, she didn't show it. Kylie felt a familiar warmth at the teasing tone of her voice.

"Way too many to count," she teased back. It crossed her mind then to offer Gretchen a glass of wine, a seat on the couch. That's what she would normally do with a woman who was picking her up to take her out.

Not a date, the little voice whispered. *Then why does it feel so much like one?* she wanted to ask.

Shaking her head free of the internal conversation, she said, "Let me just grab my shoes and we can go."

In the bedroom, she slipped her feet into flats that went well with her navy blue chinos. Glancing into the mirror, she fussed with her hair one last time, tucking it behind her ears and finger combing the ends. She decided it was a good outfit. The blue and white striped blouse was casual, but nicely tailored and her sister, Erin, had told her it fit her perfectly. Of course, in Erinspeak, that really meant it fit a little too snugly across Kylie's chest. Small gold hoops in her ears and a matching teardrop diamond necklace completed her look.

Impulsively, she reached up and adjusted her neckline so the diamond was more visible, then unfastened one more button, revealing additional collarbone, more skin, and an extra teasing wink of cleavage. She fled the room before she could change her mind and put on a turtleneck.

Downstairs, Gretchen had moved to the other side of the living room and was studying more photos. She looked up at Kylie's approach and her eyes fell directly to the exposed skin at Kylie's chest. Clearing her throat, she held up a photo of Kylie's fourteen-year-old nephew, Joshua.

"He has your eyes," she said.

"You think so?" Kylie crossed the room and stood shoulder to shoulder with Gretchen, trying to concentrate on the picture and not the hands holding it or the intoxicating scent of Gretchen's perfume.

"Definitely. They're exactly the same blue."

Kylie was touched by the statement and tried not to grin too widely as Gretchen set the picture back down on the table. "Ready?"

"After you," Gretchen said, extending her arm toward the door.

Gretchen's BMW was shining like a new penny in Kylie's driveway. Gretchen hit the remote door lock and opened the passenger door for Kylie. With a sigh, Kylie sank into the soft, deep tan leather seat and fastened her seat belt.

"Oh, I could get used to this," she commented, nestling farther into the embrace of the leather.

Gretchen got in and started the engine with a soft purr. "You like her?"

"She's beautiful. I've never been in a Beemer before." Kylie's family came from modest roots and she knew her father would never dream of spending on a car the kind of money the BMW must have cost.

"Never?" Disbelief tinged Gretchen's voice.

"Nope."

Without another word, Gretchen got out and went around to Kylie's door again, pulling it open.

Kylie crinkled her nose in confusion. "What?"

"You drive."

Kylie was hit by a sudden rush of adrenaline. "Are you serious?"

"Yes, I'm serious. Move it. You're in my seat."

Kylie didn't need to be told twice. She jumped out and quickly skirted the car to situate herself in the driver's seat. Placing her hands on the steering wheel, she inhaled deeply.

"It still smells new." She glanced at Gretchen. "Is it? Is she, I mean? New?"

"I've had her for about three months."

"Does she have a name?"

"Not yet. I'm still working on it." Gretchen gestured at the dashboard with her chin. "Come on. Reservations are at seven. You'd better get a move on if you want to zip around a little before we get to the restaurant."

Kylie felt like a little kid at Christmas. She adjusted the seat, sliding it back two settings, fastened her seat belt, smiled at her passenger, and slipped the gearshift into reverse.

❖

They pulled into Mercutio's parking lot at 7:10. Kylie put the car into park, turned off the ignition, and handed the keys to Gretchen. In the side mirror, she could see her face was still glowing from the exhilaration.

"Think they gave our table away yet?" she asked with a sheepish grin.

"Let's hope not."

"I don't care if they did. That was worth it."

Mercutio's was a well-known local establishment that was situated conveniently on University Avenue, halfway between Kylie's home and Gretchen's apartment. It was large and open, with high ceilings that sported painted ductwork and spinning fans. One side was all floor-to-ceiling windows that opened onto a large patio populated with tables and an outdoor bar.

"Do you want to sit inside or outside?" Gretchen asked as they approached the hostess.

"It's pretty warm. We should take advantage. Do you mind sitting outside?"

"Not at all." To the hostess, Gretchen said, "Hi. Reservations for two under Kaiser. We're a little late." She shot a look at Kylie that made Kylie smile.

They followed the hostess to a small, private table in a corner of the rectangular patio. Beams from the setting sun streamed across part of it and Gretchen gestured for Kylie to sit there. Strategically placed hedges and vine-covered fences provided a nice feeling of privacy in what was a fairly populated part of the city. Their table was round and glass-topped, intimate in size, and its location allowed them to observe the rest of the tables, as well as the patrons at the bar, if they so desired. Kylie decided she'd rather look at the face across from her.

"I'll bet you burn as red as a lobster in the summer, don't you?" she asked.

"My mother used to get really brown, but my dad is white, white, white. If I don't glop on at least SPF 30, I'm in trouble."

"You're like a China doll."

Gretchen raised her eyebrows. "Excuse me?"

"All dark hair and dark eyes and snow-white skin," Kylie explained. "Like a beautiful China doll."

Gretchen lowered her eyes and fussed with her napkin. Kylie

realized that she might have flustered her with the compliment, and the idea was enormously pleasing.

The waiter appeared, a young, handsome man with spiked blond hair, three earrings, and a tattoo on his wrist of some Japanese symbol. His smile was charming and his eyes sparkled as he greeted them and prepared to take their drinks order.

"Wine?" Gretchen asked Kylie.

"That would be great. Should we just order a bottle?"

Gretchen feigned shock, and then smiled when Kylie began to look slightly embarrassed. She ordered a bottle of an Italian Pinot Grigio and their waiter skittered away, promising to return with bread and dipping oil. They studied their menus in silence, both deciding on their dinner choices within only a few minutes.

"So…" Kylie leaned her forearms on the table and studied Gretchen's face. She was surprised by the sudden urge to twirl that loose ebony curl around her finger, and clasped her hands together in front of her just to be safe. "How was your visit with your family?"

"It was…interesting."

"In what way?"

Gretchen propped her chin in her hand and her elbow on the table, looking like she was honestly thinking about her answer. While she contemplated, the wine and bread arrived. The waiter poured two glasses and they digressed into placing their dinner orders.

As soon as they were alone once more, Kylie raised her glass for a toast, but Gretchen cut her off with a placating hand.

"Wait. This one is to you," she said. "To Kylie O'Brien. The best damn EAA a girl could ask for. Thank you for all your help. You are invaluable to me." Her coal-dark eyes shone and Kylie pressed a hand to her chest, touched by the words.

Their glasses met over the table, the soft pinging audible to only them. They sipped, each nodding their approval of the wine. Reaching into the basket in the center of the table, Kylie tore herself a hunk of bread and rubbed it through the garlic-infused olive oil on the plate next to it.

"Your trip home," she said, popping it into her mouth. "Why was it interesting?"

Gretchen's eyes held hers for several long seconds, as if she was trying to decide whether it was safe to talk on a personal level. She helped herself to bread and followed Kylie's moves into the oil.

"Well." She chewed. "My father has to have bypass surgery next week."

"Oh, wow."

"But nobody thought they should tell me about it. They've known for more than two weeks."

"What?"

"Yeah, they mentioned it casually over dinner on Saturday, my brother and my dad." Gretchen sipped her wine. "I'm afraid I had a little blowout with my brother in the parking lot of the restaurant." At Kylie's raised eyebrows, she nodded. "Yeah. Not cool."

"Of *course* you had a blowout. Why wouldn't you? I'd have been pissed."

"I was definitely that."

"Why didn't they tell you sooner?"

"J.J. fed me some crap about my father being worried about my move and my new job and not wanting to stress me out more."

"Hmm." Kylie chewed thoughtfully. "That makes sense." When Gretchen's eyes snapped up to hers, she quickly backpedaled. "It makes sense, but it doesn't mean it was the right call. I totally understand him not wanting to add pressure to your life. But they still should have told you."

"But see, that's where things get muddled, because my father isn't the kind of guy who worries about stressing other people out. If he did, he would have been home much more often when we were young and my mother would have had less anxiety in her life. The number one person on John Kaiser's list is John Kaiser. It always has been."

Kylie tried to imagine what her own life would have been like if her father had been unavailable, but she couldn't. Matt O'Brien had been a busy guy who worked long, hard hours, but he spent every moment of free time with his family. "He wasn't around much for you?"

Gretchen shook her head. "Not for me and not for my mom. He took my brother everywhere with him, though."

"You're close to your mom?"

"I was. She passed away ten years ago."

"Oh, Gretchen. I'm sorry."

"Thanks."

The waiter stopped by and refilled their wineglasses from the bottle sitting in a nearby ice bucket.

"So, needless to say," Gretchen went on, "I have mixed emotions about this surgery."

Kylie frowned. "What do you mean?"

Gretchen hesitated. "Part of me wants to be there and part of me thinks, 'I've got work to do. What good will it do for me to sit around a hospital for hours? It's not like he'll know I'm there. And not like he'll care.'"

Kylie nearly choked on her food. "Gretchen, you *have* to be there. You have to!"

A look of slight surprise crossed Gretchen's face. "Why? He was never there for me."

Kylie leaned across the table and her eyes bored into Gretchen's. "Because you're better than he is." She was satisfied to see Gretchen blinking, absorbing the idea. "And because if you don't go and—God forbid—something happens, you'll never forgive yourself."

Gretchen pressed her lips together and several emotions zipped across her face. It was the most animation Kylie had ever experienced from Gretchen, on a personal level, and she was inordinately pleased to have been the catalyst.

Their eyes met and held across the table.

"You should be there," Kylie stressed again.

Gretchen nodded. "You're right."

Deciding it was time to ease the tension, Kylie raised her glass. "To me being right."

A laugh burst from Gretchen's throat and she touched her glass to Kylie's just as the trendy young waiter appeared with their dinners. After he set Kylie's pasta in front of her and an enormous strip steak in front of Gretchen, he topped off their glasses and politely departed.

Gretchen speared a green bean with her fork and gazed across the table at Kylie. "I can't believe I told you all that. It's sort of...unlike me to go on about myself. I apologize."

"What in the world for? Telling somebody about yourself when they've asked you to tell them about yourself is nothing to apologize for, Gretchen. It's called having a personal conversation. People do it all the time."

"Ha ha." Gretchen slid a piece of steak into her mouth, then pointed her empty fork at Kylie. "So...tell me about you."

"What do you want to know?"

"Tell me about Angie."

"Ah. Right for the dirt, huh? I didn't expect you to be so predictable, Ms. Kaiser."

Gretchen laughed.

"Angie's wonderful. She's sweet and loving and kind. Big heart."

Gretchen arched one eyebrow. "But?"

"But we had nothing in common and no chemistry." Kylie chuckled. "We never should have been together in the first place. You know how it goes with lesbians. We had one good date, thought it must be fate and that we were meant to be together, and spent the next two years trying to figure out how to break up with each other."

They both shook their heads in amused dismay.

"Only two years?" Gretchen asked. "You got off easy."

"Tell me about it."

"How long ago was that?"

Kylie had to think for a moment. "About a year? A year and a half? Something around there."

"And nobody special since then?"

Kylie looked directly at Gretchen. "No. Nobody since then," she answered softly.

"What about Mick?"

"Mick?" The question surprised her. "Oh, no. Mick's my best friend, but we're not...I don't...oh, no." She shook her head adamantly. "We're just friends."

Gretchen put a forkful of baked potato into her mouth and studied Kylie before asking her next question. "Does she know that?"

"What do you mean?"

Gretchen cocked her head in a way that said *you're kidding me, right?* "Kylie. Come on."

"What?"

"Have you never seen the way she looks at you?"

"Mick?"

"She's crazy about you."

"No. We're friends. That's all."

Gretchen scrutinized Kylie for so long that Kylie began to fidget in her seat. Finally, Gretchen gave a resigned shrug and said, "Okay."

Kylie wondered at the fact that she seemed completely unconvinced. Maybe she'd just never experienced a friendship as close as the one Kylie had with Mick. "What about you?"

"What about me?"

"Nobody special?"

Gretchen took a sip of her wine. "No. Not in a long, long time."

Something in the wistfulness of her tone told Kylie not to pry further, so she changed the subject all together. "How'd you end up at Emerson?"

"Remember Jessica Scott?"

"The headhunter?"

"That's the one. I was at Kaplan and completely disgusted by their managerial ethics, or lack thereof. I was ready to get out and Jessica called me at just the right time. She keeps me aware of what's going on in my field."

Kylie squinted at her. "Why's she calling now?"

"She probably just wants to see how things are going. She might have heard through the grapevine that upper management was happy with our budget revisions. She might just want to say hi." Gretchen's eyes glinted and a light bulb went on in Kylie's head.

"She's your ex!"

"Not exactly."

"You've slept with her, though."

"There was a time or two. We've...kept in touch."

Kylie felt the unfamiliar tingle of jealousy well up in her gut and didn't like it. Deciding another subject change was in order, she asked, "If you could go anywhere in the world, where would it be?"

"Greece."

"Wow. You answered that fast."

Gretchen smiled. "I've just always wanted to go there."

"Why haven't you?"

"Who has time?"

"Oh, that's right. You work twenty-four hours a day. I forgot." Kylie grinned. "That's why God made vacations, Gretch."

"I know. I know. You're right." Gretchen dabbed at her mouth with her napkin. "One of these days."

"Why Greece?"

"I've always been fascinated by Greek mythology. I'd love to see all the places that show up in the stories, you know? Everything there is so old, so mystical."

"Plus, the food is great."

"You like Greek food?"

"Love it."

"There's a new little place near my apartment. I hear the baklava is to die for. We'll have to try that next time."

Kylie sipped her wine. "I'd like that."

They were silent for several long seconds. Kylie wondered if Gretchen was thinking the same thing she was: had they just made a date? Gretchen finally spoke, asking, "So, what do you think of this place?"

"I thought my opinion didn't matter to you," Kylie responded wryly.

Gretchen's cheeks colored a light pink. She bit her lower lip, as if accepting this fate. "You know what? I was a little harsh when I said that to you. Unnecessarily so. I'm sorry about that."

Kylie was genuinely taken aback. She'd been teasing, yes, but she hadn't expected an apology. "Hey, you were doing your job. You felt I was out of line. I get that."

"Still. I apologize for hurting your feelings."

"Then I accept your apology," Kylie said, touched. "Thank you." She wiped her mouth with her napkin and sat back in her chair. "Wow. That was good."

Gretchen sat forward, her forearms on the table. She looked more at ease than Kylie had seen her since they'd met. "I'm having a terrific time." She said it quietly, as though letting Kylie in on a secret.

Kylie was inordinately pleased with the remark. "Me, too."

"Thanks for agreeing to be my date for the evening."

"You're welcome. Thanks for asking me."

They eyed each other. Without letting go of Kylie's gaze, Gretchen waved for the waiter and said, "I'm going to order dessert. Want to share?"

For some reason the invitation sounded deliciously intimate. Kylie blamed the wine. "The chocolate raspberry torte looked good."

A few minutes later, the waiter dropped off an elegant-looking plate and two forks, setting the dessert knowingly right in the center of the table. He poured two cups of coffee and left them to their chocolate.

"Holy crap," Kylie said, eyeing the dessert. It was a thick triangle of rich, dark chocolate drizzled with a deep red raspberry sauce, and just looking at it made her feel guilty. "It's too pretty to eat."

"Nonsense." Gretchen picked up a fork, sliced off the tip, rubbed it through the raspberry sauce, and held it up over the table. "You first."

Kylie's heart skipped a beat before she leaned forward and took the forkful of decadence into her mouth. Gretchen's lips parted slightly in tandem with hers and she watched closely as the fork came out clean. It was an alarmingly sexy gesture that caused a spark low in Kylie's belly.

"Oh, my God." She snatched up the other fork as the chocolate melted on her tongue. "Oh, my God, that's good. Sinful. Christ." She chewed slowly, wanting to enjoy the taste for as long as possible. Hardly daring to believe they were complicit in this sensuous eating experience, she sank the fork into the torte, then held a mouthful up. "Your turn."

Gretchen's eyes grew impossibly darker, and the pangs Kylie kept feeling merged to a constant ache as Gretchen took the bite of dessert. Eyes closed, moaning softly, she held the fork in her mouth as if she couldn't bear to release it. Kylie watched in aroused fascination, worried she might choke on her own excitement as she slowly eased the fork from between Gretchen's lips. She could not believe how much of a turn-on it was to feed her.

"You're right." Gretchen opened her eyes and refocused on Kylie. "Absolutely sinful. Good Lord."

"Told you."

"Good choice." Gretchen used her fork to cut herself another bite.

Kylie was relieved they were now using their own forks, not certain she could survive another minute of feeding Gretchen without bursting into flames. Convinced her arousal had to be written all over her face, she dragged her eyes away from her date and lowered her head a little, trying to concentrate on the food. She didn't have a lot of luck.

The night air was wonderfully pleasant—not too warm, not too cool, as they sat in Gretchen's car in Kylie's driveway, both reluctant to say good night.

"I had a really nice time tonight, Gretchen." Kylie smiled warmly, and Gretchen noted how the twilight cast a bluish shadow across her face, highlighting her exquisite cheekbones.

"Me, too."

"Thank you."

"It was my pleasure."

Their eyes held and it would have been the most natural thing in the world for Gretchen to lean over and kiss Kylie softly on those full lips. It had taken every ounce of strength she could find to keep from doing just that and she was pretty sure Kylie had known it, that Kylie felt it. When the moment had passed, when it was obvious that Gretchen *wasn't* going to kiss her, Kylie's sweet, open face held an expression that was the perfect blend of disappointment and relief.

Letting herself out of the car, she bent to make eye contact with Gretchen once more. "I'll see you tomorrow."

"Sleep well, Kylie."

Gretchen watched until she was sure Kylie was safely into her house before releasing the breath she'd been holding. Then she drove home like a bat out of hell. Once she reached the lot of her building, she slammed the car into park and stared off into space for a long time, reliving the evening in her head and wondering what the hell she was supposed to do now.

"Fuck," she muttered as she slowly dropped her forehead against the steering wheel over and over and over.

❖

Back in her little house, Kylie shot the door bolt with more force than usual and marched into her living room. She flopped down onto her couch, flat on her back. She was almost used to the feeling of missing Rip, who would have jumped up to be near her. Kicking her flats onto the floor, she blew out a frustrated breath, took one of the striped throw pillows and held it over her face, then screamed as loudly as she could.

"I *cannot* have a thing for her," she said to the ceiling fan. "I can't. She's my boss. God damn it."

Chapter Eleven

It was after ten when Kylie heard the garage door open and her sister pull in. She stuck the bookmark into the Lisa Gardner novel she'd been reading and stretched her arms over her head, kicking the remaining throw pillow off the couch as she did so.

The side door opened just as she was clicking off the *Law & Order* rerun she'd had on for company.

"Hey, Ky." Erin breezed in and set her purse down on the kitchen table. She was a taller, thinner version of Kylie. "Sorry I'm late."

"No problem." Kylie didn't mind at all. She was happy to give her big sister a much-deserved break.

With three children and a full-time job, Erin didn't get much time to herself. True, her choice of outing was just a Tupperware party, but it was probably populated with women just like her who desperately needed a night away from their houses and families. With both Erin's teenagers away at friends' houses and her husband out of town on business for the week, she had just needed somebody to take care of four-year-old Becky, and Kylie was more than willing.

"She was good?"

"Always." Kylie loved spending time with her youngest niece.

"Uh-huh. For you, maybe." Erin's voice was skeptical, but she softened it with a smile. "What did you do?" She plopped down on the chair, her reddish blond hair escaping its clip little by little in rebellious wisps.

Kylie sat up. "Oh, let's see. We had lots of fun. First, we painted with the watercolors. Then we made ice cream out of Play-Doh. Then we played hide-and-seek. Then we played that memory board game — she kicked my ass, by the way." Erin chuckled and nodded knowingly. "Then came the male strippers."

"And a female one for Aunt Kylie?"

"Three, as a matter of fact. I taught Becky how to put dollar bills in their g-strings in the proper manner."

"I'm sure that's a skill she'll find useful."

"You know it."

"And she went to bed okay?"

"We read *Goodnight, Moon* four times, but that's all. She was tucked in and snoozing by eight thirty."

"Excellent. Thanks a bunch."

"How was the party? Did you actually find any Tupperware that you don't already have?" Erin's extensive collection of Tupperware was a source of humor for the entire family.

"Surprisingly, yes. A spatula. So there." Erin faked a pout before heading back into the kitchen. "I know it's late, but can you hang a little longer? Have a Coke with me or something? It's caffeine-free. I feel like I didn't get to visit with you much at the Memorial Day thing."

It was late and Kylie was tired, but she felt the same way. She and Erin hadn't always been close; with only three years between them, they used to shriek at one another when they were teenagers—pull hair, scratch, and bite. But as they grew up, and especially after Erin had had children, they'd become the best of friends and loved to spend time together. Erin was the first family member to whom Kylie had come out.

"Sure," Kylie said. "I can stay for a little while longer."

Erin poured the soda into two glasses with ice and brought one to Kylie in the living room. Dropping back into the recliner, she folded her long legs beneath her and sighed. "So, what's new, baby sis?"

"Not a lot, really. I've got to get my butt moving on my flowers. I'm a little behind in my planting. The front of my house looks bare. Otherwise, just working."

"Yeah, how's that going? The new boss must be working out. I'm sorry I didn't get a chance to meet her at Mom and Dad's."

"Gretchen. She's terrific."

"Mom said she was very nice."

"She's amazing." Kylie felt pleased that her mother had mentioned

Gretchen. "She's whipping the salespeople into shape and really cleaning things up around the office. Upper management loves her."

"How 'bout you? Is she easy to work for?"

"Very. We had a little bit of a heated conversation early on, but we got past it. She even took me to dinner last night to thank me for all my hard work, which was so cool. I mean, Jim was great, but he never treated me like Gretchen does. She's funny and smart and strong and attractive. I like her. I really like her." Kylie stopped abruptly and sipped her Coke, aware that her eyes were darting around the room instead of meeting Erin's.

"Ky?" Erin cocked her head. "What's going on?"

"Nothing. Nothing's going on." Kylie squirmed. Hiding anything from Erin was next to impossible.

"You *do* like her, don't you?"

"What? No. No, of course not. Don't be silly. She's my boss." Kylie sounded much less convincing than she'd hoped, and she knew Erin had busted her. "Damn it."

"I may not have talked with her, but I did see her. She's beautiful."

"And gay."

"You're kidding." Erin blinked in disbelief. "Shit, Kylie."

"Can you believe my luck? I finally meet somebody that I think could have potential and I can't date her."

It was the first time she'd spoken the words out loud since realizing them after their playful dinner the previous night. She wanted to date Gretchen. It was a simple fact. She admitted it to herself, and despite the futility of the situation, she felt the tiniest bit better. The workday had been great. She and Gretchen had talked about having dinner again. They'd been happy, smiling, even bordering on flirty. Gretchen would invariably reel it in and return to being professional long before Kylie ever thought about doing so.

Not surprisingly, there was no mention of chocolate raspberry torte, though Kylie was sure she'd never look at the dessert the same way again. The truth was, they'd both had quite a bit of wine. Kylie liked to fall back on that reasoning when she recalled sitting in Gretchen's car with her...the night quiet and darkening, the undeniable arousal permeating the air. She was still somewhat shocked that Gretchen hadn't kissed her, but it was probably for the best. After all, she was

Gretchen's subordinate. Gretchen was her boss. Their pairing would be frowned upon strongly at Emerson and they both knew it. If only… Kylie didn't want to think ahead, think about what could be if the situation was different.

"Does she feel the same way?" Erin asked.

Kylie colored with embarrassment. "I don't know. We have fun. She's kind of hard to read and she isn't exactly…warm and fuzzy. At least not at work."

"So…this is just a physical thing for you, then?"

"No. No, I don't think so. I mean, she's warmer and fuzzier with me than with anybody else. Other people think she's cold. I don't see her like that."

"What does Mick have to say about all this?"

Kylie pursed her lips. "I can't talk to her about Gretchen. Mick hates her."

"Why?"

"Long story."

"So, Mick thinks she's cold, too."

No, Mick thinks she's a lying, conniving bitch. She almost said it aloud, but caught herself. "Yeah."

"Well, baby sis, it seems to me that you don't have a lot of options here. A, you don't even know that Gretchen is interested in you that way, and B, she's your boss. Unless you plan on looking for a new job—which I sincerely hope you don't because you've got a lot of time into Emerson—you need to just keep it in your pants, so to speak, and go on with your life. Right?"

Kylie sighed. "Yeah." She knew Erin was right, had expected Erin to say exactly what she'd said. She just didn't want to hear it and she certainly didn't want to accept it.

"Come on, Kylie." Erin sat forward, her voice and eyes gentle. "You know yourself as well as I do and you tend to jump in with both feet. Without testing the water first. You fall hard and fast and you always have. You need to put a stop to this train of thought now, before you end up getting yourself hurt. Okay?"

Kylie nodded, feeling disheartened. "Okay."

❖

The phone call from Sarah Stevenson was exactly the kind of thing Gretchen needed to get her mind back on work. She was not the kind of person who normally let *anything*, let alone a sexual fantasy, sidetrack her, but one look at Kylie in that royal blue dress that fell just above her knees and she'd been on a fast train to Smutville. She'd spent all day Wednesday and much of Thursday morning recalling her dinner with Kylie, how much she'd enjoyed their time together, and remembering how much she'd wanted to kiss her that night. She wasn't used to such distraction and it was starting to irritate her.

Hanging up from her conversation with Sarah, she buzzed Kylie at her desk. "Call every one of our local sales reps and see if the guys in Buffalo and Syracuse can be here late this afternoon. If they can't, it's okay. I know it's last minute and they may be busy, but Sarah just closed her deal. We're having a celebration."

Out the office window, she could see Kylie's head snap around. In seconds, she was in the doorway, an enormous grin plastered across her face. "She did it?"

"She did it."

"God, Gretchen, that's…that's *huge*."

"It is. She's on her way here. Would you book her a room at the Marriott? She'll need to stay over so we can go through her paperwork thoroughly before the weekend." Gretchen sat back in her leather chair, hands clasped behind her head, enjoying the view in the doorway. "I'm trying to figure out the best way to tell Wheeler."

Kylie folded her arms and leaned against the door frame, basking in the scrutiny. "Rumor has it she's actually in her office this morning. I'd say in person is best."

"I think you're right." Gretchen sprang up and crossed the office. As Kylie moved to let her by, their bodies brushed.

"Gretchen." Kylie stopped her with a hand on her arm.

Gretchen tried not to notice the heat burning through her sleeve, but her skin seemed unreasonably sensitive.

"Congratulations. You're really making a difference around here." Kylie's voice was soft and genuine, but her gaze was steady and penetrating.

Gretchen swallowed as she felt consumed by blue. Murmuring vague thanks, she escaped to the elevator and rode up to the sixth floor, lost in her own thoughts, her hand absently rubbing her arm where

Kylie had grasped her. As the elevator door dinged its arrival at her destination, she shook herself out of her reverie and forced her focus to the office at the end of the hall.

Margo Wheeler was the vice president of sales for all of Emerson, nationwide. She was a smart, tough woman who hadn't made it this high up without a lot of effort and a lot of sacrifice. Her third marriage was dissolving rapidly. She had no children, much to her sometimes obvious dismay, and at fifty-five, never would. She did, however, have three West Highland White Terriers that she loved with all her heart. The pictures of them sprinkled throughout her office did wonders to soften the hard-edged exterior she showed to strangers.

Gretchen had actually known Margo for nearly ten years on a surface level. Their paths had crossed at many a corporate function; Margo had attempted to recruit her to Emerson on more than one occasion. They seemed to gravitate to one another during those gatherings of mostly men, sensing a kindred spirit across the room. They usually ended up in a corner with their scotches, pointing out which men were snakes and which were on their way to becoming snakes.

Margo had paved the way for women like Gretchen, dealing every day with the same double standard men always placed on women in the business world. If you were a man who was tough, no-nonsense, and didn't take anybody's shit, you were a hero, a man to be admired. If you were a woman with those same qualities, you were quite simply a bitch and in need of a good fuck by the right guy. It seemed to Gretchen that things had been that way since the dawn of time and she often wondered if they would ever change. Forward progress could be painfully slow.

She stopped at the secretary's desk outside Margo's office. A rotund, thirtyish woman with platinum blond hair and a perpetual smile sat typing at her computer.

"Hi, Connie. Did I happen to catch her in?"

"Hello there, Ms. Kaiser. As a matter of fact, you did. Can you believe it?"

Gretchen chuckled. "No."

Connie picked up her handset and pressed a button. "Ms. Wheeler? Ms. Kaiser is here to see you." Looking up at Gretchen, she said, "You can go right in."

Margo Wheeler was a plain-looking woman, not attractive and not unattractive. She was an inch or two taller than Gretchen, but her heels always made her seem that much larger, as did her air of authority. Her chestnut brown hair was pulled back off her face and in need of a coloring, the gray peeking through proudly. Gretchen was sure if she checked Margo's schedule, there was a hair appointment within the next week; Margo didn't like to appear a day older than she actually was. She always wore a tastefully expensive suit. Today's consisted of a black skirt and red and black checked jacket.

Her office made Gretchen's look like a janitorial closet. A sprawling room with a peaceful view of the wooded area behind the building, it was complete with a leather couch, matching chair, and wet bar. The smell of freshly perking coffee pervaded.

Margo stood immediately and crossed the floor with her hand outstretched. "Gretchen. Good to see you. Come in. Sit down." Her handshake was firm, her grip warm. "To what do I owe the pleasure?"

Gretchen allowed herself to sink contentedly into the leather couch. "Well, I have some good news and thought telling you face-to-face would be more fun than a phone call."

"I'm always up for good news. Coffee?"

"No, thanks. Fifteen cups is my limit and I've already reached that this morning."

Margo laughed, a loud shock of a sound that made Gretchen jump every time. "Tell me."

"Sarah Stevenson closed her deal in Albany." Gretchen let it sink in, watching Margo's face as she processed the information.

"Good Lord."

"I know."

"We're sure?"

"She's on her way here as we speak, bringing me the paperwork."

"I knew that girl had potential," Margo said softly. "You're right. This is very, very good news."

"Don't get me wrong," Gretchen said. "I know we're not even in the same league as the bigger offices. Houston is huge, and I don't know that we'll ever catch up to L.A. But I think this is a good start to getting the East Coast up to where it should be." It was important to her to let Margo know that she was aware of the shortcomings of her region. She didn't want to be projecting any hint of a false sense of security to her boss.

"You're damn right, it's a good start." Margo's voice was firm. "Don't make this smaller than it is. That account is going to bring in a lot of money for this part of the country. And if your other rep comes through...what's his name? Bergman?" Gretchen nodded. "If Bergman comes through as well..." She let the sentence dangle, watching Gretchen calculate the possibilities. "I knew hiring you was the right move, Gretchen. I knew it. I told Ed that from the start."

Gretchen felt her face color slightly at the praise. She was flattered that Margo had talked to J. Edward Emerson about her. Nothing made her prouder than knowing she was valuable in her position. It was what she lived for and the rush was exhilarating.

"Thank you, Margo. Listen, I'm putting a little impromptu celebration together late this afternoon for my staff. Just a casual thing in the conference room. Some pizza, champagne maybe. I want them to know how much I appreciate their hard work. They've really come through in the last month. It would be great if you could pop in."

"That's a fantastic idea." Margo hit a button on her phone. "Connie. Call over to Lorraine's. Have them deliver a tray of assorted sandwiches to the conference room on the fourth floor around..." She checked in with Gretchen. "Four?" At Gretchen's nod, she continued. "Four. And then call that pizza place you like so much and have a sheet pizza delivered there, too. Get some soda with that. And call Richard over in the mall and have him send five bottles of some decent champagne. Not the ridiculously expensive stuff, but not the cheap crap he gives out at Christmas, either. Charge it all to my entertainment account."

Gretchen laughed, truly not expecting such generosity. "Thank you, Margo. I really appreciate this."

"Consider it a well-deserved reward for you and your crew. Just don't let them sit back on their heels now that they've made some forward progress."

Gretchen shook her head adamantly. "Oh, no. This is just the beginning. I want them to know that." She stood to take her leave. "We'll see you in our conference room later this afternoon."

"Yes, you will. Nice job, Gretchen."

Not used to wearing her feelings visible for all to see, Gretchen had a hard time keeping the goofy grin off her face as she rode the elevator back down to the fourth floor.

❖

"I really need to get some sleep if we're going to go over all this stuff tomorrow." Sarah Stevenson was still glowing as she stood, even though the celebration had wound its way down and they'd moved from the conference room to Gretchen's office.

In addition to Sarah, there was only Gretchen, Bill and Randy—both local sales reps—and Kylie left. They all had plastic cups and Bill was finishing what had to be his seventh slice of pizza. Kylie sat on the front of Gretchen's desk, her shoes tossed into a corner and her bare feet swinging gently. Slumped comfortably in her leather chair, sipping champagne, Gretchen found her eyes wandering relentlessly to Kylie's backside just an arm's length away.

Randy stretched his arms over his head, fabricating a loudly obnoxious yawn. "I'll walk you out, Sarah."

Gretchen grinned into her cup, knowing Randy was preparing to make his move, probably in the parking lot. Sarah was miles out of his league and he would learn that soon enough. Gretchen almost felt sorry for him.

Bill looked at his watch. "Holy crap. I didn't realize it was so late. My wife's going to kill me."

The three of them gathered their things and said their good-byes. "Thanks so much for all of this, Gretchen." Sarah's gratitude was obvious and her eyes cut toward Kylie as she added, "It was a really cool thing to do."

"You've done a great job. I just wanted you to know we noticed." Gretchen walked the sales reps to the door.

"Drive safely, everybody," Kylie said from her perch. "And make some noise as you get close to the security desk so you don't give Frank a heart attack."

Briefly touching Sarah's arm, Gretchen said, "I'll see you here tomorrow morning at nine, okay? We'll get the finalities ironed out."

At Sarah's happy nod, Gretchen closed the door behind the trio, leaving her alone in the office with Kylie.

"Better lock that. We don't need the cleaning crew catching us drinking on the premises." Kylie's voice seemed loud in the now-quiet room. She held up the only champagne bottle left with any contents.

"Good point. They might want some." Gretchen grinned as she turned the lock on the knob; the blinds were already closed. She held out her cup so she could share in the last of the spoils.

Kylie continued to swing her bare feet, her shapely legs moving rhythmically as her heels thumped the front of Gretchen's desk. She was adorably rumpled, her hair tousled and her cheeks flushed, and Gretchen swallowed. She was finally beginning to come down from the high started by Sarah's phone call that morning, and she knew she was going to crash pretty soon, but she was reluctant to let go of the feeling just yet.

She realized that since her visit upstairs to share the good news with Margo Wheeler earlier in the day, she'd hardly seen Kylie alone for longer than a minute or two, and she was surprised to find she'd missed her. She wasn't sure what to do with that.

"Champagne and pizza. Quite a victory banquet, if you ask me." Kylie filled Gretchen's cup almost to the brim.

"Whoa. Are you trying to get me drunk, Ms. O'Brien?" A teasing lilt colored Gretchen's tone without her permission, and she caught a flirtatious wink from Kylie in reply. It was only with great effort that she didn't acknowledge it.

Grinning, Kylie topped off her own cup with the last of the champagne. "Depends on how far it will get me, Ms. Kaiser."

You have no idea how far you could get, Gretchen thought wryly. She'd shed her jacket hours ago and now wore only black slacks and a cream-colored silk shell. She kicked off her pumps and leaned back against the front of the desk. Kylie's swinging knee brushed her hip. Gretchen absently speculated whether the friction it caused could increase the temperature in the room, as she was suddenly very warm.

"I'm afraid champagne and pizza were the best I could do on short notice," she said.

"Well, it was a really great gesture. I think it was good of you to plan something like this. It made everybody feel appreciated. Most bosses have no idea what it means to pat their people on the back once in a while."

"I know I can be tough, but despite belief to the contrary, I'm not completely cold-hearted. I believe in rewarding my people for a job well done."

They sipped their champagne in silence, barely an inch between them in the otherwise empty office. Gretchen noticed that there were a handful of other places either of them could sit if the proximity was uncomfortable, but neither moved. The clock on the bookshelf ticked away the seconds, the minutes, its hands well on their way to midnight.

"Gretchen?" The champagne had forced Kylie's voice to a deeper, huskier register as the night went on, a fact that was not lost on Gretchen.

"Hmm?"

"Do you ever worry?"

"Ever?" The vagueness of the question made Gretchen smile. "In my life, ever?"

"No, smart-ass. When you take on a new group of sales reps. Do you ever worry that you won't be able to improve them?" Kylie blinked, those blue eyes seeming twice as wide and inquisitive as usual. "I mean, it's no secret that you've been hired here and in the past to improve the performance of a failing sales force, right? Do you ever worry that you—for whatever reason—won't live up to your reputation and *won't* be able to improve the bottom line?"

"I try not to let my mind go there," Gretchen said honestly. "Is it possible that I won't be able to shape up a sales force? Sure it is. Do I dwell on that possibility? No way. I'd drive myself crazy."

Kylie nodded, seemingly satisfied with the response. "I would worry."

"Of course you would. You're a worrier. Which is a good thing. If you're worried, then I don't have to be bothered with it. You can worry for both of us and save me the energy."

"Funny." Kylie bumped against Gretchen's shoulder affectionately. "Seriously, though. You've done an amazing job with this bunch. I mean, I didn't think they needed any improvement, but obviously I was way off base. You've really made them strive to get better." She paused, her concentration so intent Gretchen could almost hear the mental cogs whirring. "I know it's been tough and a lot of us haven't made it easy for you, but wow. I'm impressed…I'm just so impressed with you. Your drive, your determination, your strength. Plus, you're just…"

Abruptly, she stopped talking, and her eyes widened as if her brain had finally caught up with her mouth and she realized she'd very nearly crossed a line. She lowered her head and studied the contents of her cup as though wishing there were more in *it* and less in *her*.

Gretchen watched in surprised fascination as a red flush seemed to emanate from inside Kylie's dress, crawling up her chest and covering her neck and face. Curiosity warred with trepidation in Gretchen's mind, and her heart picked up speed. "I'm just…what?" she prompted softly. "Aren't you going to finish?"

"Um…no." Kylie gave a humorless chuckle. "I'd probably better not."

Gretchen continued to gaze at her and Kylie squirmed like a witness being cross-examined but did not look up.

"I'm sorry, Gretch. Ignore me. I talk too much when I've had a little alcohol."

"I don't mind listening to you talk. God knows you've got to listen to me often enough."

Gretchen wasn't drunk, but she'd also had more than her share of champagne and was feeling braver than she should. *Do not pursue this*, the voice in her head warned. *You know where the boundaries are and you know they can't be breached.* Gretchen was well aware of the direction things were headed and wondered if Kylie knew, too. She felt powerless to stop the force that seemed to be pushing her that way. She tried to focus on the inner voice, but it was muffled by the heat coming off Kylie's body, so close to hers, and the distracting scent of Kylie's musky perfume.

The unspoken hung in the air between them, almost tangibly. They each sipped their champagne and remained silent. Kylie's feet seemed to swing a little faster, her bare heels softly bouncing off the front of the desk. After several minutes, Gretchen clamped her left hand firmly on Kylie's knee to stop the sound. A small gasp escaped Kylie's lips—just the smallest intake of breath at the contact—and Gretchen turned to meet her eyes.

"I like you, Gretchen," Kylie whispered. Her tone was almost apologetic and very clearly referring to something stronger than "like." She seemed relieved to say the words out loud. "I'm sorry. I know I shouldn't."

"I like you, too," Gretchen replied, her hand still on Kylie's knee.

"I've tried to ignore it, but after dinner the other night…" Kylie made a face, then looked at her cup in disgust and set it down. "God, I should just stop talking. I sound like I'm sixteen."

"No," Gretchen assured her. "You don't." She could listen to Kylie talk all night long. Leaving her hand where it was, she turned slightly so her hip was against the desk and she could see Kylie's face better. Her thumb moved in small circles on Kylie's knee.

"I'm just trying to be honest here," Kylie said. "I don't know if bringing it up is the smartest thing to do, but I guess it's a little late to be worried about that now, huh?"

"A little bit," Gretchen conceded.

"You feel it though, don't you? This...*thing* we have going on here?"

Kylie held her breath because if Gretchen hadn't felt it, or if she chose not to admit that she felt it, she would be left twisting in the wind all alone, embarrassed and humiliated. Her heart hammered in her chest. Her mouth felt dry.

Gretchen held her gaze steadily. *Tell her no,* the voice shrieked in her head. *Tell her no, that you feel nothing, that you don't know what she's talking about.* Instead, she whispered, "Yeah. I feel it."

They kept eye contact for what felt like years, their faces so close they breathed the same air. It was Kylie who finally broke the silence.

"Gretchen." Her voice was so low it cracked.

"Hmm?"

"Either kiss me right now or stop whatever it is you're doing with your thumb, because it's driving me crazy."

Gretchen felt a surge of arousal at the pleading note combined with the throaty authority in Kylie's tone. She smoothly positioned herself between Kylie's legs, facing her, and shifted her hand so she was stroking the soft skin at the back of Kylie's knee. Because Kylie was sitting, Gretchen was actually a little taller and she silently rejoiced. With her petite frame, she was rarely taller than anyone, but this position gave her a comforting sense of power. She looked down at Kylie as she continued to stroke the bare skin beneath her hand, velvet to her fingertips.

Kylie gripped the edge of the desk, knuckles white. Her lips were parted and her breathing had grown ragged. Her blue eyes, black with desire, captured Gretchen's and held them. Gretchen pushed any other thoughts out of her head for the time being, allowing the beautiful blond woman offering herself to take up all her vision, all her focus. Moving her right hand to Kylie's left knee, she mimicked the same movement as her other hand. Kylie's eyes fluttered closed for several seconds and when she opened them, there was a determined glint.

Prying her own fingers from their death grip on the desk, she slid both hands up Gretchen's chest and neck and grabbed the sides of Gretchen's head, her fingers tangling in the silky, almost-black ringlets that tumbled around Gretchen's shoulders. Their erotically infused eye contact lasted for three more seconds before Kylie forcefully pulled Gretchen's head down into a heated, bruising kiss.

Their lips fused hungrily and Kylie groaned as she tightened her knees against Gretchen's hips and closed her fingers until she had a fistful of sleek dark hair. There was nothing tentative about the way Gretchen skimmed her hands along Kylie's thighs, then pulled on her hips, sliding Kylie's backside along the top of the desk in an effort to bring her even closer. The royal blue fabric of Kylie's dress rode farther up her thighs and whimpers and moans mingled in the air. It was impossible to tell which sounds came from which woman.

Gretchen pushed her tongue into the warmth of Kylie's mouth and very nearly succeeded in submerging herself purely in the physical. It was a talent she'd honed carefully over the years, one that allowed her to enjoy her sexual encounters entirely on a visceral level, her emotions unengaged. As she and Pete had discussed often, her ability to compartmentalize was what enabled her to have casual sex with no strings attached.

But she was certainly feeling strings now. *Why?*

Her hands itched to unbutton the row of fastenings down the front of Kylie's dress. It would be so easy. And so satisfying, she was sure. She could feel the ripple of toned muscle beneath the fabric, a testament to Kylie's athletic build. She could also feel the feminine curve of Kylie's hips, the press of Kylie's surprisingly ample breasts pushing against her. God, she wanted to see them, feel them, taste them. Why couldn't she? What was holding her back? It wouldn't be the first time she'd had sex in an office setting. And the way Kylie was kissing her—with reckless abandon and obvious desire—she certainly wasn't going to stop things any time soon.

The way Kylie was kissing her...

Gretchen wrenched herself free, leaning her forehead against Kylie's. Both women breathed heavily.

"What?" Kylie asked, touching her fingertips to Gretchen's swollen lips. "What is it? Are you okay?"

God, don't look at me like that. The deep blue of Kylie's eyes bored into hers, kind, searching, waiting.

"Kylie, we can't do this." The words were out before she could stop them, before she had a chance to chicken out.

"What?" Kylie blinked in confusion, her chest still heaving.

"We can't do this."

"Why?"

"We can't. I'm your boss. It's not right."

Slowly Kylie nodded, comprehension dawning in her eyes even as her body visibly deflated. "Yeah." The look of hurt on her face was unmistakable. "Yeah, you're probably right."

Gretchen rushed to try and make that pained expression dissipate. "It's not that I don't want to. Believe me. It's just…"

"No, no." Kylie began to pull herself together and Gretchen was amazed by how quickly the wall went up…and how much it stung to see it. "No, it's okay. You're absolutely right. I'm…this was silly."

Kylie extricated her hand from its nestling spot in Gretchen's hair and gently pushed her back several inches so she could slide off the desk. Clearly embarrassed, she smoothed her trembling hands over her dress and began to search for her shoes.

Silly? Ouch. Gretchen closed her eyes and scratched at her forehead, feeling like complete and utter shit. "Kylie…"

"No." Kylie held up a hand, cutting Gretchen off. "Really. It's okay. I had a little too much to drink and I'm sure we'll laugh about this in the morning, so just…let me get out of here without making any more of a fool of myself than I already have. All right?" She slipped her feet into her shoes, her face flushed. She wouldn't meet Gretchen's eyes.

"You didn't…" Gretchen began, unsure how to proceed. Kylie was flustered and moving quickly. Gretchen didn't want her to leave this way. She reached out to touch Kylie's shoulder, but Kylie flinched away. "Kylie, you're not a fool."

"Gretchen. *Please.*" Kylie's voice was imploring and Gretchen thought she saw tears brimming in her eyes, though Kylie wouldn't look at her directly enough for her to be sure. "Please."

Gretchen nodded once and kept her mouth shut as Kylie gathered her things and disappeared briskly down the darkened hallway. There was so much she wanted to say, things she wished she could explain to Kylie. God, there were things she wished she could explain to herself. What the hell had just happened? *What is wrong with me?*

She flopped down into her leather desk chair with the sigh of somebody who hadn't sat in years. Reaching for her abandoned cup, she downed the rest of the champagne in one large slug.

"Son of a bitch," she muttered into the stillness of the night.

❖

"Son of a *bitch*!" Kylie slammed her hand against the steering wheel over and over again as she drove. "Stupid! I'm so stupid. How can I be so fucking stupid?"

She doesn't want me.

Kylie was torn between raging anger at everybody she could think of—at herself, at Gretchen, at Rip for not being home to comfort her, at Angie for not being right for her in the first place—and devastating pain. She was sure she'd been reading Gretchen's signals correctly, *sure* of it. Kylie was thirty-seven years old; she'd been around the block a few times and could usually tell when a woman was interested in her. How had she misinterpreted things so very badly? And why did it hurt so much to realize that Gretchen wasn't really interested?

She doesn't want me.

Oh, sure, she'd used a perfectly legitimate excuse: their working relationship. It was hardly something Kylie could argue. It was unethical, plain and simple, for them to be physically involved. Or any other kind of involved. End of story. But still...

Once home and undressed half an hour later, Kylie still couldn't get her brain to shut off and leave her alone. It kept asking the same question as she washed her face and brushed her teeth. Why? Why all the—for lack of a better phrase—foreplay? Why the flirting and the dinner and the intense eye contact? Why that moment in the car after dinner when they could have so easily kissed...and both of them had wanted to? It had been glaringly obvious. Why the closeness in the office that night? Why the hand on the knee? Why all that?

Why kiss me at all?

She slipped into bed naked, covering herself with the navy blue sheet. It was after one in the morning, but she still felt wide awake and completely wired, despite the champagne. She hadn't had that much; she was such a lightweight that she was always careful about how much she consumed if she was driving herself. It had been a convenient excuse for what she'd been feeling, how she'd acted and responded. *Let her think I was drunk.*

She closed her eyes and exhaled slowly, willing her mind to ease and her body to relax. She needed to try to get at least a couple hours of sleep.

Thank God tomorrow's Friday.

At the prospect of returning to work in the morning, her eyes popped back open. *Damn it.* She'd have to face Gretchen and try to do so with her head held high in order to whitewash the humiliation she was sure she was going to feel. She briefly entertained the idea of calling in sick, but her pride won out. No, she made her bed, now she'd have to lie in it.

She rolled her eyes immediately, groaning at the unfortunate choice of words.

Tomorrow was going to suck.

CHAPTER TWELVE

G retchen Kaiser's office, this is Kylie. May I help you?"
"Hi, Kylie. It's Liz down at the front desk. I have a Pete Bromwell here for Gretchen. He says he's a little early."

Kylie's clock read 4:45. *Oh, thank freakin' God*, she thought. *This day can't end soon enough.* "I'll be right down."

She glanced over her shoulder into Gretchen's office where she was still holed up with Sarah, just as she'd been since first thing that morning. There'd been no chance for Kylie to get a minute alone with her, and she really wanted to apologize for her behavior the previous evening. She needed to get that behind her before she felt they could work together without things being weird.

Gretchen had waved to her when she arrived; Sarah was already there. Kylie had waved back, trying not to notice how good Gretchen looked in the beige pantsuit and trying to convince herself that it was *not* worry and concern she saw etched on her beautiful face.

Pushing the intercom button, she said, "Gretchen? Sorry to interrupt. Somebody named Pete Bromwell is here for you."

Gretchen swore under her breath. "Is it five already?"

"He's a little early. I'll go down and get him."

"That would be great. He's not business, he's personal, but I'd really appreciate it."

"No problem."

Kylie strolled to the bank of elevators, lost in her own thoughts, just as she had been all day long. She didn't think it was possible to be more thankful than she was for the upcoming two days off. She planned to bury herself up to her elbows in dirt and flowers, spiffing up the front of her house, hoping to take her mind off the disaster of the past week. A nice, relaxing weekend of gardening was just what she needed. It was therapy for her, something cathartic and healing for her soul that might also help take her mind off the confusion it was filled with lately.

As the elevator doors opened at the lobby level and Kylie stepped out, Mick walked briskly by, her arms filled with UPS boxes. She turned and walked backward alongside Kylie. "Hey there, hot stuff. You look luscious, as always. Happy Friday."

"Same to you." Kylie grinned, cheered as always by Mick's smiling face and ego boosts.

"Tomorrow night, babe."

Kylie shook her head and blinked, waiting for elaboration.

"You. Me. The Black Widow. We haven't been out together in over a month. Let's get a drink or two and do a little dancing."

"Maybe…"

"No maybes. I need my dance partner. I'll call you tomorrow afternoon." Mick backed into a door, pushed her way through, and disappeared.

Kylie stared after her, uncertain whether the outing was a good idea. She knew she'd be dragged out to the Widow tomorrow night whether she wanted to go or not. And she'd probably end up having a good time. *Maybe it's just what I need.*

She reached the lobby and scanned the waiting area, her eyes falling on the only occupant. She did a double take as she realized he was the sombrero man from the picture on Gretchen's desk…her ex-husband.

"Mr. Bromwell?"

He stood and held out his hand. His blue eyes were soft and kind. "Pete. Please."

Kylie put her hand in his and shook, liking that his grip was firm but not overly so, trying to make a point as many men did. "I'm Kylie O'Brien, Gretchen's assistant. She's still in a meeting, but she's wrapping it up, so why don't you come with me and I'll take you to her?"

He took the pass offered by Liz at the front desk and clipped it to the lapel of his navy blue sport jacket, then fell into step beside Kylie. "It's really nice to finally meet you, Kylie. I've heard a lot about you."

"You have?" His comment surprised her.

"Gretchen says you're irreplaceable. And believe me, it takes a lot for her to feel that way about members of her staff. You must be damn good at your job."

"Well..." Kylie was annoyed to feel herself flush with pride as she punched the button for the elevator. "She's pretty easy to work for."

"She's a great lady. I've known her for over twenty years—it freaks me out when I realize that." He laughed, a deep, warm sound that made Kylie smile. "I'm so glad she moved up here. We're having her over for dinner tonight. My wife and I live in Penfield and since Gretchen doesn't know her way around the suburbs yet, I thought it would be easier for her if she just followed me home."

"Sounds like a smart idea," Kylie said as the elevator slid upward. The ride was short and the bell announced their arrival on the fourth floor.

"Have you been at Emerson long?" Pete asked, wanting to get her talking more. He studied Kylie as they walked and she answered, thinking she was absolutely beautiful and completely understanding what he'd read in Gretchen's face when she'd spoken about her. *How easy it would be to fall for this one*, he thought. Her kind eyes and warm aura alone were enough to pull somebody in. Add to the list the unbelievable color of those eyes, the smooth, creamy complexion, the dazzling smile, and the killer figure, and Kylie O'Brien presented one hell of a package. Wait until he got a hold of Gretchen.

He was disappointed when they stopped outside Gretchen's door so soon. It opened immediately and a stunning blonde smiled as she slipped past him. She called a good-bye to Kylie over her shoulder.

"Have a good weekend, Sarah," Kylie called back. "I'll leave you two alone," she said, her eyes darting past Gretchen. "It was nice to meet you, Pete."

"You, too, Kylie. I hope we see each other again." His gaze lingered on Kylie as she returned to her desk, then he followed Gretchen into her office, eyeing her suspiciously.

She caught the look and held up a warning finger. "Not one word," she snapped at him.

❖

Kylie pulled off the blouse with an annoyed grunt and tossed it onto the bed where it joined the seven other tops that had been nixed. Sighing, she dug through the pile and pulled out the black, button-up tank top that she'd tried on first. Her shoulders had gotten quite a bit of sun during her several hours of gardening, so they looked good, prominently freckled—infinitely suckable, as Mick would say. The tank was short and showed a bit of midriff...something she wasn't used to and didn't necessarily approve of, but she had to admit looked sort of sexy.

She added a wide black belt to her low-rise jeans and strapped on a pair of black sandals that looked pretty but were comfortable enough for an evening of dancing. Topping off the outfit with some small silver hoop earrings, a matching silver necklace, and a couple of silver bangle bracelets, she was as pleased as she knew she was going to get. She scooted into the small bathroom and finger-combed her hair one last time, giving it a final spritz with the hair spray.

She was dabbing some Liz Claiborne behind each ear when she heard a quick knock and the side door open. Mick's voice called out to her.

"I'll be right down," she hollered back, giving herself the once-over in the full-length mirror on the back of the door.

I'm nearly forty years old. Why does it matter what I look like when I'm going out to a bar anymore? Who cares? She sighed and slid one more button undone before giving up, and heading down the stairs.

The look on Mick's face made all the fuss worthwhile. "Holy shit."

Kylie smothered a smile. "What?"

"You look like a million bucks, that's what. You're sexy as hell." She reached out and poked playfully at Kylie's belly button.

"Be honest," Kylie said, her face serious as she held out her arms. "Do I look like a forty-year-old who's trying to appear twenty-five? Because I hate that."

Mick's smile was warm and genuine. "Absolutely not. You look mature and...fucking hot. Is it necessary to show that much cleavage? Jesus, I'm going to have to beat them off you with a stick tonight, Ky."

Kylie was relieved. She knew Mick would tell her the truth and not hesitate to send her marching back up the stairs to change. "Well, do me a favor. Don't beat them *all* away, okay?" She pulled her driver's license out of her wallet and slid it into her pocket. "By the way, you're looking pretty damn sexy yourself, cowboy. Maybe I'm the one who needs to use the stick."

Mick wore black, tight-fitting jeans that hugged her muscled ass lovingly. Her red T-shirt was also snug, each article of clothing chosen to show off her sculpted body, the result of regular workouts with free weights. She'd gotten a haircut within the last week and it was neat and stylish, a few short strands of gray visible around her ears. Her eyes, as always, were the focal point of her face, the green seemingly more intense this evening.

Scratching the back of her neck, she mumbled a thank-you and asked, "Ready for a night of dancing?"

Pleasantly surprised to see Mick was blushing, Kylie answered, "You bet," and tucked her money in her pocket.

They headed out. As Kylie locked her door behind her, she felt good. She was looking forward to spending time with her best friend, dancing her heart out, having a few drinks, and getting her mind off a certain petite brunette with a voice she could feel in the pit of her stomach and a mouth that could kiss her in a way she hadn't been kissed in years.

Anything else. Please let me think of anything else tonight. That's all I ask...

❖

Jori's studio/apartment was a piece of art in itself, a dichotomy of home and work blended into one interesting space. Nestled above a popular restaurant on East Avenue, it was large and open, divided only by the folding Japanese-style screens placed strategically around the room, separating the two halves. Floor-to-ceiling windows on both the front and the back let in copious amounts of natural light and the high ceilings made the area seem even larger than it was.

Gretchen's gaze drifted to the large, unmade bed in one corner. It was covered with expensive sheets of deep green satin and a matching down comforter. Off that corner was the only door in the place, leading to the surprisingly large bathroom. The kitchen area lay opposite and consisted of a simple conglomeration of refrigerator, stove, sink and a handful of white cupboards all lined up like a chain gang. Jori had placed a small table and four chairs nearby for meals; the table was piled with books and mail.

The other half of the open rectangle consisted of workspace. One corner had a small stage-like block covered with black fabric and accented by a matching black fabric backdrop. Lights were mounted on various stands, all pointing at the stage. Shelves lined one wall and held books, cameras, lenses, more lights. The opposite wall was the most interesting, and it wasn't the desk that caught Gretchen's eye. She had never had a chance to look at the dozens of pictures Jori had mounted on the wall; the two or three times they'd been there, they'd always moved straight to the bed.

This time, she lingered as Jori finished dressing, taking in the art of the woman with whom she'd been having sex. The thing that surprised Gretchen the most about the pictures was that they weren't Jori's professional prints. These seemed to be more candid, photos of her friends and family, and for some reason, Gretchen's heart warmed just a little. She spotted Mick in several, and there was a crowd shot of an outdoor gathering from at least twenty years ago, judging from the clothing worn by the subjects.

With closer scrutiny, Gretchen picked out Kylie's mother among the group and realized she was looking at the O'Brien family cookout from nearly two decades before. Smiling, she moved along the wall, and then her breath caught in her throat as she stopped in front of a black and white, eight-by-ten, lovingly framed photograph of Kylie.

It was definitely candid, a head shot in semi-profile; Kylie seemed unaware she was being photographed at all. She stood outdoors somewhere, her face tilted up toward the sky, exposing her long throat, making her seem impossibly vulnerable. The creamy skin begged for fingertips, and an unseen wind blew her dark blond hair off her face, revealing one adorable ear decorated with a diamond stud that glinted in the sunlight.

Even in a photo without color, it was completely apparent that Kylie had the bluest eyes you could imagine. Her mouth quirked slightly in a smile that seemed to house a secret, like she knew something the rest of the world didn't and she *might* share, if coaxed in just the right manner…there was something very intimate about the shot and it tugged at Gretchen low in her belly. She found it hard to breathe and she was unable to move her feet. She stood imprisoned, and wet her lips as she stared in wonder.

"Gorgeous, isn't it?" Jori's voice startled Gretchen, so close to her ear.

"She is...er...it is. Very. When did you take it?"

"Oh, five or six years ago, I think. A bunch of us went hiking up near Cayuga Lake. It was a beautiful fall day and I sort of stumbled upon Kylie all alone, looking off into the distance. I think she was looking at a hawk or an eagle or something. She was so...breathtaking, I couldn't *not* take the shot, you know? I'm not even sure she knows I did to this day."

"Were you...?" Gretchen hesitated, not sure how to pose the question niggling at her. "Did you two...you know...ever have a thing?"

Jori chuckled and a bit of sadness was apparent in its rhythm. "Me and Kylie? Nah." She looked down at her feet for several long seconds. "Not that I wouldn't have wanted to, though, especially back then. But I'm a big girl now, big enough to know that she's way out of my league."

Gretchen cocked her head, surprised at the remark. Her face must have said so, because Jori grinned widely.

"Oh, come on, Gretchen. You know it's true. She's the kind of woman who deserves *way* better than somebody like me or you, right?" Jori walked across the room to the little table and picked up her keys, unaware of the pained expression Gretchen knew had parked itself on her face. "Are you ready to go?" she asked without looking back. "I hear dinner calling my name."

Gretchen blinked several times and gulped down the bitterness rising in her throat. She purposely did not look back up at the photograph. "Sure. I'm ready."

Chapter Thirteen

The Black Widow was jumping, much to the surprise of many of its patrons. Women's bars didn't have much of a reputation in Rochester other than being the businesses most likely to close down within the first six months. Somehow, the Widow had managed to stay open and keep a crowd for the last five years, withstanding the changes in the weather as well as the changing landscape of the city. It was located far enough downtown to be considered "in the city," but not far enough to be considered "in the bad part of town." The owners had gotten it just right.

The crowd was a mix of ages. It was going on eleven o'clock, so the younger college-age lesbians were beginning to show up. Their appearance was radically different from the older crowd that had appeared earlier—tattoos, piercings, and shaved heads versus jeans, T-shirts, and neat, practical haircuts. The older crowd was playing pool. The younger crowd was doing shots.

Kylie garnered looks from both crowds. She didn't really seem to notice, though Mick always did. Mick was also aware of the envious glances she received from the people who didn't know them personally and assumed Kylie belonged to her. Those were her favorites.

"What do you want to drink?" Mick had to put her mouth very close to Kylie's ear in order to be heard over the thrumming bass of the dance music. Not that she minded; being so close allowed her to get a satisfying lungful of Kylie's evocative perfume.

"Vodka tonic," Kylie responded, glancing around as Mick pushed her way to the bar and put in her order with Christy, the bartender.

She stifled a yawn and chuckled inwardly at herself for being such an old fart. *I go to bed by ten every night. Why should a Saturday be any different?* The DJ seemed to be playing a nice mix of eighties music, though, so she was pretty secure in the fact that she'd wake up once she got dancing. It was good to be out.

"Here you go, hot stuff." Mick handed her the drink. "What do you think? Music sounds good. It's not that rap shit that all sounds the same."

Kylie nodded, sipping from her glass and sending an appreciative smile back at Christy behind the bar. "Damn, that girl knows how to mix a drink."

"Only for those of us who are special." Mick grinned.

"I don't know how you do this so often," Kylie commented. "I'm ready to fall asleep."

"You're such a lesbian." Just then, the DJ decided to play "Vogue" by Madonna, and Mick took Kylie's drink and set it on a nearby table next to her beer. "Come on," she ordered. "This'll wake you up."

Mick was right. Within an hour, Kylie was dancing her heart out, pleasantly buzzed and on her way to drunk, though thinking about changing to Coke soon. Mick was a fantastic dancer but Kylie was a bit more self-conscious, so she just held onto Mick and let her lead. Her friend's strong, solid form was comforting and Kylie gripped her shoulders without hesitation.

They did their own version of dirty dancing, Mick's thigh tucked between Kylie's legs, her hand across the small of Kylie's back where bare skin peeked out under her cropped shirt. Because of the difference in their heights, Mick enveloped Kylie and the picture they made was quite a sexy one. Spectators—both subtle and overt—were abundant.

One song blended into the next until Kylie needed to drink and rest. Laughing, she wiped the sweat from her upper lip and led Mick off the dance floor. She picked up her drink from the table where Mick had placed it and took a long swallow. When her eyes drifted to the far end of the bar, her smile faltered and she nearly choked as the mouthful of vodka and tonic water went down the wrong pipe.

Jori was cheerfully chatting with Christy, her arm draped over the shoulders of none other than Gretchen Kaiser. Despite the fact that she was frustrated by their presence, Kylie couldn't help but let her eyes roam over Gretchen's form, from the snugly fitting jeans to the white, short-sleeved button-up top to the mass of hair she itched to dig her fingers into. Gretchen looked absolutely edible.

Damn her.

Slugging back the remainder of her drink, Kylie grabbed Mick's arm and pulled her toward the dance floor.

"Hey, Jori's here," Mick commented even as she was being led in the opposite direction.

"Yeah, I know."

Mick noticed Jori's date, then looked back at Kylie, apparently taking in the fact that Kylie wasn't looking toward the bar at all. She followed obediently and did her best to keep Kylie dancing with her back to the rest of the crowd. Kylie knew she was showing stress rather than fun and that she was dancing like she was doing a job rather than enjoying herself. But she had no ability to do anything else. All sense of enjoyment had disappeared.

They danced for nearly a half hour with no conversation—and very little smiling on Kylie's part—until a familiar voice interrupted their individual thoughts.

"Excuse me, ladies, but can I cut in?" Jori bumped her hip into Kylie's, taking her place as Mick's dance partner.

"Sure," Kylie said, before Mick could protest. "I need another drink anyway."

She left the two of them boogying to "Brand New Lover" and headed for the bar. She pushed through the crowd and ordered another vodka tonic from Christy. When she reached for her money, Christy waved her off.

"Nope. You're paid for." She used her chin to point across the bar. Gretchen gave a small wave.

Crap. Kylie held up the glass in silent thanks, then turned her back to the bar, and Gretchen, and downed half the glass's contents in three swallows, suppressing a shudder as she did so. She was working diligently on the rest of it when that rich, molten voice sounded dangerously close to her ear.

"Work up a thirst on the dance floor, did you?"

Chills ran pleasantly up Kylie's spine and she closed her eyes for the briefest of seconds to revel in the feeling. When finally she turned and met Gretchen's deep brown gaze, her eyes seemed softer than usual. Kylie couldn't keep the smile from her face.

"Hi there," she said.

"Hi yourself," Gretchen replied, a hint of relief coloring her tone, detectable even over the pounding dance music.

Gretchen had pressed herself close to Kylie in order to be heard and Kylie could feel the heat emanating from both their bodies, mingling thickly in the air. "Thanks for the drink," she said, holding up her glass. She grimaced with embarrassment when she realized it was empty.

Gretchen chuckled and motioned to Christy as they stood in slightly awkward silence while they waited for another drink. The pounding bass beat of the music stopped abruptly and a slow number began. To Kylie's alarmed delight, Gretchen held out her hand.

"Dance with me?"

If she hadn't been drinking, Kylie might have been able to summon up the strength to refuse. She might have politely declined. She might even have snorted a laugh in Gretchen's face. As it was, though, she was powerless...against Gretchen's eyes, her voice, against the small, strong hand hovering, waiting to lead her to the dance floor. She didn't hesitate at all. She put her hand in Gretchen's, trying not to swoon at the warmth, the solidity of her grip, and allowed herself to be escorted toward a far corner of the small dance floor. The zone was dimly lit and occasionally slashed with red and blue light, ideal for keeping a low profile.

Kylie paid no attention to the fact that Jori barely noticed them. She paid no attention to the look of concerned annoyance that Mick shot in their direction. Her eyes were lowered, watching nothing else but the sway of Gretchen's slim hips, the rolling of her behind as she strolled ahead.

They were very nearly the same height again, Kylie's sandals and Gretchen's ankle boots with the heel working in their favor. When Gretchen turned to face her, Kylie swallowed. She felt suddenly submerged in Gretchen's presence, as if Gretchen's physical hold on her was the only thing keeping her from drowning. Gretchen lifted their joined hands and nestled them to her chest; Kylie could feel the softness of the white shirt and the steady beating of Gretchen's heart beneath it. The exposed skin of her back tingled unbearably as Gretchen slid her other hand into position, her thumb rubbing small, lazy circles.

When Gretchen tightened her arm and gently pulled their bodies closer together, Kylie was barely able to stifle the gasp that forced itself from her parted lips. Her heart was pounding, and Gretchen's mouth was but three inches from hers. She rested her own hand on Gretchen's shoulder, feeling possessive and possessed in equal measure. Like she belonged there.

I never want to leave this spot. Ever.

They swayed together easily, comfortably, barely even registering what song was playing. Kylie had thought she had so much to say to Gretchen, but she couldn't seem to find her voice and then she didn't want to. She was afraid of breaking the spell. She wanted to stay like this forever, swaying in Gretchen's arms, held tightly and feeling protected. For that moment, there was no job, no rules or ethics. There was only the two of them and the heat surrounding them.

Gretchen's eyes hadn't left Kylie's lips since they began moving to the music and it took every ounce of strength Kylie had to prevent herself from leaning forward a hair, from pushing her own mouth into Gretchen's, but she promised herself she'd let Gretchen make the move. She was in no hurry to end up in the same state of embarrassment she'd experienced on Thursday night at the office. From the look on Gretchen's face...the hooded eyes, the parted lips, the tongue darting out to moisten them...Kylie suspected she wouldn't have to wait long.

"Hey, break it up," Jori said playfully, startling them both so much that they actually jumped. "I've got somebody I want you to meet."

It was only as Jori was dragging Gretchen away by the arm that Kylie noticed the music had changed; the slow song was gone and the pumping bass beat was back. She followed Gretchen's retreating form, noticed the apologetic grimace that crossed her face, and blew out a frustrated breath. Gretchen and Jori disappeared into a large group of people at the end of the bar. Kylie headed to the other end where her drink and Mick were waiting. Her vision blurred slightly and she realized she was drunker than she originally thought. And God was she turned on. *Damn you, Gretchen.*

"That was interesting," Mick commented, a gleam of irritation shining in her eye.

"What was?" Kylie slugged back half her drink, glad Mick was driving.

"That dance." Mick narrowed her eyes as Kylie finished the rest of her drink. "Easy there, Ky. You're going to have a hell of a headache in the morning."

"Whatever." Kylie watched across the bar as Gretchen smiled politely at the handful of people surrounding her and Jori. Jori's arm was draped over her shoulders again and it made Kylie grind her teeth.

She laid down a five for the drink Christy brought her, not paying any attention to Mick's silent direction to Christy that she'd had enough. She once again nearly choked on the two large swallows she took as she watched across the bar. Then she did choke on the third and everything in her stomach threatened to heave up onto the surface in front of her as Jori caught hold of Gretchen and kissed her on the mouth.

Kylie's world was spinning. Setting down her drink, she turned to Mick and gripped her arm tightly. "Take me home."

"What? Now?"

"Take. Me. Home."

Mick's green eyes suddenly filled with concern as she saw the tears welling up in Kylie's.

"Please, Mick?" She could hardly focus. All she could think about was getting out before she burst into humiliating sobs.

"Okay. Let's go."

❖

After Kylie's third attempt at getting the key into the lock, Mick took the keys from her and slid the correct one home. She pushed the door open and stood aside, letting Kylie enter ahead of her. Shaking her head, she followed her into the living room. Kylie rarely drank enough to get this drunk; she was quite careful about it because she tended to be self-conscious about the Irish stereotype. She only drank in excess when she was upset.

"What's going on?" Mick asked gently.

Kylie hadn't turned any lights on. Only the glow from the streetlights outside shining through the open living room windows made it possible for them to see one another, both bathed in a soft orangey glow. She stepped close to Mick.

"Hug me?"

"You got it." There was nothing Mick could deny her best friend, especially when she used that soft, pleading, feminine voice. She wrapped her arms around Kylie and pulled her close, resting her chin on the top of the blond head and trying not to feel anything beyond the closeness of their friendship.

Kylie rubbed her cheek against Mick's chest, feeling protected by the strong, muscled arms holding her. It wasn't quite the same feeling of protection she'd gotten from Gretchen, but... Shaking that thought angrily away, she looked up at Mick. "Kiss me."

Mick blinked at her, clearly taken aback. "What?"

"I said kiss me. Now." Kylie grabbed the back of Mick's head and pulled her down.

"Ky, what the—" Mick's protests were silenced when Kylie's lips met hers. She grabbed Kylie's forearms, fully intending to withdraw, but Kylie's lips were so soft, so sweet, so insistent. There was nothing she could do, no way to resist.

Mick moved her hands to either side of Kylie's face and kissed her back, tenderly at first, tentatively, exploringly. It wasn't long before she couldn't refuse the desire to taste Kylie's mouth more fully and she expertly slid her tongue into the warmth that waited for her. Kylie moaned and pushed her body more firmly against Mick's taller one. There was no sound but the soft smacking of their lips.

Maybe it was the flashback of Kylie and Gretchen dancing earlier. Maybe it was Kylie's sudden change in behavior. Maybe it was that the current situation was bordering on a wish coming true and Mick was a skeptic. Whatever the reason, Mick suddenly wrenched her mouth from Kylie's, breathing raggedly, her heart pounding in her ears.

"Wait. Ky, wait. What are you doing?"

Kylie pulled at Mick's head, her arms still wrapped around Mick's neck. "Mick. Just kiss me. Please? Just..." Their mouths met again and this time, Kylie pushed *her* tongue into Mick's mouth.

Mick whimpered, feeling completely ambushed. The sweetness of Kylie's mouth, the intensity of her desire, made it hard for her to put up any kind of a fight. She'd dreamed of this, of kissing Kylie, of being wanted by Kylie. She'd fantasized endlessly, had masturbated to just this scenario countless times. And now it was happening. And it was so wrong.

She pulled away again, making sure to hold Kylie at arms' length. "Kylie. Wait. Please. Just...wait."

"I don't want to wait," Kylie pleaded. Even in the dark, Mick could tell she was inebriated and out of focus. Mick reached for the lamp on the nearby end table, but Kylie stopped her, tugging at her arm. "No! No, leave the lights off. Please. Leave them off and kiss me again."

And at that moment, things were suddenly, painfully clear to Mick.

She flashed again on Kylie and Gretchen dancing; she flashed on Jori kissing Gretchen and Kylie's immediately reaction of flight. She swallowed hard, allowing the anger seeping in to push the hurt out...at least for the time being.

"This is about Gretchen, isn't it?" It was more a statement than a question.

The combination of expressions on Kylie's face told Mick she was trying hard to pretend that Mick hadn't hit the nail on the head, but she was too drunk to pull it off.

"What is it about her? Huh?" Mick stepped closer to Kylie, who seemed to shrink a bit. "Why her?"

"I don't know." Kylie's voice was just above a whisper.

"Did you figure if you left the lights off, you could pretend I was her?"

Kylie's silence was answer enough.

"Fine." Mick grabbed Kylie's face in her hands and held her firmly, hissing, "Is this what you want?"

She crushed their mouths together, thrusting forcefully into Kylie's as she held her prisoner. Kylie tried to escape by stepping back, but Mick followed and there was a loud crash as Kylie's backside hit the table against the wall and the framed pictures on it fell flat.

Kylie struggled feebly, pushing against Mick's chest, fighting not only Mick, but the growing excitement burning in her belly. She'd had way too much to drink, and Mick was much stronger than she was, and before she knew it, her butt was on the table, her back against the wall, her arms crossed in an X and pinned over her head by one of Mick's large, strong hands. Mick stood between her spread knees, and Kylie felt surrounded. Mick's size difference had always made her feel sheltered and safe. Now she felt trapped, caught. The combination of fright and arousal scared her even more.

"Is this what you want?" Mick snarled again, her mouth close to Kylie's ear. "Do you want her to fuck you right here on this table? Hmm?"

The comment angered Kylie, but she groaned as Mick's large hand closed over one breast and squeezed. Mick's mouth trailed a hot, wet path down the side of Kylie's neck where she bit and nipped the sensitive skin there, alternately using her teeth and tongue as she listened to the change of pace in Kylie breathing. Grasping a handful of Kylie's shirt, Mick yanked hard and the buttons popped, the shirt suddenly falling open, revealing heaving breasts held lovingly in black lace.

"She doesn't deserve you," Mick murmured, covering the lace with one hand and kneading firmly, first one breast, then the other. "She doesn't deserve these. *I* do."

Kylie struggled against the hand that pinioned her, the disparaging comment about Gretchen, and her own helpless arousal. Her bracelets jangled against each other as she tried to free her hands. Mick's fingers zeroed in on her rapidly tightening nipples and captured one through the fabric of the bra. Kylie knocked the back of her head into the wall, her groans of aroused protest swallowed by Mick's mouth as it covered hers once more.

Mick's head swam. The stimulation of touching Kylie's body had eclipsed her anger, though that anger was still very present. Kylie's warped view of Gretchen Kaiser made her crazy and she wanted nothing more than to open Kylie's eyes. *Why can't you see me?* She didn't realize right away that she was voicing her thoughts aloud. She was only aware of Kylie's body heat, of her sweet-smelling skin, of her slim wrists, of her pliant, sensitive breast, of her meager attempts to resist.

"She doesn't deserve you," Mick repeated, trailing her mouth around Kylie's neck and throat. "Why do you think she does? What do you see in her? She doesn't care about you. If she did, would she have been kissing Jori tonight? Why can't you see what's right in front of your face?"

"Mick," Kylie whispered, her voice strained. "Stop it."

"I'm right here. *I* am *right here*," Mick insisted, nipping at Kylie's collarbone as she slid her hand around behind and skillfully unfastened Kylie's bra.

"Stop." Kylie squeezed her eyes shut, her internal battle raging, her mind sobering quickly.

"I'd do anything for you, Kylie Jane. Don't you know that?" Mick slipped her hand under the fabric that now hung loosely over Kylie's breasts and caught one bare handful of flesh, groaning at the warm, honeyed feel of it. "Oh, God. Anything."

Kylie twisted her hands in another attempt to free them, but Mick held tightly and dipped her head lower. Catching a nipple between her lips, Mick sucked gently, then more firmly. Kylie gasped.

"Mick..."

Mick switched to the other breast, giving equal time. Kylie squirmed, heat shooting through her body like an electric jolt from her breasts to her groin.

"I'd treat you like a queen," Mick whispered. She let her free hand travel down Kylie's bare side and around over her smooth, quivering stomach. When she pressed it determinedly into Kylie's crotch, Kylie whimpered. "God, you're so wet. I can feel it through your jeans." She moved the heel of her hand in a slow, circular motion, grinding against Kylie and keeping her held firmly against the wall. "See? See how good it can be between us? Gretchen can't do this to you."

But Gretchen did do it. Kylie's brain was clearing rapidly and the mention of Gretchen's name kicked her into high gear. She redoubled her efforts and struggled in earnest. "Mick. Stop it. Please." Her voice was strong. "Right now."

Mick seemed to be ignoring her and used Kylie's struggles against her, pushing more securely into her, holding her against the wall like a pinned butterfly.

"Please, Mick. I mean it. Let go."

"Just relax, Ky. I'll make it good."

"No. Mick, please..."

"I promise."

Frightened now, Kylie managed to get her knee in between them enough so she had a little leverage and she pushed against Mick's hip as hard as possible. *"Stop it!"*

The sharp cry was enough to get Mick's attention and she visibly jerked as if waking up from a dream. She stepped back in surprise, releasing Kylie's wrists. Chests heaving, the two of them faced each other, blinking in confusion, hurt, and anger.

Mick spoke first, her voice a pained, ragged whisper as she watched Kylie rub feeling back into her hands. "It'll never be me, will it?"

Kylie swallowed, looking at her lap. "Mick..."

"She'll hurt you."

Kylie sighed. "She might."

"I do everything for you. Anytime. You call me, I come running." Bitterness and perplexity were starting to seep into Mick's voice and anger began to resurface in her green eyes.

"I know."

"I fix your house. I take you out when you're lonely. I help you bury your dog. I massage your fucking feet, for Christ's sake."

Kylie said nothing.

"God, you're so selfish, Ky. And so blind. You're so blind." Mick's anger was now being fueled by the underlying hurt and it was hard for Kylie to watch, knowing she had caused it and that there was nothing she could do to make things any different. "That bitch will rip your heart out, you know."

Kylie felt a spark of annoyance and slid gingerly off the table to her feet. She wrapped her arms around her torso in a feeble attempt to cover herself. "Maybe you should go."

Mick's eyes flashed. "Sure. Things are getting uncomfortable now, aren't they? I say something you don't want to hear and now it's time for me to go." She ducked down so she could catch Kylie's eyes with her own. "Why her? Honestly, why?"

"I don't want to discuss this with you." Kylie tried to step around Mick, but Mick blocked her path.

"Why not? I'm your best friend, aren't I?" Sarcasm laced her tone. "What's the deal? Are you just hot for her?"

"It's time for you to go, Mick."

"That can't be it. You don't do one-night stands. What do you think she's got to offer you?"

"Please. Just go."

"She's been here for less than three months and she's already fucked both Christy and Jori. What makes you think you're any different?"

Kylie's face hardened. "Get out."

"She just wants to get into your pretty little black lace panties, Kylie." Mick wasn't letting up. "That's what she does. And then she'll probably fire you."

"Get out. Now."

"You're nothing but a piece of ass to her. Why can't you get that through your skull?"

"Because I'm in love with her!" They stood staring at one another in the dark, Kylie's admission echoing off the walls of the living room. "I'm in love with her." The truth of the statement made her eyes well up with tears, and she looked down at the floor. "Christ."

"Then you're a fool."

Kylie snapped her head back up and she stared at Mick in painful shock. "Why would you say that? Why can't you be happy for me? Support me? Why would you hurt me like this?"

Mick's eyes never left her face, and Kylie was surprised to see unshed tears sparkling in them. She'd never seen Mick cry before in all their years of friendship.

Mick's voice was barely audible. "Because you've been breaking my heart every day since we were seventeen. And the fact that you've never even noticed is what hurts the most."

Mick turned and walked away. Kylie heard her snatch her car keys off the kitchen counter and then the door closed behind her. The SUV's engine turned over in the driveway and less than five minutes after Kylie's admission of love for Gretchen, Mick was gone, possibly forever. The weight of the realization was achingly heavy and forced Kylie down on the floor.

Only a few seconds passed before a sob ripped up through her chest and out. Kylie wrapped her arms around herself, rocking and crying, big, stinging tears burning their way down her cheeks. She noticed the various fabric hanging from her upper body and tore it all off with an angry, pained growl, winging both the shirt and bra across the room with all the strength she could muster. The flying material didn't have the same force as something like flying dishware might have, but it still made her feel the tiniest bit better.

Looking to her right, she noticed Rip's big, fluffy dog bed still in its place in the corner. She crawled to it and curled up, the comforting scent of her faithful companion surrounding her like a blanket. Still wearing her jeans and sandals but naked from the waist up, she fell asleep.

Chapter Fourteen

A hospital waiting room on Tuesday morning was the last place in the world Gretchen wanted to be. It was true that she was proud of herself for being there—it was a big step for her to miss a day of work if she wasn't on her own deathbed—and if she wasn't mistaken, her father had seemed to be genuinely pleased to have her at his side before they wheeled him into surgery very early. The doctors went over all the risks that stem from having any kind of surgery, then to this type of heart operation in particular. But they reassured her and J.J. that everything would be fine and all they could do was make themselves comfortable and wait. They'd be informed when he was out of surgery and recovering in ICU.

Gretchen had already made several laps around the hospital, exploring different floors, becoming familiar with both the gift shop and the cafeteria. After several hours, she was bored out of her mind.

As had happened more times than she cared to count over the past three days, her thoughts had turned to Kylie. She'd called in sick yesterday, leaving a message on Gretchen's voice-mail at the ungodly hour of four thirty in the morning. Her voice had been hoarse and scratchy and she'd simply said she was feeling like crap and thought it would be a good idea for her to stay home. She wished Gretchen a safe trip to Poughkeepsie and said she had access to her work e-mail from home, so she'd be sure to at least keep up with that.

Out of curiosity, Gretchen had gone back through Kylie's old personnel files and confirmed her suspicions: Kylie had taken exactly three sick days in the past five years.

Gazing unseeingly at the toneless walls of the hospital waiting room, she thought about Saturday night. That dance had been the most erotic, tantalizing thing she'd experienced in years and she could have killed Jori for interrupting. At the same time, she knew it was probably a good thing; she'd been inches from kissing Kylie and she was frustrated with herself over the mixed signals she'd been sending. She wanted to taste Kylie's lips again so badly...she'd thought of nothing else all day Sunday and it took every bit of willpower she had not to call Kylie up just to say hello.

What the hell is going on with me?

Across the waiting room, J.J. was engrossed in a six-month-old issue of *Sports Illustrated.* Next to him, Jenna stared out the window, her legs crossed. Gretchen told them she was going for a walk.

"Another one?" J.J. sounded irritated.

"I can't just sit here. I'm going nuts."

He nodded. "Okay. It'll probably be another hour or two anyway."

Jenna smiled. "I'll come find you if we hear anything."

"Thanks. I'll be back." She headed down and out into the parking garage where she was allowed the use of her cell phone. Seeing that she had a voice-mail message, her heart rate picked up speed, hoping that Kylie had called. Even if she was cluing Gretchen in on some problem, it would be worth it to hear her voice.

She dialed in her code and was disappointed to hear Pete's voice, sending his love and his best wishes for her father. She immediately felt guilty over her reaction. *Jesus, I am such a bitch.*

She wandered back through the lobby of the hospital and out the front door where she discovered an unoccupied bench. She took a seat, leaning her head back and soaking in the warmth of the sunshine. It was rather hot out, but the air-conditioning in the hospital had been worse than it usually was at Emerson, and she was freezing. She felt the steady warming of her bones and she sighed at the feeling.

Glancing back down to the cell phone in her hand, she debated for several minutes before rolling her eyes in self-disgust and dialing. The phone was picked up on the second ring.

"Gretchen Kaiser's office, this is Kylie. May I help you?"

She sounded tired, but Gretchen smiled anyway. "How are you feeling?"

Kylie's voice changed only slightly, as if she struggled to keep herself on a professional level. "Better. Thanks. How's your dad?"

"So far so good. He's not out of surgery yet, but soon."

"That's good."

The silence stretched between them. Gretchen bit her lip. "Everything okay there?"

"Everything's fine."

"No crises?"

"None."

"Any messages I should know about?"

"Nothing I haven't taken care of."

The silence resumed. Gretchen watched the cars drive along the road in front of the hospital, knowing there was so much more she should tell Kylie and having no idea how to say any of it.

"Okay." She quietly exhaled her frustration. "I'll check back in with you later on."

"Okay."

After a couple more seconds of silence, she said good-bye and snapped the phone shut. *Well, that was fun.*

Her subconscious took her back to the dance on Saturday night and when she closed her eyes, she could almost feel Kylie's body in her arms again, feel the closeness of her breath, the warmth of her hand. God, she'd felt good. Gretchen couldn't remember the last time she'd been that in sync with somebody...couldn't remember the last time she'd felt desire of *that* intensity. It had been surreal.

She cursed aloud. Whether it was the Fates, dumb luck, destiny— whatever put her in this position, the position of wanting something she couldn't have—she hated it. Hated the unfairness. Hated the anger that burned in the pit of her belly whenever she thought about it.

"Hey."

A hand on her shoulder startled her and she looked up into Jenna's brown eyes and released a breath of annoyance.

Jenna smiled. "Sorry about that. I didn't mean to scare you."

"What's up?" Gretchen asked, noting the laugh lines around Jenna's eyes and the sudden absence of the worried expression she'd carried all morning.

"He's out. He's in recovery. Everything went fine."

Gretchen was shocked by the wave of relief that washed over her. "He's okay?"

"Yeah." Jenna's smile was enormous as she nodded.

"Thank God."

"Yeah."

❖

It was nearly six o'clock that night before anybody could actually see John Kaiser, and then it was only for a few minutes at a time. Gretchen stood next to the hospital bed as her father gradually swam up from the depths of anesthesia and pain medication. His skin was a sallow gray and he seemed impossibly small under the hospital-issue bedding. Her eyes took in the various tubes and wires connecting him to all the beeping equipment and bags of liquid. She'd never liked science and hated to admit to her squeamishness; the sight of blood turned her stomach. But she paid close attention to everything the doctor said, even though she was sure that Jenna had taken actual notes.

J.J. and Jenna had finally allowed Gretchen to shoo them down to the cafeteria after spending the entire time of the surgery, as well as the six hours of recovery time, in the cramped, stuffy waiting room. Gretchen was now alone with her father and she felt a little awkward just standing there, so she was glad to see his eyelids fluttering. His eyes opened, a watery brown that was completely out of focus for several long seconds as he obviously tried to once again comprehend his whereabouts.

She waited patiently until his face cleared before she spoke. "Hi, Dad."

His eyes flicked to his right and his gaze settled on her. Relief seeped onto his face and the corners of his mouth turned up in a vague smile. His voice was hoarse and raspy. "You're still here."

The three words surprised her. "I'm still here."

"Didn't expect…you'd stay."

Gretchen pressed her lips together, unable to stave off the guilt as she closed her hand over his. His skin felt papery thin, the bones far too easy to feel beneath it. His frailty squeezed her heart in a vice grip. "Well, I did."

"I'm glad." His eyes fluttered again as if his eyelids were heavy and he was having trouble holding them open. "Gretchen?"

"Hmm?"

"Live life."

Gretchen leaned closer. "What was that, Dad?"

"Live it. You're supposed to *live* it." Within a few seconds, he was asleep once more.

Gretchen shook her head, remembering that the doctor had said her father would probably be somewhat incoherent for several hours. Taking in his fragility once more, she swallowed the unexpected lump that had formed in her throat and bent forward to place a soft kiss on her father's forehead.

"Sleep well, Daddy," she whispered.

❖

For the first time since her mother died, Gretchen had actually hesitated to leave her parents' house. The feeling annoyed her even now, two days later, as she sat at her desk in her office and went through Thursday morning's e-mail.

Kylie had been right: there were no crises, no emergencies that hadn't been handled while she was away, and she honestly wasn't sure how she felt about that. True, it was really only a day and a half that she'd been gone, but she didn't like being out of the loop even that long. She'd gotten back into the office yesterday afternoon, cleaned up her accumulated e-mail and returned a few phone calls, but otherwise, things were running smoothly. She was almost disappointed.

A rap on her door frame pulled her thoughts back to the present and she looked up to see Margo Wheeler standing in the entryway. Her navy blue skirt and jacket were a smart combination and her hair had been recently colored and styled. She looked very classy.

"How's your father doing?" She smiled expectantly at Gretchen.

"He's good. Thanks for asking."

"I'm surprised to see you back so soon." Though her tone held only surprise and no accusation, Gretchen stiffened at the feeling of defensiveness that prickled down her spine.

"There's not really a lot I can do there, you know? He's going to be in the hospital for a while longer and my brother and sister-in-law live close by and have things under control, so…" She trailed off under Margo's scrutiny and glanced down at the open file on her desk, fiddling with the corner of the paper.

"Well, still. If you feel the need to go back for a few days, feel free. We certainly don't expect you to have all your focus on work when a family member is ill."

"I appreciate that. Thanks, Margo."

Wheeler held her gaze for a few seconds longer and looked as though she had more to say. Seeming to think better of it, she simply walked away down the hall. Out the window of her office, Gretchen caught Kylie's eye for a split second before the EAA looked away.

Kylie.

She'd been nothing but professional and competent. She'd handled things quickly and efficiently while Gretchen was away. She'd briefed Gretchen thoroughly upon her return and it was almost as if Gretchen had never been away. Other executives Gretchen knew would give their right arms for an assistant as valuable as Kylie O'Brien.

Her proficiency was making Gretchen miserable.

Am I insane? I am. I'm completely mad, aren't I?

She missed Kylie. She was loath to admit it, but it was the God's honest truth. She missed the humor, the friendliness, the honesty. She missed the conversations they had in the past, conversations about *real* things, meaningful things. And she missed the physical closeness... Lord, how she missed that. At least when they were friends, Gretchen could inadvertently brush against Kylie or touch her fingertips as Kylie handed her something. Now even those types of occurrences were taboo...Kylie would certainly see through them and Gretchen knew she couldn't keep doing the come closer/stay away dance she'd been doing recently. It wasn't fair to Kylie.

I have to maintain my professional distance. It's the ethical thing to do. In the next breath, she put her elbows on her desk and dropped her forehead into her hands. *I blew it. I completely blew it.*

She'd had a fantastic working relationship with Kylie, but she'd been unable to keep her hands to herself and she'd ruined it. Now everything was different. There was no going forward and they couldn't go back to the way it had been. It was like they were stuck in some sort of Façade Limbo, like they had to continue on with the motions of their jobs, but they were stuck in time, unable to grow and unable to regress, eternally pretending everything was just fine.

During their briefing yesterday, Kylie had answered any questions Gretchen had tossed at her, and even answered them with a smile. But the smile hit Gretchen like a slap the first time she saw it. It didn't reach Kylie's eyes. It was almost forced, like it was for show only, and Gretchen hated that this was what she'd reduced the two of them to. She'd never felt so frustrated in her life.

❖

Mick growled aloud and slammed her office phone back into its cradle with viciousness. Yet again, she had almost called Kylie to say hi, ask her to lunch, see what she was doing later. And yet again, she had chickened out at the last minute.

She had never expected that she'd miss Kylie this much, that she'd feel her absence so deeply. It was as if she now had a big hole in her life, in her soul. Kylie had been a part of her for twenty years.

She glowered at the ham sandwich she'd brought for lunch. She knew she should eat it, but she hadn't been hungry for days. She had no appetite, no energy, and she'd apparently lost the ability to smile as well. Every night this week, she'd gone home, popped open a beer, flopped onto the couch, and channel surfed until she fell asleep. She was beginning to feel like a slug, her muscles practically begging her to get her ass to the gym.

"Hey, Mick." One of her staff, Carl, handed her some papers. "Here are the instructions for that mail project for HR next week." Carl turned to leave, hesitated, and turned back to his boss. "Are you okay?"

Mick knew her feelings had to be blazing from her eyes for a split second before she was able to rein in her annoyance and realize he was just showing concern. "Yeah, I'm fine."

"You sure? You look kind of…sad lately."

Though touched by his concern, the last thing Mick wanted to do was get into personal stuff with one of her subordinates. Still, it was nice of him to be worried. "I'm good, Carl. Thanks for asking."

He studied her for a second or two, then gave a half-smile and walked away.

I am so not *good. I feel like shit and I want to talk to my best friend about it. But I can't because everything is so fucked up.*

Her mind wandered back to Saturday night, how incredible Kylie's body had felt, how soft her lips had been, how surprisingly, tantalizingly aggressive she was. It had been a fantasy-turned-reality. Before she had a chance to revel in the memory, the image changed and Mick saw Kylie's anger and hurt all over again. The wounded expression on her face was unforgettable. Then there was Mick's own pain as Kylie told her to get out.

They'd had arguments before; they'd had disagreements; they'd even gone without speaking for a day or two. But nothing like this. This was bad. Lines had been crossed by both of them. Mick missed Kylie something awful, but the last couple of days had also helped her realize that she needed to let go of certain feelings she had for her. And the only way she could possibly do that was to stay away from her. For days or weeks…maybe even for months. For however long it would take.

She wondered how she would possibly survive.

❖

Friday morning brought nothing for Kylie but relief that the week was over. She wanted to spend the weekend with her niece, talking baby talk and watching cartoons and kiddie movies, and not thinking about anything that mattered. Not work. Not Mick. Certainly not Gretchen. She dropped her sunglasses and her keys into the top drawer of her desk and sat down to check her e-mail.

Her stomach rumbled and she knew she needed to find some coffee. Breakfast would be better…certainly a smarter choice, but she couldn't seem to eat lately. She had laughed bitterly the previous evening after she'd made herself some pasta and eaten three whole bites before setting it aside. The only times she had ever lost her hearty Irish appetite, and effortlessly dropped weight, had been when she was going through breakups. Diets never worked for her, only women who broke her heart.

So who did I break up with? Mick or Gretchen?

She chuckled bitterly, maddeningly tired of the whole thing. She wanted to crawl into a hole and sleep until years had gone by and it was safe to emerge again.

She'd called Erin the previous night in the hopes that her sister's wise outlook on life would make her feel better, but she hadn't been able to bring herself to lay out the full story. She'd told Erin it was difficult to work with Gretchen, given the attraction she had for her, but that she was managing. She said she'd had a fight with Mick, but she was sure it would blow over.

Lies and half-truths. They were all she seemed capable of these days.

Kylie sweetened her coffee in the fourth-floor kitchen, stirring it absently as she stared out the window.

"Hi, Kylie." Brandy Charles worked a couple cubicles over from Kylie and they'd been friendly for years.

"Hey, Brandy. How are you?" As Kylie met Brandy's soft hazel eyes, she realized they hadn't spent any time together in months.

"I'm great. Hey, I was thinking about you last night."

"You were? Why?"

"My mom's breeder said she found a male she really liked and Destiny had a litter about a month ago. There are still a few not spoken for. You immediately came to mind."

Kylie's heart warmed and her eyes welled. Brandy had mentioned her mom's Australian Shepherd breeder when she saw Kylie's pictures of Rip soon after they first met.

Seeing the threat of tears, Brandy immediately backpedaled in a panic. "Oh, God. I'm sorry, Ky. I didn't mean to upset you. I know Rip hasn't been gone for very long. God, I'm an idiot…"

Kylie laughed, one tear making its way down her cheek. "No. No, Brandy." She laid a hand on her friend's shoulder. "It's okay. You didn't upset me at all—it's really sweet that you thought of me, actually. I think I must be PMSing today. My emotions are really close to the surface." It wasn't a complete lie.

"You don't look so good," Brandy said, her worried gaze combing Kylie's face.

The sympathy was almost too much. Suppressing tears, Kylie fought off the misery wreaking havoc with her sense of herself and surprised Brandy by giving her a big hug. "You know, we haven't done happy hour in ages. Are you free next Friday?"

Brandy's eyes lit up. "I think I am."

"Good. Let's plan on hitting the Park Bench right after work next week. And bring the number for that breeder, okay?"

"You got it."

Kylie felt a bit lighter as she returned to her desk, hot coffee in hand. She stroked her fingertips over a picture of Rip, thinking that he was and would always be irreplaceable in her heart, but it might be time to think about another puppy. She recalled how adorable he'd been when she first got him…a big puffball of soft, silky blackness. She'd fallen in love with him in six seconds flat. She looked forward to feeling that again.

Maybe I'll get a different color this time. The blue merles are so pretty. Or even the red tricolored ones are cool looking…

She was evicted from her thought process by a hand on her shoulder. Jumping at the intrusion, she looked up into the concerned brown eyes of Margo Wheeler.

"Ms. Wheeler." Kylie could not contain her surprise. Margo Wheeler didn't often bother conversing with the support staff aside from the mandatory pleasantries exchanged at celebrations, award ceremonies, and department-wide meetings. Her orders, changes, or requests were normally passed down through the ranks. Kylie sat up straighter and smoothed her hand over her burgundy dress slacks. "What can I do for you?"

As she looked more closely at Margo's expression, she knew something was wrong. Her mind quickly rewound the past week or two. *Did I screw something up? Was I rude to any clients? Did we miss a deadline?* Another, more horrifying thought struck her. *Oh, God, did somebody see me and Gretchen in her office last week?* She braced herself for impact.

"Gretchen won't be in today." Wheeler's voice was hushed, gentle. "She called me early this morning. Her father passed away last night."

"*What?* Oh, my God." Kylie covered her mouth with one hand, letting the words sink in. "But…he was doing okay. Gretchen said everything went fine. I don't understand."

Wheeler nodded. "His surgery did go fine, but apparently, there was a blood clot of some sort…I can't remember the medical term for it."

"Pulmonary embolism," Kylie whispered, remembering the doctor's verdict when her grandmother died in the hospital six years earlier.

"That's it. Took everybody by surprise, I'm afraid."

"Oh, poor Gretchen."

"I know. She asked me to be sure and let all of you know she'd be out for a couple days."

Kylie could only nod as the shock settled over her. Wheeler patted her awkwardly on the shoulder and left without another word.

"Oh, poor Gretchen," Kylie repeated.

She sat back in her chair and stared off into space. Recalling Gretchen's indecision about being present the day of her father's surgery, Kylie sent up a silent prayer of thanks, knowing that if Gretchen had chosen *not* to go and this had happened, she might never forgive herself.

The business day at Emerson continued to buzz all around her, but Kylie was unable to focus on anything but Gretchen, wishing she could be with her during this time, knowing that however tough a person was, they could always use some friendly support during emotionally trying situations. She wondered if Gretchen had somebody to stand with her, and immediately thought of Jori.

Discomfort settled like a rock in the pit of her stomach. She held the phone stiffly, appalled by the thought of talking to someone Gretchen had slept with—even if Jori was a dear friend. Her fingers shook slightly as she dialed.

The voice on the other end was groggy. Kylie said hi and Jori mumbled, "Kylie? What's up?"

"I'm sorry. Did I wake you?"

"Is it before noon?"

Kylie grimaced. "Um, yeah. It's about ten."

"Then you woke me."

"Sorry. Listen, I was wondering if you were heading to Poughkeepsie today."

Jori was silent for several seconds, then yawned. "I'm going to New York, but not until tomorrow."

"Is that when the services are?"

"What services? No, I've got a shoot in Manhattan."

Kylie frowned, realizing they were on completely different pages. "Jori, you know that Gretchen's dad died last night, right?"

"Oh. Yeah, she left me a voice-mail. We were supposed to meet up tonight and do dinner and she needed to cancel. That's too bad."

"Yeah, it is. I know they weren't close, but I think she was really relieved that he'd come through the surgery okay."

Jori grunted, Kylie assumed in agreement.

"Do you have any details on the service? What time will you go? I'd like to send some flowers." *I really wish I could be there for her,* she thought. But the idea of standing off to the side while Jori supported Gretchen was just too much to bear.

"Oh, I'm not going."

Kylie blinked and took several seconds to register what Jori had said. "What do you mean you're not going? Why not?"

"It would be a little awkward, and you know me. I don't do well at funerals and things."

"Jori. You *date* her, for Christ's sake. The least you can do is stand next to her at her father's funeral."

"Jesus, Ky, you sound like my mother or something." Jori's tone held an edge of defensiveness. "I don't date her, okay? We're not like that. She doesn't owe me anything and I don't owe her. We have an understanding."

"An understanding. Terrific." Kylie shook her head, trying hard to comprehend that type of arrangement and failing miserably. "So... you're not going. At all."

"I told you. I've got a shoot."

"Wow. Your priorities are admirable." She took a deep breath, trying to remain calm. "Okay. Fine. Do you at least know where it is or have any details?"

"Nah. I haven't spoken to her yet."

This time, Kylie's grip on her anger slipped and she let it burst through. "You haven't even *called* her? For Christ's sake, Jori." She was flabbergasted and didn't bother trying to hide it.

Jori had the good sense to at least sound a little embarrassed. Kylie could almost see the shrug and had a crystal clear visual of fifteen-year-old Jori. "I just thought she probably had a lot of other stuff going on."

Kylie couldn't take it anymore and ended the call quickly, afraid she'd say something to her old friend that she might regret later. *I've already destroyed one friendship this week. I don't need to lose another.*

She sat back in her chair and sipped her now-cold coffee, unable to get the image of Gretchen all alone for the burial of her father out of her mind. John Kaiser lived in Poughkeepsie, she knew that much. Maybe she could find the local paper online and get information that way. She had already entered a few words into her Google search when a thought hit her and she bit her bottom lip.

After several long minutes of debate, she went into Gretchen's office and sat at her desk, sinking into the soft leather and inhaling the lingering scent of Gretchen's perfume. She took a deep breath, opened the e-mail program on Gretchen's computer, and scanned the list of contacts until she found the entry she was searching for.

Chapter Fifteen

Pete was worried about Gretchen. It was normal for someone to be upset about the death of a parent. It was normal for that person to seem a little numbed or lost, even a person usually in control of things. Gretchen, however, seemed completely shell shocked. He'd never seen her like this and it made him a little apprehensive for her.

When he'd seen her for the first time since the news and given her a hug, she'd put her arms around him, but barely squeezed. His wife Allyson said she'd gotten the same reaction. Gretchen had hardly said two words other than voicing her opinion of funeral home technicalities to help out poor J.J., who was an absolute mess.

John Kaiser hadn't wanted endless hours of services. Instead, he'd requested—according to J.J.—a small memorial service and then an immediate burial, all in the same day. Pete admitted to the benefit of getting everything done and over with, but he almost wished, for Gretchen's sake, that there was a little more to the public good-bye process. Maybe it would help her become unstuck.

The memorial service had been nice, though Pete abhorred referring to anything that had to do with death as "nice." He hated hearing people walking away from the open casket at a wake saying, "He looks good, doesn't he?"

No, he doesn't look good, he always had the urge to scream. *He's dead!*

But the speech given by the local priest had been gentle and kind. Gretchen's uncle had given a glowing, often humorous eulogy, during which Gretchen had stared straight ahead from the front row, her face showing no emotion whatsoever. Conversely, on her left, J.J. had tears rolling down his ruddy cheeks, Jenna holding his hand tightly from the chair next to him, their two older kids on the next two chairs, looking sad and uncomfortable.

Pete had watched from the corner of his eye, keeping track of Gretchen during the entire service. He wasn't sure what he'd been waiting for. A complete breakdown? Maybe a sob? One small tear? He didn't know. But he kept her in his sights, just in case. She had shaken hands with the endless line of John's former coworkers and clients; at one point before the service, the line had run out the door of the funeral home and down the block and the service itself had been standing room only. John Kaiser knew a lot of people, that fact was indisputable.

The ride from the funeral home to Poughkeepsie Rural Cemetery was quiet, and he could practically feel Allyson's swirling thoughts from the seat next to him as he maneuvered their car so they followed the hearse and limo in a line down the street.

"Gretchen doesn't look so good," she said softly. Her creamy smooth face was clouded with worry and he felt that old familiar urge to hug her to him and make everything all better.

"I know."

"What can we do for her? There must be something we can do." Tears filled her big blue eyes and her voice cracked. "I hate seeing her like this."

"Me, too, honey." Pete had scanned the crowd all day, had kept his eyes peeled and his proximity close to Gretchen, but he hadn't seen what he was looking for and he began to think he was holding out hope for something that just wasn't going to happen.

"Do you think she'd let us stay with her tonight? We could do that, couldn't we?"

Gretchen was staying at her parents' house, despite J.J. and Jenna's offer to stay with them and the kids. Pete didn't like the idea of her being there alone, but he was 99.9 percent sure she would refuse Allyson's offer and claim that she'd be fine, that she preferred to be alone.

"I doubt she'll go for it. You know how she is."

Allyson mulled that over for several minutes. "Well...maybe it will be good for her to be alone. Maybe that's when she'll allow herself to grieve. I mean, I know they weren't close, but...he was still her father."

Pete nodded as they turned into the gated entrance of the cemetery. He hadn't been there in years, but he was continually awed by the age, by the feel of history that always struck him whenever he passed through the large stone pillars. He parked in a line with the other cars and walked a short way to the freshly dug grave next to Emma Kaiser's as the funeral home employees positioned the casket nearby and laid a large bouquet of white roses on top.

Pete and Allyson stood behind Gretchen, each of them laying a hand on the shoulder of her black dress. Pete felt her stiffen slightly as she turned around and met him with hollow, haunted dark eyes. Her pain stabbed him deep in the gut, but he didn't know what to do for her so he squeezed her shoulder and left his hand there throughout the service.

The blessing was short and sweet and the priest mentioned that the family wished to express its thanks by inviting everybody to J.J. and Jenna's home for coffee and pastries. J.J.'s cheeks were still wet as he pulled a red rose from a nearby arrangement and stepped forward to lay it upon his father's casket. Jenna followed him, an audible sob issuing from her chest, then the children. Gretchen didn't move and stood as if riveted to the ground. The crowd began to slowly disperse and make their way back to their cars.

J.J. stopped next to his sister, kissed her sweetly on the cheek, and headed for the limo. Jenna did the same, unable to hide her worry, and squeezed Gretchen's hand before following her husband. In a few short minutes, there were only Gretchen, Pete, Allyson, and the funeral home workers left.

"Gretchen?" Pete said softly. "Ready to go?"

Gretchen cleared her throat and spoke to him for the first time in hours, though she stared straight at the casket and didn't turn to meet his eyes. Her voice was hoarse. "I think I'm going to stay here for a little longer."

"You don't have a car, sweetheart."

"I know. I've got my cell. I can call a cab when I'm ready."

Pete pursed his lips. "Can we wait for you?"

"It's okay, Pete. Thanks, though. Jenna will be looking for you two."

"You're sure?" Allyson asked. It was clear that this idea didn't sit well with her.

Gretchen nodded.

Pete took a deep breath and let his eyes wander the cemetery as he searched his brain for a way to not leave Gretchen alone there. When his gaze fell on the figure standing near a tree a dozen feet away, relief flooded his heart.

"As long as you're sure," he said. Allyson looked at him as if he was insane for agreeing to leave her there alone, but he leveled a reassuring gaze at her behind Gretchen's back and she refrained from comment.

As they headed to their car, they passed the woman leaning on the tree, and Pete gave her a nod and a heartened smile of thanks. Allyson took in the woman's blond hair, simple black skirt and white blouse, and tear-stained face and smiled sympathetically.

When they were safely past her, she whispered, "Who was that?"

"If my instincts are correct, that, my dear, was the person who's going to help Gretchen get through this." He broke into a genuine grin for the first time all day.

Allyson furrowed her brows in confusion and he gave her time to put the pieces together. "Wait..." Her eyes widened. "That was *her*? She came all the way down here?"

Pete nodded with satisfaction. "Kylie O'Brien. In the flesh."

"Oh, thank God," Allyson muttered.

"Tell me about it."

They got in their car and Pete turned the key in the ignition but didn't shift into gear right away. Instead, he and Allyson watched as Kylie approached Gretchen from behind and stopped a foot or two away from her. Gretchen turned and her face registered a crystal-clear combination of surprise, joy, and relief. It didn't look to Pete like Kylie said a word; she simply opened her arms.

"Oh, my God." Allyson's gasp was audible next to him as she watched Gretchen step into Kylie's embrace without a second thought. Gretchen's smaller body began to shake with sobs.

"Told you," Pete said, his voice quiet and proud. He shifted the car into drive and pulled away.

❖

Gretchen wasn't sure how long she stood wrapped up in Kylie, how long she'd cried in Kylie's arms, but she knew she never wanted to let go. She felt relieved. She was warm, safe, protected.

Loved.

"I can't believe you're here," she mumbled against the soft, silky fabric of Kylie's white blouse.

"I'm a little late. Sorry."

"How did you find me?"

Kylie smiled against Gretchen's hair and tightened her arms around the small frame. "MapQuest is a beautiful thing."

"How did you even know?" Gretchen pulled back far enough to become lost in the emotional blue of Kylie's eyes. "I mean, I should have called you. I'm so sorry I didn't."

Kylie used her thumb to wipe away the tears on Gretchen's cheek. "Wheeler told me. As for getting the right time and information…" Her eyes twinkled. "I had a little help."

"You called Pete."

"I did."

"He's a good guy."

"He cares a lot about you."

Gretchen nodded. She turned back to the gravesite, her palm sliding down Kylie's arm and finding a comfortable grip on her hand. The funeral home employees who were left tried hard to look as though they were paying no attention to the two women, not wanting to intrude, so they busied themselves arranging and rearranging flowers and such. Gretchen knew she needed to let them get on with their jobs. She took a deep breath as she gave her father's casket one last look.

Bye, Daddy.

Turning to Kylie with a lump in her throat and the irritating threat of more tears, she asked, "Did you drive or fly?"

Kylie grimaced sheepishly. "I thought I could probably use the drive time to do some thinking." She pointed. "My car's right there."

Gretchen voice was a hoarse whisper. "Can you drive me home?"

"Of course I can."

Once situated in the car, Kylie was forced to drive one-armed, as Gretchen surprised her by once again grasping Kylie's hand, lacing their fingers together. They didn't say much, Gretchen giving directions here and there, but her grip on Kylie's hand remained tight and secure. She felt almost afraid to let go.

Gretchen watched out the window as they zipped along the streets, feeling somehow annoyed at the people who carried on with their mundane tasks on their regular day. Couldn't they see this was no regular day? She wanted to scream at them. Instead, she gripped Kylie's hand tighter.

She still couldn't believe Kylie was here, that she'd taken the time to drive all the way to be here for her, despite the fact that she'd never even met Gretchen's father. *What did I do to warrant such caring from her?*

Rather than try to answer the question, she squeezed her eyes shut and tried to claw her way out from under the pile of thoughts and feelings that threatened to smother her. Her head was too full and she felt like she might simply collapse into a pile of mush any minute from the weight of it all.

They pulled into the driveway of Gretchen's father's house after about twenty minutes. As she awkwardly shifted into park with her left hand, Kylie asked, "Are you sure you don't want to go to your brother's place?"

Gretchen shook her head. "I just…don't want to be around all those people right now."

"Well, I've reserved myself a room at the Holiday Inn for the night and I have my cell. Please don't hesitate to call—"

"What?" Gretchen interrupted her. "No. No, you don't have to stay there. You can stay here."

Kylie wrinkled her nose. "Oh, I don't want to intrude, Gretchen. I know you want to be alone and I…I understand that."

"No, no." Gretchen pressed her lips together as she gathered her thoughts and chose her words carefully. "I don't want to be around *those* people. But I'd be really grateful if you'd stay here. Tonight. With me." She stared at her lap, feeling twelve.

Kylie suppressed a grin, thinking that vulnerable actually looked good on Gretchen. "If you're sure," she said with gentleness, looking down at their still-linked hands.

"I am."

"Okay, then."

They got Kylie's duffel bag out of the trunk and Gretchen led her into the house. Kylie looked around, trying without much difficulty to picture a young version of Gretchen wandering around, studying, following all the rules like a good girl.

"You can put your bag in here," Gretchen said as she headed up the hardwood stairs. She opened a door at the top and entered the inviting lavender bedroom of her childhood.

Kylie noticed Gretchen's bag on the floor at the foot of the bed and decided not to comment on the fact that she was being put in the same room. She made a mental note to deal with that later. Her eyes fell on the trophy shelf in the corner and she walked over to it with a smile.

"Wow," she commented. She ran her fingertips lightly over the metal, wood, and crystal and was reminded of all the "adult" awards in Gretchen's office back in Rochester. "You were a gymnast?"

"Until I was fourteen. Tore the tendons in my knee."

"And that was it, huh?"

"That was it."

"Well, that sucks." Kylie tried not to think about how heartbreaking a blow that must have been for a girl so young. Her eyes traveled over the academic awards, sensing that Gretchen had simply focused her efforts elsewhere. "You were quite an accomplished kid."

"Yeah, well, I didn't have much of a social life. I was too busy trying to impress my dad with that stuff." Gretchen's voice held a trace of bitterness. "Fat lot of good it did me."

Kylie turned to look at Gretchen, who had kicked off her heels and was now even smaller than Kylie was used to her being. "This is the part where I'm supposed to reassure you that your father was definitely impressed, but I don't think that's going to make much difference to you right now, especially since I never even met the man. So I'll just tell you this: *I'm* impressed."

Gretchen's face softened. *God, I'm glad you're here.* "Thanks," she whispered.

Kylie crossed the room and stood in front of Gretchen, studying her carefully. With Kylie still in her pumps and Gretchen in her bare feet, Kylie seemed to tower over her, emphasizing her recent vulnerability. She touched a hand to Gretchen's cheek and ran a thumb over the dark circle beneath her eye.

"When's the last time you ate something?" she asked with tenderness.

Gretchen shrugged. "Yesterday morning? I haven't been very hungry."

"I understand that. But you need to eat. Tell you what. Let's both get out of these clothes and into more comfortable ones and I'll see if I can't whip us up a little something. Okay?"

Gretchen didn't want to admit to the need to be taken care of, at least for tonight; it just wasn't in her nature. But it was such a relief to hand over the reins, no matter how uncharacteristic a move. She weakly nodded her assent and turned to her opened bag.

Kylie rummaged through her own bag, pulled out a gray Provincetown T-shirt and an old pair of navy blue gym shorts, and went into the adjoining bathroom to change, closing the door behind her with a quiet click. Ignoring the lingering scent of Gretchen's perfume that hung in the air of the small room, and resisting the urge to examine the brands of shampoo and soap in the shower, she changed quickly and exited.

In the bedroom, Gretchen was sitting on the edge of the bed, still clad in her black dress and staring off into space. Kylie approached her slowly, squatted down in front of her, and laid a hand on one knee.

"Gretchen?" She looked up into the drawn face and watery eyes. "You okay?"

Gretchen said simply, "I had time, you know."

"Time for what, sweetheart?"

"Time to fix things. With my dad. Time to talk to him, to try to iron out the issues. He wanted to, I think. My brother was right. I was too selfish, too stubborn. Just like him."

Kylie took in a deep breath, searching for the right words to say and having a harder time than she expected. "Everybody has regrets when somebody dies, Gretchen. I think that's a normal reaction. We all have things we wish we'd said or done differently."

Gretchen nodded, her gaze finally focusing on the younger woman who was trying so hard to make her feel better. She brushed her fingers through the front of Kylie's hair. "I know."

Kylie smiled, loving the feeling of connectedness Gretchen's touch instilled in her. "I'm going to go loot the kitchen. Get changed and come on down, okay?"

"Yes, ma'am."

Kylie squeezed her hand and left the room. Only then did Gretchen allow one lone tear to spill over and track down her pale cheek. She focused on it, forced herself to feel the warmth of it as it left a line down her face. Crying wasn't something she did often, and the sensation was practically foreign to her. She was tough and strong. *Tough, strong people don't show emotion.* She learned that from watching her father, who rarely showed any emotion other than stoicism.

But she was so tired. Being tough and strong and stoic was exhausting. Had John Kaiser been this tired?

She sighed as if the weight of the world was upon her shoulders, then stood up and removed the black dress. She changed into soft cotton drawstring pants in a baby blue with pink stripes and a simple, snug white tank top. Examining her pale, drawn face in the bathroom mirror, she sighed again, thinking, as she reached for a plastic hair clip, that she looked every bit as old and tired as she felt. She pulled her unruly hair back and fastened the clip at the base of her neck.

The smell of food hit her the second she opened the bedroom door and she salivated immediately. The rumbling of her stomach was loud enough to surprise her and she actually smiled at the sound.

Okay. Apparently, I'm hungry.

Kylie was humming softly as she flitted around the kitchen, searching cupboards and the fridge for various items required to create her culinary masterpiece of cheese omelets. Gretchen stood in the doorway, unseen for several minutes, just watching her.

Kylie's toned legs were showing signs of a summer tan, and something about the fact that she was barefoot made her seem even sexier. The T-shirt was worn and it clung to her body lovingly with no undergarment to hinder it. Rebellious strands of hair had been tucked haphazardly behind her ears and as Kylie stood at the stove monitoring the progress of the eggs, Gretchen had the almost irresistible urge to hug her from behind. Instead, she gritted her teeth and cleared her throat as she entered the kitchen so as not to startle her.

"Smells terrific," she commented.

Kylie smiled at her and Gretchen didn't miss the way Kylie's eyes quickly slid over her body before she redirected them back to the frying pan. "Nothing says 'comfort food' like eggs and a glass of milk." She gestured with her chin at the small table in the corner of the kitchen. "Sit."

"I didn't realize how hungry I actually am until I smelled food." Gretchen pulled out a chair, noting with a gentle smile that Kylie had set it for the two of them and that it seemed perfectly natural. She propped her chin in her hand and watched the artist at work. "Do you cook often?"

"Not really," Kylie said as she expertly flipped the omelet in the pan. "I like to cook, but it doesn't make much sense to go to the trouble for just one person. I eat a lot of cereal," she said with a wink.

Gretchen grinned. "Me, too."

Kylie slid the omelet onto a plate and cut it in half, the melted cheese spilling out as she did so. She transferred one half to a second plate and delivered both plates to the table. Gretchen's gaze never left her as Kylie settled herself down in her own chair and picked up her fork. When she looked up, their eyes met and held.

"Okay?" Kylie asked.

"Okay," Gretchen nodded.

They ate in comfortable silence. When they finished, Kylie stood and cleared their plates.

"No," Gretchen protested. "You cooked. I clean. It's only fair."

"Gretchen." Kylie's voice was gentle, but with a firmness to it that stopped Gretchen in mid-rise and caused her butt to drop back into her chair. With a tenderness that Gretchen hadn't heard in what felt like ages, Kylie said, "Let me take care of you. All right?"

Gretchen swallowed the lump in her throat that threatened more tears and nodded.

"Thank you," Kylie said, and began loading the dishes into the dishwasher. Once the counter was wiped down and she was drying her hands on a dishtowel, she turned back to Gretchen. "What else do you need? Coffee?"

Gretchen looked up at the clock. It was seven in the evening and still light out. "Do you think...?" she began, then looked down at her hands, clasped on the table in front of her. "This is going to probably sound a little weird."

Kylie smiled that gentle smile of hers and stepped close to Gretchen, leaning a hip against the table. "Hit me."

"I want to curl up on my bed and watch TV with you. Is that silly?"

"It's not silly at all. As a matter of fact, I think it sounds perfect." Kylie tossed the towel onto the table and held out her hand. "Let's go."

Gretchen was annoyed once again to feel her eyes welling with tears as she placed her hand in Kylie's and allowed herself to be led up the stairs to her own bedroom.

It was a warm evening and Kylie opened the windows wide as Gretchen used the bathroom, letting in the balmy summer breeze. She pulled the bedspread down and folded it neatly along the foot of the bed, loving the softness of the creamy ivory sheets underneath. She found the TV's remote on the dresser and held it in her fist as she crawled along the bed, impressed with the firmness of the mattress. She propped up an ample supply of pillows and arranged herself against the white wooden spindles of the headboard.

She was flicking through the notable selection of cable channels when Gretchen came out of the bathroom. Her hair was free of the clip, her cheeks were pink from scrubbing, and she smelled like soap. She looked utterly exhausted.

"Come here." Kylie opened her arms.

Again, Gretchen didn't even hesitate. She crawled along the bed and burrowed into Kylie's embrace, pushing her face into Kylie's neck, curling up against Kylie's side, feeling an overwhelming sense of relief as she felt Kylie's arm wrap around her and tighten, pulling her closer.

"Comfy?" Kylie asked, placing a sweet kiss on top of Gretchen's head.

Gretchen could only nod, afraid if she tried to speak, the unfamiliar combination of emotions within her—grief, regret and loss mixed with intense desire, safety, and love—would cause the dam to break and she'd become a blubbering mess. Worse, she was afraid if she started to cry again, she wouldn't be able to stop this time, possibly ever. Instead, she swallowed hard, draped her arm over Kylie's stomach and reveled in the alien sensation of being protected.

"Let me know if you see something you want me to stop on." Kylie was channel surfing like a pro. "I have a bad habit of just constantly flipping through and I don't stop long. Just say something, okay?"

Gretchen nodded again, finding herself more engrossed in watching Kylie's hand on the remote than what was actually on the screen…the delicate blue latticework of veins in her wrist, the feminine shape of her fingers, the evenly filed fingernails. She watched as Kylie's thumb pushed the channel button at regular intervals. It was almost hypnotic, and it wasn't long before Gretchen's eyes drifted closed.

Chapter Sixteen

When Gretchen's eyes popped open, it was dark and she had no idea of the time. Vague remnants of a dream clung to the outer edges of her mind, but she couldn't grasp any solid memory of it.

Live life.

It was spoken in her father's voice, which was odd enough to begin with since she rarely dreamed of him. The rest was foggy. Those two words were the only bit of the dream she was sure of.

Live life.

She blinked, allowing her eyes to focus in the dark. The windows were still open, the sounds of crickets chirping and far-off, late-night traffic floating in on the gentle night breeze. Bluish shafts of moonlight streamed in through the open curtains and soon she remembered where she was. And why. Before the grief could crash down on her, she heard the words once more.

Live life.

Meaning what? She inhaled gradually, taking in a large lungful of fresh air, loving the familiar smell of her childhood home, the familiar comfort of being in her old room. Unfamiliar, of course, was the feel of the warm body next to her. She turned her head slowly until she was gazing at the beautiful and relaxed form.

Kylie was on her side facing Gretchen, her knees bent slightly. The sheet covered her up to her waist and her blond hair was tousled on the pillow. She had one arm curled up, her fingers resting in a loose fist against her forehead. Her breathing was deep and even, her full pink lips parted slightly. Gretchen had to fight the urge to reach out and stroke them with a fingertip.

The sudden rush of desire that flooded her body took her completely by surprise, so much so that she immediately sat up in the bed hoping to calm her ragged breathing and racing heart. She felt sweat bead on her upper lip and she swiped at it with the back of her hand, blinking in confusion. *What the hell is wrong with me?*

Her sudden movements startled Kylie awake and she, too, sat up. "Gretchen?" Her voice was a concerned whisper. "Are you okay?"

Gretchen turned to look at her in the moonlit darkness. Kylie thought Gretchen's eyes seemed nearly as black as night. She waited for Gretchen to answer, wondering if she was still asleep and having a bad dream. She reached out and lightly touched Gretchen's hand.

"Sweetheart? What is it?"

"I…" Gretchen began, but couldn't seem to form any other words. Her eyes bored into Kylie's, then traveled the length of her body, causing Kylie to shift under her gaze. She reached out, touching her fingertips to Kylie's cheek, her breath catching at the softness, the warmth. "I…"

"What, Gretchen? Do you need something?" Kylie's voice was laced with worry. "Talk to me."

Live life.

Reaching out with a suddenly determined expression on her face, Gretchen curled her fingers around the hem of Kylie's T-shirt and pulled it up and over Kylie's head. The move was so unexpected, Kylie simply went along with it before she could think clearly, lifting her arms to help. Then she could only blink in response and watch as Gretchen tossed the shirt to the floor.

"I need *you*." Gretchen's voice was a commanding hiss tinted with a note of pleading.

Her eyes raked over Kylie's naked torso so intensely, Kylie was sure she could feel it just as tangibly as a touch and she shivered.

"I need *you*," she said again, and watched as Kylie's breasts rose and fell with the quickened pace of her breathing.

Kylie tried to swallow her surprise, along with her rapidly growing arousal, as she sat topless in front of Gretchen, feeling practically devoured by her eyes alone. "Gretchen…"

Gretchen grasped Kylie's chin in her hand. The steeliness in her eyes eased and when she spoke this time, it was no more than a whimper. "Kylie. I need you."

"Are you sur—" Kylie was unable to complete the sentence before Gretchen's mouth covered hers.

Gretchen's grip on her chin tightened, then her hand slid around to the back of Kylie's head as she pushed forward, holding Kylie's mouth to hers, the kiss moving from gentle and tentative to demanding in a matter of mere seconds.

Live life.

The words sounded in Gretchen's head and she surged harder into Kylie, pushing her onto her back and groaning at the feel of the warm bare skin beneath her. *God. So soft.* She forced herself to slow down, wanting to savor every single second. Kylie's belly quivered as Gretchen ran her palm over it. Then Kylie's fingers dug into Gretchen's mass of dark curls, pulling her closer as she deepened the kiss, her tongue pushing, delving for more. Gretchen grasped at Kylie's hip, feeling the hindrance of the shorts and pulling at them.

"Off," she muttered, yanking at the fabric.

Obediently, Kylie lifted her hips off the bed and allowed Gretchen to pull her shorts and panties free. They joined her T-shirt in a heap on the floor.

Gretchen balanced herself on her forearm above Kylie and stared, allowing her eyes to travel down the length of the naked body beneath her. The beauty of this woman made a lump form in her throat and tears to spring into her eyes. She swept her gaze back up until crystal blue eyes intercepted her own, studying her intently, darkened with desire but still tinted with worry.

Gretchen smiled at her to alleviate any concern. "You are so beautiful," she said reverently, with disbelief, and ran her hand slowly up Kylie's thigh, her hip, her side, and gently cupped one breast.

She stroked the softness of it with the tips of her fingers, measured the surprising heft of it in her palm, and ran her thumb over the nipple, watching it tighten under her touch, feeling Kylie's breath hitch just a little. She repeated the move and felt Kylie squirm beneath her. The third time, she watched Kylie's face and a surge of wetness dampened her panties as she witnessed Kylie bite down on her bottom lip and her eyes drift closed. Gretchen dipped her head and ran the flat of her tongue over the same now-hardened nipple.

"Oh, my God," Kylie rasped as her body arched.

Loving the reaction, Gretchen licked the other nipple just as slowly and gently as the first. Kylie groaned and the fingers she'd tangled in

Gretchen's hair closed into a fist. For Gretchen, the almost-pain of her grip only ratcheted the excitement upward.

Shifting her position, Gretchen settled herself fully upon Kylie, nestling her hips between Kylie's legs, her weight mostly on her own forearms. The warm, silky wetness that slid along her abdomen between her short tank and the top of her pants was not lost on her as she looked down into Kylie's flushed face.

This is life. This woman is life.

She kissed Kylie's mouth thoroughly and seductively, then moved lower and set to work bathing Kylie's breasts unhurriedly with her tongue. First one, then the other, then back, she worshipped the velvety skin, the pebbled areola, and the hardened nipples, taking her time as if she had forever and a day.

Kylie squirmed, arched, and groaned below her, squeezing her eyes shut and groping blindly for the headboard until she located one wooden spindle and wrapped her fingers around it. She'd never been so aroused in her life, and Gretchen had barely touched anywhere below her belly.

Gretchen sucked one nipple into her mouth, flicking it with her tongue and then raking her teeth across it, coaxing a whimper from Kylie. She knew immediately that she could spend the entire night doing just what she was doing, but there was so much more to touch, to feel, to taste. She ran her tongue off Kylie's breast and along her side, following up the arm that was extended over Kylie's head to the elbow, leaving a hot, wet trail. The stretch made her pelvis push into Kylie's center.

Kylie gasped. "Oh, God. You're trying to kill me, aren't you?"

Gretchen didn't answer. Rather, she brought her mouth crashing down onto Kylie's and at that moment, she was the only important thing in the world, this woman beneath her. Even as Gretchen sank into the kiss, even as she let her hands drift and roam and explore the gloriousness of the body she ravaged, she knew in the back of her mind that something was different. Something big. She'd had a lot of sex in her day...a *lot* of sex. And with the exception of Diana so long ago, that's all it ever was: sex. Release. Satisfaction. But this was different. Kylie was different.

Gretchen focused every iota of concentration and energy she possessed on Kylie. At that moment, her sole purpose in life was to make Kylie feel beautiful, wanted, and loved.

Kylie pulled at Gretchen's tank top, but Gretchen caught her wrist, muttering, "Later," through their kisses. Her fingers moved lower and sank into the wet warmth that awaited her between Kylie's legs. Kylie inhaled sharply, hissing Gretchen's name and inclining her hips, silently asking for more.

Gretchen focused on keeping her movements slow and even, but she knew Kylie didn't have long. *Let's just get this first one out of the way,* she thought, her anticipation almost too much to bear. She kissed Kylie again as she slipped her fingers inside, stroking firmly, rhythmically, her thumb moving against the swollen flesh beneath it.

In a matter of seconds, Kylie wrenched her mouth from Gretchen's and threw her head back into the pillow, a long, low groan issuing from deep in her throat. Gretchen watched in awe as she kept the movements of her hand steady, stunned by Kylie's beauty and how it made her feel.

She slowed her rhythm in time with Kylie's breathing until Kylie clasped her wrist and stopped her altogether. Gretchen gently withdrew her fingers. Kylie's inner walls were still twitching periodically.

"My God," Kylie whispered, her hand over her eyes.

Gretchen smiled widely, her main realization that she wanted more. She wanted to give more. She wanted to take more. She was far from finished with this woman. She *never* wanted to be finished with this woman. Lowering her head, she tenderly licked at Kylie's nipple until it tightened obediently and Kylie whimpered.

"Gretchen…wait…oh, my God." Kylie was astonished to feel yet another rush of wetness between her thighs as Gretchen gently bit down on her oversensitive breast. She'd barely had time to catch her breath and Gretchen was cranking up the heat again. Very successfully.

Gretchen couldn't get enough. She wanted to taste every single inch of skin that covered Kylie's body, from the top of her head to the tip of her toes and everything in between. The salty sweetness of her was intoxicating and Gretchen felt like a drunk in a liquor store as she licked, nipped, and savored. The combination of Kylie writhing beneath her, grasping at her, and moaning made Gretchen feel like she might spontaneously combust from her own fiery arousal. Her cotton pants were soaked through, the crotch stuck to her, but she didn't want to leave Kylie's body even long enough to shed her own clothing.

She tasted her way down Kylie's torso, taking a split second here and there to glance up at the object of her worship. Kylie was completely at her mercy, one hand over her head and seemingly fused to the wooden spindle of the headboard, the other tangled in Gretchen's hair. Her head was thrown back into the pillow, exposing her long, elegant throat, and just for a moment, Gretchen contemplated going back upward specifically to lick that sexy column of flesh. She continued her path down, though, her desire to know what Kylie truly tasted like winning out. She settled herself between Kylie's legs, and with a hand on each thigh, she pushed them farther apart.

"Spread your legs for me, Kylie." The tone of the command was so low, she barely recognized her own voice.

Kylie did as she was told, quickly opening herself as far as she could, her rapid breathing giving away her impatience. Gretchen closed her eyes and inhaled deeply, the musky scent of Kylie's arousal causing her mouth to water. She slipped her hands under Kylie's backside and around to her hips where Kylie let go of Gretchen's hair and instead, grasped her wrist and held tightly. Gretchen rubbed her cheek against the baby-smooth skin of the inside of Kylie's thigh, reveling in the joy such a simple sensation could bring her. She repeated the same movement on the other thigh, going back and forth until she could wait no longer. She stroked her tongue along the satiny wet skin between Kylie's legs, the taste of her making Gretchen moan in tandem with Kylie's cry.

Kylie shifted, trying to push herself more firmly into Gretchen's mouth, but Gretchen held fast with her hands on Kylie's hips, determined to set the pace. She had no intention of teasing Kylie yet, but she didn't want to rush either. She took her time, exploring every fold, every hidden crevice and each different spot that caused Kylie to twitch, melt, or groan. She made mental notes, cataloging what reaction each touch inspired, what Kylie seemed to like most, when the contact was too firm and when it was not firm enough. Such research could become her life's work and Gretchen would die a happy woman. She knew that with all her heart and she suddenly felt it welling up from within her...a phrase so foreign and unfamiliar it nearly choked her with its accuracy.

I'm home.

At that very moment, Kylie came violently, arching up off the bed as her hand left Gretchen's arm and instead clamped the back of Gretchen's head, holding her in place. Gretchen's eyes looked up the length of Kylie's body and watched her orgasm, then slowly relax, and the overwhelming splendor of what she saw made her emotions surge higher. As Kylie's hand slipped away from Gretchen's head, Gretchen's chest filled with warmth, a feeling completely unfamiliar to her. Before she had time to analyze what was happening, a sob ripped up through her and tore its way from her throat. She climbed up to her knees, her hands on either side of Kylie's waist, and was unable to stop the tears.

"Gretchen?" Kylie blinked, her breathing still ragged. "Honey? What is it?"

Gretchen was horrified by her own weeping and she clamped a hand over her mouth in an attempt to control herself.

"Oh, God, sweetie. Come here." Kylie pulled Gretchen down on top of her and, meeting no resistance, wrapped her arms around the shaking shoulders. "I'm so sorry. I was worried that this was a bad idea. I should have known..."

"No," Gretchen managed to croak out. "No. It wasn't." She sniffed, then pushed herself up far enough to make out Kylie's face, seeing the worry there. "I..." She gazed around the dark room looking for a clear thought to grab a hold of. "I don't know how to put this into words..."

Kylie reached out and lovingly tucked Gretchen's wild hair behind her ear. "Just talk to me," she said softly. "Tell me what you're feeling."

Gretchen's eyes found Kylie's and locked onto them and she swore she could feel energy and courage pouring into her. "I buried my father less than twenty-four hours ago, but...I've never felt so...*complete* in my whole life like I do here with you tonight."

This time, Kylie was the one filled with emotion. Her eyes welled and one tear spilled over as she swallowed audibly. "Oh, Gretchen," she whispered and pulled her close, wrapping her up and holding her as tightly as possible.

Gretchen burrowed into Kylie's neck and inhaled the sweet smell of her. She pulled the sheet up over their entwined bodies. She never wanted to leave this spot. Ever.

❖

Sunlight streamed through the open windows, forcing Kylie to either turn her head in the other direction or have her eyes lanced by the cheerful but irritating rays of brightness. She didn't open them right away, instead listening and feeling in order to reacquaint herself with her surroundings.

She was lying on her stomach, the light sheet covering her backside and one leg, but other than that, she was completely naked and exposed. A Cheshire cat grin spread itself slowly across her face as she gradually recalled the activities of the previous night, the pleasant soreness in her thighs reassuring her that it was no dream. When her brain replayed for her Gretchen's emotional breakdown, she realized she was alone in the bed. Only then did she open her eyes.

The sound of water running registered in her ears and she barely had to move her head at all to see into the small adjoining bathroom. Gretchen's back was to her and she was still clad in the small white tank top and striped drawstring pants. She was bent over the sink washing her face, and the sight of the cotton stretched over her petite but shapely ass sent a shot of desire through Kylie that surprised her with its intensity.

She got up immediately and padded naked across the floor to the bathroom. When Gretchen stood up straight, water dripping from her face, Kylie was right behind her. Gretchen gasped in surprise, then relaxed and smiled in the mirror at the reflection of the gorgeous woman at her back.

"Good morning," she said, her low voice quiet in the stillness of the room.

"Good morning to you, you beautiful creature." Kylie's arms encircled Gretchen from behind and she hugged her tightly and studied her still-wet face in the mirror. She planted a soft kiss on the exposed part of Gretchen's shoulder. "How do you feel?"

Gretchen nodded. "I'm doing okay. How 'bout you?"

"My legs are sore."

Gretchen pressed her lips together in a feeble attempt to suppress a grin. "Really? Huh."

Kylie tightened her grip, rubbing her cheek against Gretchen's hair, marveling over the feel of the compact body in her arms, its muscles surprisingly tight. "And I realized something."

"What's that?" Gretchen was effectively trapped between the edge of the sink and Kylie's body, giving her a combined sense of unease and arousal. Kylie's lips skirted along the ridges of her ear and sent goose bumps across her arms.

"I realized that I barely got a chance to touch you last night." It was scarcely a whisper, but erotic chills shot down Gretchen's spine.

Kylie slipped a hand under Gretchen's tank top and moved upward, capturing one small breast and kneading it firmly. Within seconds, the tight nipple was pushing into her palm.

"Oh." It was the only word Gretchen could manage to form coherently.

She was shocked by how quickly her body was responding to Kylie. It wasn't that she was usually slow to arousal, it was that this time, it was virtually immediate. She gripped the edges of the small vanity with both wet hands as Kylie's lips traveled along the side of her neck, lapping up the trickles of water before fastening onto the juncture of her neck and shoulder. She bit down firmly.

Gretchen gasped. "God…"

"I know you like to be the one in control, Gretchen, but every so often, you're going to have to give that over to me." Kylie's tone was conspiratorial, as if she was letting Gretchen in on a little secret.

Gretchen was astonished to find herself completely at the mercy of the woman behind her, the same woman she had unrelentingly dominated the night before.

Kylie's fingers pulled at the drawstring of Gretchen's pants. "Understand?"

Gretchen nodded quickly, a groan escaping her lungs as Kylie's hand slipped into her pants and dipped down into the slickness that signaled just how much she understood.

Kylie whimpered as her fingers sank into the warmth. "Oh, my God," she whispered with awe in her voice. Gretchen was already soaked. "Do I do this to you?"

"You have no idea."

Kylie worked both hands at once, kneading Gretchen's breast and rolling her nipple at the same time and in the same rhythm she used to stroke the liquid silk between Gretchen's legs. Gretchen dropped her head back onto Kylie's shoulder, her eyes drifting shut at the sensations that were washing over her.

Kylie's tongue explored the whorls and folds of Gretchen's ear, dipping in and around, sucking the soft lobe into her mouth. She was completely absorbed by the feel of this woman in her arms. Gretchen's body was small, smaller than most would expect given her large personality and her penchant for controlling things. But everything was taut…her belly, her arms, her rear end.

Kylie had always thought Gretchen had a dancer's body, but

actually feeling the dichotomy of the strong, sinewy muscle covered with soft, velvety skin was more amazing than she'd even imagined. She suddenly felt like she couldn't get enough. Gretchen was breathing heavily against her, her hips rocking subtly with the rhythm of Kylie's fingers between her legs. Kylie picked up the pace, watching Gretchen's face in the mirror.

"Gretchen," she whispered into the ear next to her lips. "Gretchen. Look at me." She kept her rhythm steady as Gretchen opened her eyes and blinked, her entire body moving with Kylie. Their eyes locked in the mirror and Gretchen reached up and grasped the back of Kylie's neck. They stayed that way for several long, blissful minutes, their eyes boring into one another as Kylie's fingers moved deftly, lovingly, speeding up and then slowing down depending upon Gretchen's facial expressions.

"Kylie," Gretchen croaked at last, not sure how much more teasing she could take. "Please." She caught her bottom lip between her teeth and tightened her grip on Kylie's neck. "Please?"

Kylie smiled tenderly at Gretchen's reflection, allowing the image to burn itself into her brain. "Okay," she whispered into Gretchen's ear as she applied heavier, steady pressure. "Come on, love."

Kylie's adjusted touch, combined with the intensity of their stare and the sound of Kylie's voice in her ear, finally pushed Gretchen off the precipice on which she'd been perched. She ground her teeth together, a low growl erupting from her chest as she pushed her head back into Kylie's shoulder and squeezed her eyes shut.

Kylie suppressed a wince as Gretchen's fingernails dug into her neck as well as the forearm that snaked up Gretchen's shirt. As Gretchen's body began to relax, Kylie tightened her grip to keep her from sliding to the floor.

"Good Lord," Gretchen said, her voice an exhausted sigh. "That... you...I don't think I can stand up anymore."

Kylie chuckled. "Then let's get back into bed, shall we?" Gretchen followed obediently and when they reached the edge of the mattress, Kylie turned to her, grasping the tank top and tugging it gently over Gretchen's head. "I want to feel your skin against me, not your pajamas."

Gretchen stepped out of her pants and crawled under the sheets with Kylie, opening her arms so Kylie could settle her head on Gretchen's shoulder. A few more limb adjustments and they were completely wrapped up in one another.

Kylie sighed in contentment. "Oh, this is nice."

Gretchen tightened her grip, reveling in the unfamiliar feeling of satisfaction. "Yes, it is." *I never have to move again.*

They were quiet for a long while, the hypnotic sound of their breathing the only noise in the room. Just when Gretchen began to think Kylie had fallen back to sleep, she spoke.

"Gretchen?"

"Hmm?"

"What will you do now?"

Gretchen took a deep breath and let it out slowly. "I think I'm going to stay here for a while longer. I have to go through my father's papers with J.J. There are issues with the house. You know. Things like that."

Kylie nodded against her, surprised but silently pleased that Gretchen wasn't immediately running back to the office. "I think that's a good idea. Work can wait. You have more important things to deal with." She paused, then added, "I wish I could stay here and help you."

Gretchen placed a soft kiss on Kylie's forehead. "So do I. But it's not a good idea for both of us to be gone from the office at the same time. The field reps will panic." She felt Kylie's throaty laugh vibrate through her body.

"That's an understatement. God forbid I'm not at Jason Bergman's beck and call. He's liable to have a nervous breakdown."

Gretchen smiled and they burrowed closer to one another, reluctant to allow any space between their bodies. Kylie suppressed a frown, her mind awash in the events of the past twenty-four hours. There was so much she wanted to say to Gretchen, so much she wanted to ask. *What was last night? Was it a one-time thing or is there something more here for you like there is for me? If I leave you here, when will you be back? And when you are, what will I be to you?*

But fear of the answers kept her lips fused closed and her voice box achingly silent. After several long minutes, she realized that Gretchen had fallen back to sleep. She swallowed her anxiety and tightened her arm around Gretchen's midsection, determined to enjoy and remember every second of this closeness that she could…just in case.

CHAPTER SEVENTEEN

K ylie was feeling too many emotions at once and she found that fact to be both exhausting and annoying. It was Wednesday and she'd discovered, much to her dismay, that it was nearly as difficult to *not* call somebody as it was to work up the nerve *to* call them. What was worse was that all she wanted to do about her situation with Gretchen was to talk it over with her best friend. But Mick had been avoiding her like the plague and Kylie had no idea how to fix the mess she'd helped create.

On one hand, she completely understood Mick's evasion. *I'd do the same thing in her shoes.* Thinking back on that night, Kylie shook her head in self-disgust. At the same time, she was angry at Mick, too. *Am I a mind reader? How was I supposed to know how she felt? In twenty years, she never said a word!*

This internal discussion had gone on endlessly. Combined with her Herculean efforts to not call Gretchen twenty-seven times a day, her forced reassurance of the sales reps who called to offer Gretchen their condolences, and her attempts to keep her mind at least somewhat focused on her job, Kylie felt like she was going insane. *Two of the most important people in my life and I can't figure out a way to talk to either one of them.*

Her departure from Poughkeepsie on Sunday had been hard. She'd had to continually remind herself not to cling to Gretchen like lint as she hugged her good-bye. She'd wanted promises; she'd wanted professions of love. She'd gotten neither and she'd made neither and it was more frustrating than she'd imagined it could be.

She'd spoken to Gretchen on Sunday night, dutifully as requested, to let her know she'd made the drive safely and arrived home in one piece, but it was late and they were both tired, so the call had been brief. They'd also talked on Monday evening. It, too, had been a short conversation, as Gretchen was emotionally drained from her trip down memory lane going through her father's things and not in a terribly conversational mood. Understandably so. Kylie had wished her a good night and hung up, trying not to let her disappointment overwhelm her.

On Tuesday afternoon, Gretchen had called the office to make sure everything Emerson-related was running smoothly. It was, Kylie reported. She told Gretchen not to worry, that everything was well under control and to take whatever time she needed. Gretchen had thanked her and ended the call. By Wednesday morning, Kylie was ready to take the bridge.

Later that day, when Kylie returned from grabbing a quick sandwich, there was one message from Gretchen. Kylie was annoyed that she'd called during the lunch hour. *The best chance of avoiding me,* she thought bitterly. Still, she played it six times just to hear Gretchen's voice.

"Hi, Kylie, it's me. Just checking in, making sure no crises have developed." There was a long, uncomfortable pause. *"Look...I'm really sorry. I'm not in a very good place right now and I...I need to think about...I have to...Christ, I don't even know what I'm saying. Just...just give me a call if something comes up that needs my attention."*

Kylie felt a wave of dread at the implications of the message. *She needs to think? She's not in a good place?* Neither of those statements boded well. Gretchen sounded so tired. Kylie wished she could be there to help. She also wished Gretchen would ask for her help...for her presence...for anything at all, but for the first time, she began to seriously doubt it was going to happen. The thought was more than she could bear.

The phone rang and her heart skipped a beat, as it had been prone to doing all week, a fact that was beginning to irritate her. She snapped it up.

"Gretchen Kaiser's office, this is Kylie. May I help you?"

"Hi, Kylie, this is Jessica Scott returning Gretchen's call. Is she in?"

Kylie was confused. Returning Gretchen's call? "No, I'm sorry, Ms. Scott, she's not. She's—"

"Oh, wait," Jessica interrupted. "I see she actually left me the Poughkeepsie number. It would be nice if I paid attention once in a while, huh?" Her laughter peeled across the line and Kylie winced as if it was fingernails on a chalk board. "I'll call her there. Sorry to have bothered you."

"No problem," Kylie muttered to the dial tone. Her brain instantly replayed the conversation she and Gretchen had had about the infamous Jessica Scott when they'd had dinner together.

"She probably just wants to see how things are going. She might have heard through the grapevine that upper management was happy with our budget revisions. She might just want to say hi."

"She's your ex!"

"Not exactly."

"You've slept with her, though."

"Yes. We've...kept in touch."

A mix of jealousy and panic rose within her and threatened to choke her where she sat. Gretchen had called Jessica from Poughkeepsie? *She called her? But not me? Well, she called me, but not exactly to chat. Why Jessica? Why...*

Her thought process stopped abruptly when she remembered the other thing Gretchen had said about Jessica.

"I was ready to get out and Jessica called me at just the right time. She keeps me aware of what's going on in my field."

Kylie rubbed at her temple with her fingertips. Was Gretchen looking for a new job? Already? Without even talking to her about things first? The idea was almost more than she could bear. She felt like a lead blanket had just been dropped over her shoulders and the air seemed to completely abandon the room.

After all that had happened between them, how could Gretchen close her out this way? They'd made love—no, they'd made *passionate* love—but it had been more than that. Hadn't it? They'd made a connection, a solid, emotional connection, and Kylie had been sure they were on a path to... She searched the air for the right words. Something more? It was vague, but frighteningly accurate.

She avoided thinking too much about any kind of a future with Gretchen, but she knew deep down that's exactly what she wanted. She thought Gretchen had wanted it too, but now, she wasn't so sure. Gretchen's message left her uncertain. The uncertainty made her angry.

She wanted to call Gretchen, call her right now and ask her what the hell was going on. But she thought of Gretchen's deep, throaty voice on her voice-mail, of how utterly exhausted she sounded, how hard it must be to sort and sift through an entire life's possessions of your dead parent, and she just couldn't do it. She couldn't bear to call and burden her with more.

Instead, she stared straight ahead at nothing with no idea what to do next.

No idea at all.

❖

God, I hope I'm doing the right thing.

It was the clearest thought in her mind as Gretchen hung up the phone. Her timing was lousy, but if she was going to make a change in her attitude—hell, in her life—this was the only way to do it. She knew she needed to talk to Kylie, really *talk* to her. But her head was just too full and it was all she could do to keep it from exploding in a mess all over the living room walls.

She flopped herself onto the couch to wait for J.J. They were both so exhausted. Gretchen felt like she'd been through an emotional wringer over the last week and just when she thought she was done with the tears or the pain or the regret, she'd stumble across another memory and the floodgates would burst open yet again.

As worn out as the process was making her, J.J. was in much worse shape. He was taking their father's death extremely hard and there was actually a little part of Gretchen that was jealous, envious that she didn't have a close enough relationship with her father for his death to devastate her. Despite the fact that she'd been way more affected than she'd expected to be, that jealousy made her feel ashamed. *What kind of person envies another's pain?*

She briefly thought about eating, but her stomach churned in protest. The refrigerator was packed full, people stopping by all week and dropping off casseroles and pasta and loaves of bread so she and J.J. wouldn't have to worry about cooking. They'd picked a little bit, but the kids had eaten most often.

She looked at the pictures adorning the table across from her. She and J.J. in their adolescence, looking awkward and gawky, her mother smiling at the camera in a rare moment of relaxation and carefree happiness, her parents' wedding picture. She squinted at that one, trying to find evidence that they weren't as happy as they looked, but she failed. Her mother's cheeks were rosy and her eyes sparkled. Her father was smiling like he was the luckiest guy in the world. Gretchen wondered when it all went downhill, when he decided his job and his business friends were more important than this woman he obviously adored the day he married her.

Live life. You're supposed to live *it.* She heard John Kaiser's deep, rumbling voice in her head and wondered if it was a lesson he'd learned too late...and if so, did he regret it? Did he regret the gymnastics tournaments he'd worked through? Did he regret not being home when Gretchen had announced she was the valedictorian of her high school graduating class? Did he regret that he wasn't present the day his wife had finally given in to the cancer and had passed into the next world? Did he regret that he'd given his daughter so little of his attention that she'd moved away without a backward glance? Did he regret that the two of them had never sat down and talked through their differences, their decisions, their anger?

They were all questions Gretchen would never have the answers to, and that was a very hard pill for her to swallow. She wasn't the kind of person who took things on faith alone—truth be told, she had precious little of it—and right now, she was having a very difficult time knowing these queries would swim around in her head forever.

When J.J. arrived twenty minutes later, Gretchen was still sitting in the living room lost in her own thoughts. He gave her a wave and a weak "hey," then leaned against the door frame between the living room and dining room and studied her. She looked even more tired than he felt. He'd never seen his big sister seem so small before. Her face was drawn and her eyes looked inexpressibly tired. Her old sweats and ratty T-shirt hung on her as if they were three sizes too big. Her hair was pulled back off her face, but it was out of control even in its clip, sticking out at all angles.

It was disconcerting for him; she'd always been so strong, so larger-than-life to his younger self. He'd always trusted her to take care of things. Seeing her so lost and unable to control the happenings around her shook him up much more than he cared to admit. Not to mention the fact that he never expected her to take the loss of their father so hard.

It wasn't like the two of them were very close at all, nor had they been in years. He'd expected her to be sad, but not this distraught. He suspected it was more guilt and regret than grief that was bogging her down.

"Sleep okay?" he asked softly as he entered the room and sat down beside her.

She shrugged. "You?"

"Eh."

"J." Gretchen didn't look at her brother as she spoke his name, but he turned to face her anyway.

"Hmm?"

"Am I like him?" Her voice was so small and so frightened, J.J. got his first sense of what she must have sounded like when she was six years old. He swallowed, knowing what she meant and knowing the answer, but unsure as to whether she wanted the truth.

"What do you mean?" he stalled.

"You know what I mean. Work has always come first for me, hasn't it?"

He remained silent, sensing that she just wanted to vent and needed him to listen. He nodded and she continued.

"I thought..." She squinted, concentrating as though trying to figure out a riddle. "I thought if I could be like him, if I could be as successful and respected in my field as he was, he'd finally sit up and take notice, you know? That he'd point at me and say to his friends, 'That's my girl right there. Isn't she something? Chip off the old block, that one.' But he never even looked. And I kept trying and kept focusing until I didn't even care if he noticed anymore. It just became who I was. I worked. I succeeded. It's what I did. God, I treated Diana just like he treated Mom."

J.J. pressed his lips together, his heart breaking for his sister. He'd liked Diana very much. He'd seen what was happening so long ago and he'd even tried to tell Gretchen, but she'd been unable to accept his words. Diana hadn't been as strong as their mother. Or maybe she'd been stronger. Gretchen turned to him then and there was such fear in her dark eyes that he wanted to scoop her into his arms and protect her.

"I don't want to end up like him," she whispered. "I don't want to make those mistakes. I don't want to shut the important people out of my life and end up alone."

A tear spilled over and down her porcelain cheek and at that moment, J.J. did wrap his arms around her. It was the only thing he could think of to help her.

"It terrifies me, J." she muttered into his chest.

"I know." He pressed his cheek to her hair and tightened his grip on her. "Gretchen, if you don't want to be like that, then don't." He said it as if it was the simplest piece of advice in the world.

And in a way, it was.

Chapter Eighteen

K ylie lay on the couch late Saturday afternoon watching *Ferris Bueller's Day Off* for the thirty-fifth time in her life. She could recite every line and it reminded her fondly of high school. Whenever she was channel surfing and came across that film, she stopped and watched the rest, whether it had just started or it was almost over.

Muttering lines with the actors, she could actually smell the approaching thunderstorm on the breeze drifting in through the open windows, and she felt the tingle of excitement. She'd briefly entertained the idea of turning on the air-conditioning, but the sound of the rain soothed her, despite the mugginess of the air, and she didn't want to close the windows. Summertime thunderstorms were one of her favorite things.

She burrowed farther into the throw pillow, getting comfortable in anticipation despite her pounding head. Taking another long slug from the bottle of water on the coffee table, she waited for her second dose of Motrin to kick in, glad she'd chosen a gray and rainy day on which to be hungover.

Going out the previous night with Brandy had been a great idea. They'd had a lot of fun...until the fourth martini. Try as she might, Kylie couldn't get Gretchen out of her head after that. More accurately, she couldn't get the fact that Gretchen hadn't called *at all* on Thursday or Friday out of her head.

Apparently, she'd thought she could wash that reality away with copious amounts of vodka and vermouth. Thank God Brandy had pooped out early and was ready to head home by ten. One more of those deadly concoctions and Kylie would be in infinitely worse shape than she was now.

The good news was she'd gotten the name and number of the breeder Brandy had mentioned the previous week. Glancing at the basket of Rip's toys, Kylie sensed that by the time the latest litter was ready to leave the mother—about three more weeks—Kylie would be ready to at least go look at the puppies. Rip had been gone for nearly four months and Kylie's life felt empty without a dog.

She was contemplating the possibility of some tomato soup and a grilled cheese sandwich when the phone rang. She wasn't really up for chatting, but something in her nature didn't allow her to let it ring. She'd never been one to screen her calls, and therefore got nabbed by telemarketers on a regular basis.

"Hello?" she answered without emotion.

"Kylie?"

Kylie sat up, recognizing Gretchen's voice immediately. To punish her for her too-quick movement, her head swam and her stomach churned. She bit back a groan. "Hi."

"Hey. How are you?" Gretchen sounded unsure, like she was treading carefully. *And she should be.*

"I'm fine. And you?" Kylie tried to remain cool, to stay neutral, despite the twittering Gretchen's voice could cause in the pit of her stomach.

"I'm hanging in there. Hey, listen. What are you up to?"

"Today?"

"Right now."

Kylie glanced at the cable box. It was 4:27. She had no plans at all, though she almost wished she did. She also hadn't showered and was still in her pajamas. "Um...I'm sort of in the middle of something right now, but I'll be done by five." She grimaced and punched the couch cushion next to her, annoyed at how easy she made things for other people, Gretchen in particular.

"Do you mind if I stop by your place? We need to talk."

We need to talk. The most dreaded words in the history of relationships, and Gretchen had just said them.

Kylie closed her eyes, inhaled deeply, and slowly let it out. "Sure," she said, resigned. "You know where to find me."

"Great. See you at five."

Kylie stared at the phone in her hand for several minutes after they'd hung up. She'd had a feeling things would end up like this, so she wasn't at all surprised. There was a pain in her chest, though, a steady, pounding ache, and she swallowed hard, willing it back down, knowing if she let it go, it would tear up and out and she'd end up a blubbering mess on her own living room floor.

The last thing in the world she wanted was for Gretchen to know how much this was going to hurt her. She needed to stay strong, unaffected, at least until she could get Gretchen out of her house. She tidied the couch, took her water bottle into the kitchen, and then headed upstairs to take a quick shower, not quite sure why she was even bothering.

Not quite fifteen minutes later, she was clean and dressed, having donned an old pair of navy blue shorts and a yellow tank top emblazoned with University of Rochester across the front. Both articles of clothing were over ten years old and worn to the perfect softness. She combed her wet hair back away from her face and momentarily wondered if she should bother drying it. But the air was sticky and the thought of the heat from the blow dryer was enough to deter her. She spritzed on some perfume, then rolled her eyes at herself. *Like Gretchen's going to care what I smell like while she's letting me down easy.*

As she headed downstairs, her stomach growled. Thinking she was finally ready to eat something, she pulled an ice cream sandwich from the freezer and plopped back down on the couch to continue watching TV while she waited for Gretchen. She hoped they could get this over with quickly, like ripping off a Band-Aid. She was determined to be fine while Gretchen was here; she'd let the sting hit her later, when she was alone.

Kylie was eating the last bite of her ice cream when the doorbell rang and she licked her fingers clean on her way to answer it. She took a deep breath before opening the door. The sight before her nearly caused her to choke.

Gretchen stood on the doorstep in the rain. She was dressed simply in khaki cargo shorts and a black T-shirt and she looked positively delicious. Kylie had no control of her own eyes as they roamed down over Gretchen's bare legs, then back up.

Gretchen smiled uncertainly. "Hi."

Kylie blinked. "Hi."

Gretchen's smile faltered ever so slightly as they stood staring at each other. "Um…can I come in?"

Kylie shook herself. "Oh. Yes. Sorry." She stepped aside and let Gretchen enter.

"It's good to see you," Gretchen said, fidgeting as she stood in the foyer.

"It's good to see you, too. You look great." Kylie grimaced as soon as the words left her mouth, chiding herself for letting them slip.

"So do you." Gretchen took in the sexiness of Kylie's wet hair and then scanned her figure. She wondered how it was possible for a woman to wear crappy old clothes and look this alluring. She pulled her attention back up to Kylie's face. "Can we talk?"

"Sure." Kylie studied her as Gretchen shook the raindrops out of her loose hair. She ground her teeth against the familiar tingle that made her itch to dig her fingers in and grab a handful of the dark curls. She bit the inside of her cheek, completely annoyed at herself for being sucked in so easily. "Come and sit down."

Gretchen followed into Kylie's living room. She sat on the couch and patted the spot next to her, inviting Kylie to sit close. Kylie sat, leaving plenty of space between their bodies, not trusting herself to be in close proximity.

"You know what?" Gretchen felt strangely exposed as Kylie's blue eyes blinked expectantly at her. "Could I have a glass of water?"

"Water?" Kylie noticed the slight tremble in Gretchen's hands and forced herself to hold back a sarcastic and bitter grin at the thought of Gretchen being nervous about cutting her loose. "Sure. Be right back."

A couple minutes later, they sat again facing each other. Gretchen took a large gulp of her water, and then set the glass down before she spilled it all over the couch. She took a deep breath and studied her lap for several minutes. *How is it possible for this to be so damn hard?* When she looked up and met Kylie's eyes, her heart warmed. In the depths of the blue, beneath the veneer of anger and hurt, she saw worry, concern, and love...so much of it. Gretchen felt courage pour into her and she briefly wondered how Kylie managed to do that to her—help her through hard times the way she did, with nothing but her eyes.

"I've made some changes this week," she began and then suppressed a grimace. *All right, not exactly my strongest opening.* Now, she had no choice but to run with it.

"Okay," Kylie said, drawing out the word.

"I've had a lot of time to think."

"Mm-hmm." Kylie flashed on the phone call from Jessica Scott that had come earlier in the week and her heart clenched.

"And I realized a lot of things about myself."

Kylie nodded. Gretchen looked so nervous, and it was so unlike her to look so nervous, Kylie almost felt sorry for her. *God, just tell me,* she thought with a hint of irritation.

"So, I made some calls."

Kylie could take it no longer. "And you're leaving Emerson," she blurted.

Gretchen blinked in surprise. "Yes. How'd you know that?"

Kylie looked out the window at the darkening sky, unable to bear looking at Gretchen's face. This was harder than she'd thought it was going to be, the ache in her chest intensifying and eclipsing her anger, much to her dismay.

"Jessica Scott called for you last week and said you'd called her from Poughkeepsie. I put two and two together."

Gretchen felt blindsided by the turn the conversation had taken. "And...how do you feel about that?"

"About you leaving?"

"Yes."

Kylie shrugged. "Hey, you've got to do what you've got to do, right?"

Gretchen was surprised by the nonchalance in Kylie's shrug. "I suppose that's true."

"The company will miss you." Kylie was still gazing out the window. "You were good for the sales force. They'll be sad to see you go."

"The company will miss me," Gretchen repeated softly. "Oh."

Suddenly Kylie's head whipped back around. "Can I just say something?"

"Of course you can."

Kylie felt the strange combination of deflation and anger as she spoke. "I'm sorry, Gretchen. I won't say I wish things had happened differently, but I feel bad. I feel responsible. At the same time, I wish you had the balls to face this instead of running from it. I..." Her voice trailed off as if she'd run out of steam. Finishing quietly, she added, "I'm really sorry that things ended up like this."

Gretchen shook her head, confusion written all over her face. "The balls to face...ended up like what?"

"Ended up with you being so uncomfortable working with me that you had to leave your job." There was an unspoken *duh* at the end of her sentence that almost caused Gretchen to burst into laughter.

"Kylie." Gretchen was smiling widely now, a fact that Kylie found unrelentingly grating.

"What?" she snapped.

"I left my job so I could continue to see you. To date you." She amended quickly, "If you want to, of course." She waited for what seemed like hours, watching as Kylie's mouth opened and closed several times, no sound escaping. "You look like a fish doing that. Please say something. Say anything."

"You want to date me?" Kylie's voice was small, like that of a disbelieving child.

"Yeah. I do. Very much." Throwing caution to the wind, she added, "Actually I...I want to do more than date you."

"You do? Why?"

"Why? *Why?* What kind of a dumb question is that?" Gretchen's smile took any sting out of the words, but Kylie pressed on, the sternness of her voice matching that of the expression on her face.

"But...you just disappeared on me, Gretchen. I mean, I know you had stuff to deal with at your dad's, but...you were just gone. It hurt. After the time we spent together last weekend, it hurt a lot. I didn't know what to think."

Gretchen wet her lips. "I know. I'm sorry. I really am. I had so much to sort through, Kylie. I was confused about so many things... things about my father and things about you. I wanted to talk to you so badly."

"And instead you left me a cryptic, I-need-time-to-think message on my voice-mail."

"I know. I shouldn't have done that."

"No, you shouldn't have," Kylie said.

"I just wanted to talk to you so badly."

"But you didn't."

"But I *couldn't*. Don't you see?" Gretchen inched closer and took Kylie's hands in her own, studying them, remembering how they felt on her, how those fingers could be both gentle and demanding at the same time. She focused on the words in her head. "I had to do some serious soul searching and I had to do it on my own, with no outside influences...not even yours, much as I wanted it. It was the only way to make sense of what was going on in my head. It was the only way to come to honest, unbiased conclusions about what I was feeling."

Kylie was quiet for several seconds, but her eyes never left Gretchen's face. It was as if she was expecting answers to appear directly on Gretchen's skin. "And what conclusions did you come to? About what you were feeling?"

Kylie looked so sweet and so beautiful, Gretchen thought she might melt into a puddle right there on the couch. She felt so overcome with emotion that the next words slipped from her mouth before she had time to even think about editing them. "I'm in love with you, Kylie. I'm so in love with you I can barely see straight. No pun intended." She took a deep, relieved breath. "There. I said it."

Flashing a nervous grin, Gretchen felt as if an enormous weight had just been lifted and she was suddenly light as a feather. She inhaled again and said it once more for good measure. "I'm in love with you." She watched with enormous affection as Kylie's impossibly blue eyes welled and one tear spilled over from each eye, rolling down her flushed cheeks. "Please tell me those are tears of joy," she whispered.

Kylie could only nod, her throat closed up by emotion.

Gretchen held her arms open. "Come here."

Kylie threw herself forward into the waiting embrace. "I love you, too," she murmured into Gretchen's shoulder and felt Gretchen's hold on her tighten.

Suddenly, a huge crash of thunder rocked the house. Gretchen chuckled at the timing. "I hope this isn't the part where you begin to laugh maniacally and I realize I've just sold my soul to the devil."

Kylie's shoulders shook as she laughed, but instead of a verbal answer, Gretchen felt warm lips on her neck, nibbling gently and working their way up to her ear. Kylie held Gretchen's face in her hands as she pulled back and looked her in the eyes. A flash of lightning colored the room an eerie gray for a split second.

"I love you, Gretchen," Kylie whispered. "I have for a long time." Without waiting for a response, she pulled Gretchen closer and kissed her slowly and deeply, trying to convey all she was feeling into that one action.

Gretchen let herself sink into the kiss, allowing her entire being to center on the unbroken connection of mouth to mouth, focusing all her energy on the wonderfully intense heat that suddenly ignited between them.

The lightning flashed again and was followed a few seconds later by another crack of thunder and the sound of harder rain spattering the house. The two women on the couch barely flinched, so lost in one another were they. Their easily paced kissing didn't last long, though, as Kylie began pulling at Gretchen's clothes, her arousal increasing dramatically the longer her lips were fused to Gretchen's.

"You're overdressed," she complained. "Take these off. Now."

Gretchen arched an eyebrow, as she had just been thinking the same thing about Kylie. She tugged at the shoulder strap of the yellow tank. "Maybe we should take this up to your bedroom."

Kylie nodded, then yanked on the neckline of Gretchen's T-shirt and fastened her mouth to the exposed collarbone before sliding up to her throat. Gretchen groaned, slipping her fingers into Kylie's still-wet and shockingly soft hair. Holding her head in place, Gretchen dropped her own head back as the sensations of whatever Kylie was doing with her mouth shot straight to her groin.

Somehow, she managed to stand, pulling Kylie up with her. She divested Kylie of her tank top. As if in a duel, Kylie grabbed Gretchen's T-shirt and pulled it over her head until they both stood in their bras and shorts, breathing heavily and staring at one another. Their mouths found each other once again and they performed the nearly impossible feat of kissing and walking at the same time, making it halfway up Kylie's stairway before losing their balance.

Gretchen found herself on her back on the steps, the carpeting rough on her bare skin. She kicked off her shoes, hearing them tumble down several stairs. Kylie was on top of her, wrenching at the button of her shorts, her tongue deep in Gretchen's mouth, chasing all other thoughts from her head.

Kylie wanted nothing more than to have Gretchen completely naked under her hands, but the steps were hindering her progress. She wrenched her mouth from Gretchen's, who whimpered at the loss of contact, and pulled her to her feet. Leading her quickly by the hand, she led her up the rest of the stairs and down the hall until they finally fell backward once again the second they hit the edge of Kylie's bed.

The windows were open and a stiff, hot breeze was blowing through the room, carrying with it the smell of rain and ozone. The two finally naked women wrestled for top position, clamoring all over one another with hands, lips, and teeth. Gretchen was much stronger than she appeared, but she was no match for Kylie's taller, more muscular frame and before long, she found herself flat on her back, Kylie straddling her hips and pinning her arms over her head.

Both of them breathed raggedly, their chests heaving, their skin slick with sweat, the air charged with the heady combination of sex, desire, and love. Their gazes held, the connection electric. Kylie switched her grip so she held Gretchen's wrists in one hand while she allowed the other to roam Gretchen's body. Her eyes never left Gretchen's as her fingertips skimmed along the pale, soft skin of Gretchen's shoulder, her chest, down the center of her torso, and then her palm flattened over the quivering abdomen. There was a slight paunch there and it made Kylie smile with affection. *As it should be.*

She reversed her path and moved back up to catch one small breast in her hand. Gretchen squirmed beneath her as Kylie kneaded the flesh, liking its compact size. She felt the pink nipple tighten beneath her palm and she focused in on it, capturing it with her finger and thumb, rolling it and tugging it gently until Gretchen bit her bottom lip and her eyes fluttered closed. When Kylie bent forward and took it in her mouth, Gretchen growled and pushed her head back into the pillow, twisting her wrists in Kylie's grip.

"God, Kylie. You're driving me crazy."

"Get used to it," Kylie replied, biting down and then smiling as Gretchen's entire body flinched.

The thunder rolled on relentlessly, as did Kylie's mouth. By the time she had freed Gretchen's hands and her head was tucked securely between Gretchen's thighs, Gretchen thought her entire body might simply implode. When she tried to participate in the directing of things by digging her fingers into Kylie's hair, Kylie stopped her ministrations just long enough to command, "Let me," and grasped her wrists firmly, holding them to the mattress at Gretchen's sides.

Relinquishing control was not something Gretchen did eagerly and she actually struggled a bit, but Kylie held tightly. When she tugged on Gretchen's wrists, it caused her mouth to push more firmly into Gretchen's center and she used that maneuver to her advantage, enjoying the gasp it forced from her partner. It happened three times before a guttural groan erupted up from deep in Gretchen's body and escaped from her throat as the orgasm took her, full force. She arched her back, slamming her head back into the pillow and hissing Kylie's name, her hands fisted in Kylie's grip.

Kylie held tightly, her mouth still moving, still tasting, but her eyes watching Gretchen's body. The display was a most magnificent performance, dazzling in its sensuality, and made more beautiful by the flash of lightning that sizzled through the room.

"Okay," Gretchen whispered, her voice ragged and breathless, her chest heaving. "Okay. Stop. Stop. Christ."

Kylie smiled and released Gretchen's hands. She placed one last, gentle kiss on the warm, slick flesh beneath her lips, causing Gretchen's hips to jerk in response.

"Please," Gretchen begged. "Come up here."

Kylie did as she was asked, feeling more satisfied than she had in ages. She kissed Gretchen sweetly on the mouth, lingering only a little before Gretchen wrapped her arms around her and pulled her down.

"Oh, God," Gretchen moaned as Kylie settled her weight. "You're so warm."

Kylie burrowed in and sighed in happiness as she felt Gretchen's arms tighten around her. She slid a little to the side so her full weight wasn't crushing Gretchen, and threw one leg over hers. She settled her head on Gretchen's shoulder. She could feel Gretchen's wetness on her knee and she fought hard to keep from pushing into her. Gretchen pressed a kiss to Kylie's forehead and they lay in silent contentment for a long while. Kylie was just about to drift off when Gretchen spoke.

"Kylie? You asleep?"

"Yes," Kylie answered wryly.

"Can we talk a little?"

"You can talk as much as you want. You have no idea what your voice does to me."

"Oh yeah?"

"If you weren't such a great sales manager, I'd suggest a career in the wonderful world of phone sex."

Gretchen smiled. "I'll file that away for later. Maybe I'll call you sometime and you can rate me."

"You're on."

"Kylie, I…" Gretchen faltered and seemed to be searching for the right words.

Kylie lifted her head. "Oh, Gretchen, you're not dumping me already, are you?"

"What?" Gretchen's eyes widened in surprise. "No! No, of course not."

Kylie settled back down. "Thank God."

Gretchen chuckled. "I guess I've sort of given you the right to expect that, haven't I?"

"You do seem to like to check out during the afterglow, so to speak."

Gretchen grimaced, realizing the validity of the statement.

"Is that when you panic?" Kylie's voice was soft and without accusation.

Gretchen nodded. "Yeah. I think so."

"Are you panicking now?"

"No." Gretchen inhaled and let the air out slowly. "But I am worried."

"About what?"

"About a lot of things."

Kylie drew small patterns on Gretchen's stomach with her fingertips. "Name a couple."

Gretchen cleared her throat. "Well, let's see." She paused, trying to determine exactly how honest she should be and decided on 100 percent. "I'm worried that I'll screw this up. I'm worried that I'm not what you think I am. I'm worried that I'm going to hurt you."

Kylie smiled. "You're so predictable. Do you know that?"

Gretchen turned to face the woman in her arms, her face showing a combination of insult and puzzlement. "I'm predictable?"

"It's not meant as a jab, sweetie. I just mean that I'm not the least bit surprised that you're worried about these things."

"You're not?"

"No. You're a perfectionist and a control freak." She laughed at the mock anger that crossed Gretchen's face. "Oh, come on. I'm not telling you anything you don't already know. All I'm saying is, given your personality type, it would be very strange for you *not* to be worried about those things."

"Oh." It was the only answer she had to respond to such an accurate assessment.

"And for what it's worth, I worry, too. So there."

"Yeah? About what?"

"The same things you do. I don't want to screw this up. I don't want to hurt you. And I want to be everything you want me to be, everything you think I am, but I'm sure that I won't."

Gretchen absorbed the information in silence.

"All we can do is our best, right?" Kylie asked.

And just like that, the simplest answer was the right one. Gretchen nodded and tightened her arms around Kylie. She pulled the sheet up to cover them lightly. They lay in each other's embrace and listened to the sound of the rain falling gently around them, the thunder a distant, rumbling memory moving east.

"I love you, Gretchen," Kylie whispered, just before she let go completely and allowed sleep to claim her.

❖

Kylie felt like she was underwater, the sound muffled, her body throbbing as she debated pulling herself into wakefulness. She was so warm and comfortable in this place, a sensual tingle buzzing through her, making her limbs seem exhaustedly heavy and feather-light at the same time. Then the tingle became stronger, more of a pulse that settled directly between her thighs, a delicious aching need that had an unmistakable rhythm.

She pulled herself up from the depths with effort and opened her eyes to three wonderful realities: Gretchen's body stretched along the length of hers, Gretchen's mouth fastened onto and sucking one of her breasts, and Gretchen's fingers between her legs, sending little shocks of pleasure throughout her body as if controlling her completely from that nerve center.

"Oh, my God," she whispered as she tried to focus in the darkness of the room. "Gretchen."

"I'm sorry," Gretchen whispered back as she looked up, her fingers never ceasing their movement. "I couldn't help it. I woke up and I was watching you sleep and you were just so damn beautiful, I had to touch you." She didn't sound the least bit regretful and her eyebrow arched wickedly as she continued, "And you were *so* wet."

Kylie could respond with nothing more than a whimper, and then Gretchen's mouth covered hers in a searing kiss. Tongues battled, pressure increased, and Kylie was rushed to the edge before she was even fully awake, her body refusing to wait for her. Her muscles tensed and strained as she teetered, waiting for release. Her body arched, and Gretchen felt the delicious pain of Kylie's fingernails on her back.

"I love you," she hissed into Kylie's ear, giving her a final push with her fingers, her voice, and her heart.

The erotic cry ripped from Kylie's chest was almost enough to send Gretchen over right behind her. *God, I love that sound.* She watched and listened, awed by the effect Kylie's climax had on her, how it filled her so completely with love and passion and confidence. She wished with every ounce of her being that it would always be this way and she knew instinctively, deep inside, that it was actually possible. With Kylie by her side, anything was possible.

They lay together in the aftermath. No more words were spoken as Kylie struggled to catch her breath. Gretchen kissed her neck, her cheek, her forehead, and withdrew her fingers gently. She wrapped them up in each other until they were nothing but a mass of tangled, exhausted limbs, heaving lungs, and racing hearts covered with a midnight blue cotton sheet.

Chapter Nineteen

"S tephen Jenkins's office, this is Kylie. May I help you?"
   "What are you wearing?"
"Who is this?"
"Funny."
"Why are you harassing me at work?" Kylie did her best to hide the smirk, knowing Gretchen could hear it anyway. "I have very important things to do, you know."
"Are you wearing the black silk set or the blue one?"
"I think you're single-handedly keeping Victoria's Secret in business."
"If you didn't look so damn edible in their stuff, I wouldn't be forced to buy it. Just tell me which color. Please?"
"If you had come over last night, you'd know, now wouldn't you?" Kylie adopted a teasing tone to take any sting from the words.
"Touché. I'm sorry, sweetie." Gretchen's voice sounded truly apologetic. "I really needed to get my monthly sales figures in order and I knew if I was anywhere near you, there would be no work getting done. Not to mention I needed some sleep."
"Are you saying I'm a distraction?"
"The biggest."
"And I prevent you from getting any sleep?"
"You have no idea."
"Well, I'm sorry about that."
"Liar."
Kylie laughed because it was true. She was still learning the effects she had on Gretchen, physically as well as emotionally. She

chuckled inside because Gretchen had the exact same effects on her; she just didn't realize it yet. All Gretchen had to do was look at her and Kylie could completely lose her train of thought. She could be speaking to other people and if Gretchen glanced her way, she'd falter in mid-sentence, totally forgetting what she was going to say. It was unnerving…and devastatingly sexy.

She was well aware that their "newness" would eventually wear off—or at least tone down a little—and they *would* be able to actually sleep when they were together. She vividly recalled three nights ago when they'd made love on Gretchen's kitchen floor, unable to wait even long enough to make it to the bedroom. Clearing her throat, she pressed her lips together and looked around in embarrassment, wondering if any of her colleagues could read her filthy mind.

"What time are you picking me up tonight?" she asked, thinking a change of subject was definitely in order.

"About six thirty." Gretchen's voice softened. "Nervous?"

"A little. Yeah."

"No need, love. Pete already adores you and Allyson is the sweetest woman on the face of the earth. You two are going to hit it off and I'm going to have to drag you out of there kicking and screaming when it's time to go."

"You think so?"

"I'm sure of it."

"Okay." In truth, Kylie was looking forward to their first dinner with friends as a couple. It had been several weeks and they were taking things very slowly, but dinner with Pete and Allyson was a big step for Gretchen; Kylie knew that. They were a part of Gretchen's life that she didn't share with many people. The ramifications were not lost on Kylie. "How's your day going?"

"Really well. It's still a little weird being at a small company like this. I keep expecting the usual corporate bullshit and politics, but there really isn't any. It's kind of nice."

"You seem a lot more relaxed, you know." Kylie had noticed almost immediately the change in Gretchen. She was not nearly as tightly wound. "This new job agrees with you."

"I think there are other factors involved."

Kylie felt her heart warm. "Maybe."

"Listen, sweetheart, I've got another call coming in so I've got to go. I'll scoot to your place in a bit and let Jake out during lunch, okay?"

Kylie couldn't hide her surprise. "Are you sure you have time? I can do it."

"No, no. It's okay. I want to. If you don't mind."

"Mind? Of course not. Brandy asked me to lunch anyway."

"Tell her you're spoken for."

Kylie laughed. "She's straight, honey."

"Yeah, well, we're all straight until we're not. Gotta run. Hey, you didn't tell me which color. Blue or black?"

"That's for me to know and you to find out."

"Tease. Bye."

"Bye." Kylie returned the phone to its cradle with a smile.

She still couldn't believe how well things were going. They had their issues, it was true. Gretchen still had trouble letting go of work at the end of the day, even though she now worked for a much smaller company with a lot less demand and she was enjoying it immensely. Every so often, Kylie had to remind her to leave the office at the office. It was something they were working on, something that would take time, but something that was definitely worth the effort.

Jake was another surprise. An eight-week-old puppy wasn't always the easiest way to introduce dogs to somebody who'd never had one, but Gretchen had taken to the white, black, and brown speckled Australian Shepherd immediately. She'd gone with Kylie to pick him out and had held him the entire hour-long ride home. They'd definitely bonded, Gretchen and Jake, and Kylie loved to watch them together.

She had only given Gretchen a key to her house a week ago, and the fact that Gretchen wasn't at all hesitant to use it was still a shock to her. Kylie had her own issues—like waiting for the other shoe to drop. Things were working out so well, so unbelievably well, that part of her was convinced it would all fall apart before long. It wasn't like either of them had great track records. It seemed far more likely that they'd crash and burn than be together forever.

Erin constantly scolded her for her inability to relax and enjoy the ride. Knowing she had a tendency to overanalyze things, she consciously tried to prevent herself from doing so, but it wasn't easy. She tried not to worry, not to dwell, but it scratched at the back of her mind in fairly regular intervals, the doubt, the uncertainty. *But isn't it*

normal to worry at least a little? Is anybody ever 100 percent certain of
their life, of their relationship, and where they're headed?

Her thoughts were interrupted by a touch on her shoulder that
made her jump. She turned her head to find Margo Wheeler pulling her
hand away as though she'd been burned. They both laughed.

"Sorry about that, Kylie. I didn't mean to startle you." Margo
looked sharp in a deep green skirt and jacket and ivory silk shell, her
hair pulled back smoothly.

"No problem. That's what I get for daydreaming."

"I just wanted to see how things were going with Steve. Two new
bosses in the space of three months is a lot for any admin to handle."

Kylie smiled. "It's great. He's great. He's very nice. He's efficient.
The reps seem to really like him."

"Good. He's spoken highly of you as well, so it looks like the fit
is right."

Kylie nodded.

"Well, then. Carry on." Margo took a step away, then turned back,
a twinkle in her eye. "Do tell Gretchen I said hello."

"I will."

Kylie felt her face heat up as Margo continued down the hall.
Gretchen had told Kylie that she'd been completely honest with Margo
when she handed in her resignation, and Kylie was by no means
closeted, but it was a little strange to know that Margo Wheeler *knew*.

Shrugging, she glanced at the clock. It was going on noon and
Brandy would be by any minute. Kylie answered a phone call for Steve,
then put her phone on voice-mail and opened her Outlook to jot off a
quick e-mail before she left. She was just about to start typing when a
rap sounded on the frame of her cubicle. Expecting Brandy, she looked
up and couldn't hide the surprise that crossed her face as she saw Mick
standing there.

They hadn't spoken since that disastrous night in Kylie's living
room, and she missed her friend terribly. Kylie had wanted to call
dozens of times, had even gone so far as to dial the phone and get Mick's
answering machine on several occasions, but she had no idea what to
say. Before she realized it, over a month had gone by and the two of
them had been doing a commendable job of avoiding each other at
work as well as home. Kylie chided herself for being such a coward.

Dressed in her usual well-pressed khakis and polo shirt, her hair
recently trimmed, Mick looked as neat and as put-together as she

always did. She also looked a little nervous, shifting her weight from one foot to the other.

"Hey," Kylie said, happiness tinting her voice. She wanted to get up and hug Mick but thought that might be pushing things. Instead, she favored her with a big, genuine grin. "It's good to see you. How are you?"

"I'm good, Ky." Mick ventured a small smile. "I'm really good. How are you doing?"

"Great. I'm great."

Mick gestured over her shoulder at Gretchen's old office. "The new guy? How's he? You like him okay?"

Kylie nodded. "Yeah. Yeah, he's been terrific. Very nice. Very competent."

"That's what I hear. People seem to like him."

They both nodded like bobble-head dolls. The conversation stalled, neither knowing how to keep it going. Finally, Mick took a deep breath and looked down at her booted feet.

"Listen, Ky, I'm having a little get-together at my place this weekend. Nothing huge. Just a dozen or so friends, the usual crowd. If you're not busy, maybe you and, um, Gretchen can stop in, have some wine, eat some food." She looked down the hall, at the wall, anywhere but at Kylie's face. "If you're not busy," she repeated.

Kylie felt a lump form in her throat and for a moment, she couldn't speak. She knew Mick well enough to know how hard the invitation was for her to present, and she took it for exactly what it was: an olive branch. It told her that Mick missed their friendship as much as she did. It certainly didn't make everything magically all better, but it was a start. Kylie was proud of Mick for taking the first step…something she hadn't had the courage to do.

Shifting sideways slightly in order to catch Mick's clouded green eyes, she said, "It sounds like fun. We'd love to come."

Mick's face lit up into a real smile this time. "Good. Saturday night, anytime after six." She gave Kylie a small wave and escaped before she could feel any more exposed.

"See you then," Kylie said to her disappearing friend. She shook her head with a smirk, thinking how strange life was and how things had a funny way of working out when you least expected it. For the third time, her thoughts were interrupted when Brandy appeared at her side, eager to go.

Kylie grinned up at her. "Let me just send off this quick note." She turned back to the e-mail she'd begun just before Mick arrived. It was to Gretchen in her new office. Kylie typed one word.

Black.

Grinning, she hit the Send button.

"You're awfully smiley lately," Brandy observed, affectionately bumping her with a shoulder as they walked down the hall.

"Yeah?" Kylie asked, knowing it was true.

"Very. You seem happy."

"I am."

Gretchen's face filled Kylie's mind, dark hair flying, rich brown eyes twinkling, and Kylie suspected her smiling wasn't going to end anytime soon.

About the Author

Georgia Beers was born and raised in Rochester, New York. After high school, she attended college in Pennsylvania at Mansfield University, where she earned a bachelor's degree in mass communications. Always believing she wanted to be involved in television or radio somehow, she tried her hand at both after graduation and decided rather quickly—and much to her own horror—that she didn't like either one.

For as long as she can remember, Georgia has written stories. After discovering the Internet and the surprisingly large world of writing that exists on it, she met a fellow writer in the year 2000 to whom she felt close enough to share her first attempt at a manuscript for a novel. One thing led to another, Georgia was introduced to a publisher, and the next thing she knew, she was an actual honest-to-goodness novelist. To this day, she still has trouble believing it.

It's now 2006 and Georgia is currently at work on her fourth novel, *Fresh Tracks*, as well as various short stories and a script for a short film. She still resides in Rochester with her partner of twelve years, Bonnie, and their two dogs.

Her published works include two lesbian romances, *Turning the Page*, 2001, and *Thy Neighbor's Wife*, 2003 (Regal Crest Enterprises), as well as numerous selections in anthologies: *Milk of Human Kindness: Lesbian Authors Write about Mothers and Daughters* (RCE), *Infinite Pleasures* (Intaglio), and *Stolen Moments: Erotic Interludes 2* (BSB). Upcoming works include "Diva," a short story in the erotica anthology *Erotic Interludes 4: Extreme Passions*, Bold Strokes, 2006, and *Fresh Tracks*, a romance from Bold Strokes, 2006.

Books Available From Bold Strokes Books

The Traitor and the Chalice by Jane Fletcher. Without allies to help them, Tevi and Jemeryl will have to risk all in the race to uncover the traitor and retrieve the chalice. The Lyremouth Chronicles Book Two. (1-933110-43-0)

Promising Hearts by Radclyffe. Dr. Vance Phelps lost everything in the War Between the States and arrives in New Hope, Montana, with no hope of happiness and no desire for anything except forgetting—until she meets Mae, a frontier madam. (1-933110-44-9)

Carly's Sound by Ali Vali. Poppy Valente and Julia Johnson form a bond of friendship that lays the foundation for something more, until Poppy's past comes back to haunt her—literally. A poignant romance about love and renewal. (1-933110-45-7)

Unexpected Sparks by Gina L. Dartt. Falling in love is complicated enough without adding murder to the mix. Kate Shannon's growing feelings for much younger Nikki Harris are challenging enough without the mystery of a fatal fire that Kate can't ignore. (1-933110-46-5)

Whitewater Rendezvous by Kim Baldwin. Two women on a wilderness kayak adventure—Chaz Herrick, a laid-back outdoorswoman, and Megan Maxwell, a workaholic news executive—discover that true love may be nothing at all like they imagined. (1-933110-38-4)

Erotic Interludes 3: Lessons in Love ed. by Radclyffe and Stacia Seaman. Sign on for a class in love...the best lesbian erotica writers take us to "school." (1-9331100-39-2)

Punk Like Me by JD Glass. Twenty-one-year-old Nina writes lyrics and plays guitar in the rock band Adam's Rib, and she doesn't always play by the rules. And oh yeah—she has a way with the girls. (1-933110-40-6)

Coffee Sonata by Gun Brooke. Four women whose lives unexpectedly intersect in a small town by the sea share one thing in common—they all have secrets. (1-933110-41-4)

The Clinic: Tristaine Book One by Cate Culpepper. Brenna, a prison medic, finds herself deeply conflicted by her growing feelings for her patient, Jesstin, a wild and rebellious warrior reputed to be descended from ancient Amazons. (1-933110-42-2)

Forever Found by JLee Meyer. Can time, tragedy, and shattered trust destroy a love that seemed destined? When chance reunites two childhood friends separated by tragedy, the past resurfaces to determine the shape of their future. (1-933110-37-6)

Sword of the Guardian by Merry Shannon. Princess Shasta's bold new bodyguard has a secret that could change both of their lives. *He* is actually a *she*. A passionate romance filled with courtly intrigue, chivalry, and devotion. (1-933110-36-8)

Wild Abandon by Ronica Black. From their first tumultuous meeting, Dr. Chandler Brogan and Officer Sarah Monroe are drawn together by their common obsessions—sex, speed, and danger. (1-933110-35-X)

Turn Back Time by Radclyffe. Pearce Rifkin and Wynter Thompson have nothing in common but a shared passion for surgery. They clash at every opportunity, especially when matters of the heart are suddenly at stake. (1-933110-34-1)

Chance by Grace Lennox. At twenty-six, Chance Delaney decides her life isn't working so she swaps it for a different one. What follows is the sexy, funny, touching story of two women who, in finding themselves, also find one another. (1-933110-31-7)

The Exile and the Sorcerer by Jane Fletcher. First in the Lyremouth Chronicles. Tevi, wounded and adrift, arrives in the courtyard of a shy young sorcerer. Together they face monsters, magic, and the challenge of loving despite their differences. (1-933110-32-5)

A Matter of Trust by Radclyffe. JT Sloan is a cybersleuth who doesn't like attachments. Michael Lassiter is leaving her husband, and she needs Sloan's expertise to safeguard her company. It should just be business—but it turns into much more. (1-933110-33-3)

Sweet Creek by Lee Lynch. A celebration of the enduring nature of love, friendship, and community in the quirky, heart-warming lesbian community of Waterfall Falls. (1-933110-29-5)

The Devil Inside by Ali Vali. Derby Cain Casey, head of a New Orleans crime organization, runs the family business with guts and grit, and no one crosses her. No one, that is, until Emma Verde claims her heart and turns her world upside down. (1-933110-30-9)

Grave Silence by Rose Beecham. Detective Jude Devine's investigation of a series of ritual murders is complicated by her torrid affair with the golden girl of Southwestern forensic pathology, Dr. Mercy Westmoreland. (1-933110-25-2)

Honor Reclaimed by Radclyffe. In the aftermath of 9/11, Secret Service Agent Cameron Roberts and Blair Powell close ranks with a trusted few to find the would-be assassins who nearly claimed Blair's life. (1-933110-18-X)

Honor Bound by Radclyffe. Secret Service Agent Cameron Roberts and Blair Powell face political intrigue, a clandestine threat to Blair's safety, and the seemingly irreconcilable personal differences that force them ever farther apart. (1-933110-20-1)

Protector of the Realm: Supreme Constellations Book One by Gun Brooke. A space adventure filled with suspense and a daring intergalactic romance featuring Commodore Rae Jacelon and the stunning, but decidedly lethal, Kellen O'Dal. (1-933110-26-0)

Innocent Hearts by Radclyffe. In a wild and unforgiving land, two women learn about love, passion, and the wonders of the heart. (1-933110-21-X)

The Temple at Landfall by Jane Fletcher. An imprinter, one of Celaeno's most revered servants of the Goddess, is also a prisoner to the faith—until a Ranger frees her by claiming her heart. The Celaeno series. (1-933110-27-9)

Force of Nature by Kim Baldwin. From tornados to forest fires, the forces of nature conspire to bring Gable McCoy and Erin Richards close to danger, and closer to each other. (1-933110-23-6)

In Too Deep by Ronica Black. Undercover homicide cop Erin McKenzie tracks a femme fatale who just might be a real killer...with love and danger hot on her heels. (1-933110-17-1)

Stolen Moments: Erotic Interludes 2 by Stacia Seaman and Radclyffe, eds. Love on the run, in the office, in the shadows...Fast, furious, and almost too hot to handle. (1-933110-16-3)

Course of Action by Gun Brooke. Actress Carolyn Black desperately wants the starring role in an upcoming film produced by Annelie Peterson. Just how far will she go for the dream part of a lifetime? (1-933110-22-8)

Rangers at Roadsend by Jane Fletcher. Sergeant Chip Coppelli has learned to spot trouble coming, and that is exactly what she sees in her new recruit, Katryn Nagata. The Celaeno series. (1-933110-28-7)

Justice Served by Radclyffe. Lieutenant Rebecca Frye and her lover, Dr. Catherine Rawlings, embark on a deadly game of hide-and-seek with an underworld kingpin who traffics in human souls. (1-933110-15-5)

Distant Shores, Silent Thunder by Radclyffe. Dr. Tory King—along with the women who love her—is forced to examine the boundaries of love, friendship, and the ties that transcend time. (1-933110-08-2)

Hunter's Pursuit by Kim Baldwin. A raging blizzard, a mountain hideaway, and a killer-for-hire set a scene for disaster—or desire—when Katarzyna Demetrious rescues a beautiful stranger. (1-933110-09-0)

The Walls of Westernfort by Jane Fletcher. All Temple Guard Natasha Ionadis wants is to serve the Goddess—until she falls in love with one of the rebels she is sworn to destroy. The Celaeno series. (1-933110-24-4)

Change Of Pace: *Erotic Interludes* by Radclyffe. Twenty-five hot-wired encounters guaranteed to spark more than just your imagination. Erotica as you've always dreamed of it. (1-933110-07-4)

Honor Guards by Radclyffe. In a wild flight for their lives, the president's daughter and those who are sworn to protect her wage a desperate struggle for survival. (1-933110-01-5)

Fated Love by Radclyffe. Amidst the chaos and drama of a busy emergency room, two women must contend not only with the fragile nature of life, but also with the irresistible forces of fate. (1-933110-05-8)

Justice in the Shadows by Radclyffe. In a shadow world of secrets and lies, Detective Sergeant Rebecca Frye and her lover, Dr. Catherine Rawlings, join forces in the elusive search for justice. (1-933110-03-1)

shadowland by Radclyffe. In a world on the far edge of desire, two women are drawn together by power, passion, and dark pleasures. An erotic romance. (1-933110-11-2)

Love's Masquerade by Radclyffe. Plunged into the indistinguishable realms of fiction, fantasy, and hidden desires, Auden Frost is forced to question all she believes about the nature of love. (1-933110-14-7)

Love & Honor by Radclyffe. The president's daughter and her lover are faced with difficult choices as they battle a tangled web of Washington intrigue for...love and honor. (1-933110-10-4)

Beyond the Breakwater by Radclyffe. One Provincetown summer, three women learn the true meaning of love, friendship, and family. (1-933110-06-6)

Tomorrow's Promise by Radclyffe. One timeless summer, two very different women discover the power of passion to heal and the promise of hope that only love can bestow. (1-933110-12-0)

Love's Tender Warriors by Radclyffe. Two women who have accepted loneliness as a way of life learn that love is worth fighting for and a battle they cannot afford to lose. (1-933110-02-3)

Love's Melody Lost by Radclyffe. A secretive artist with a haunted past and a young woman escaping a life that has proved to be a lie find their destinies entwined. (1-933110-00-7)

Safe Harbor by Radclyffe. A mysterious newcomer, a reclusive doctor, and a troubled gay teenager learn about love, friendship, and trust during one tumultuous summer in Provincetown. (1-933110-13-9)

Above All, Honor by Radclyffe. Secret Service Agent Cameron Roberts fights her desire for the one woman she can't have—Blair Powell, the daughter of the president of the United States. (1-933110-04-X)